AF615318

THE OTHER SHEEP

Also by **Delma Luben**

The Protocol Officer Handbook
Poems for Poets and Writers
The Universal Experience
Living, Learning, Love
The Freedom Nation
The Writing World
Glorious Autumn

THE OTHER SHEEP

An Historical Adventure Saga Based on Scripture

Delma Luben

Aventine Press

First Edition

Published by Aventine Press
1023 4th Ave. #204
San Diego, CA 92101
www.aventinepress.com

ISBN: 1-59330-333-5

Printed in the United States of America

To contact the author: dlubn3@yahoo.com

DEDICATION

To my sons, Hal and Lyn,
who inspire me,

and to the memory
of their father.

ACKNOWLEDGMENT

The author wishes to publicly thank Esther Manville for her inestimable editing expertise and tireless assistance in preparation of the manuscript—and the nearly endless series of re-writes. Her professionalism, and cheerful dedication, resulted in a significant contribution, and are greatly appreciated.

INTRODUCTION

After a lifelong study of world religions, including the revelations, and the lives of those chosen to receive them, I have ascertained this simple truth: Our Father in Heaven sends holy guidance and higher wisdom to His earthly progeny periodically and continually….

History reveals that new truths and information for promotion of progress in health, happiness (and how to live in harmony) are sent in increments, to different people in different places at different times—to all generations of all nations, color, ethnicity, and persuasions—for all are equal in the eyes of The Father….

And from these revelations the receivers, or their followers, initiate new religions, each including the same rudimentary instruction—to love our Maker and one another. In the tenets of every organized religion can be found a wording of The Golden Rule. But because of the inherent human inability to believe, or even read what is sent to others, we miss the reality, fail to see the whole picture—and kill the new receiver as an enemy of truth (our truth)—the *whole* truth being beyond comprehension of the finite mind.

However, people who look for truth only in their own scriptures *will* read about God's dealings with others when they are presented as entertainment. Myriad scriptural accounts have been novelized for the general public. But to the best of my knowledge (except for a partial narrative simplified for children) not this one—**despite a great potential for movie epic or mini series.** So, after waiting nearly twenty years to find it done by others I decided to write it myself.

I offer you *The Other Sheep.*

THE BIBLE:

"And I have other sheep which are not of this fold."

— John 10:16

THE BOOK OF MORMON:

"Ye are they of whom I said: Other sheep I have which are not of this fold."

— 3 Nephi 15:21

THE URANITA BOOK:

"Also must you remember that I have sheep not of this flock, and that I am beholden to them also."

— Part 1V, 140:6

CHAPTER I

Lehi quickened his pace. That voice. He strained his ears, then spoke unconsciously, "Jeremiah has returned!"

He began to run, a middle-aged man—after working in his fields all day.

This June afternoon, like many times before, Lehi had taken the long way home (through the city to the travelers gate marketplace) in the hope that there would be a prophet on the platform, rather than a politician, irate citizen, or salesman hawking wares. And each time hoping desperately that it would be Jeremiah.

Since the fiery prophet's exile myriad diviners had expounded from the marketplace platform, more than in all the years before. But if they were God's messengers, they were of lesser caliber. Most, like priests, seemed more concerned with the letter of the law than the quickening of the spirit; many stirred the people to anger; but none of them set souls afire like Jeremiah.

Strongly believing in the possibility that voice is given to many, even unto outsiders, Lehi would listen to them all, weigh their words, and give them benefit of doubt. But he *knew* that Jeremiah spoke for God—and with that same inner certainty awaited the day the great prophet would return to the holy city.

Could this be the day?

Buoyed up by the fire in the voice, snatches of familiar phrases, and wishful thinking, Lehi fairly flew down the cobblestone street, his graying head jutting forward, pulling his aching body, while his mind raced back….

Years ago, mourning that Jerusalem was not the same shining city of his youth, watching the black tar of iniquity spread, he had prayed *even with all his heart on behalf of his people* that heaven would send a messenger. And when finally came that fledgling, humble friar from a nearby village (whom God electrified) he felt that his prayers had been answered.

But big-hearted Jeremiah, believer of good in the wayward people, labored tirelessly, speaking God's words of damnation and pointing out pathways to righteousness and reform, to no avail. Soon his very name became synonymous with denunciation. However, the chosen messenger could not but continue the message: *Repent, or Jerusalem must be destroyed.*

For that dire prediction, constantly, in the temple court, the teeming streets, and this same marketplace, God's spokesman became the number one enemy of the privileged as well as the backsliding majority. Like the transgressors of common law Jeremiah was put into stocks, and thrown into a dungeon. By royal command forbidden to preach, by royal hand his sermons destroyed. The king personally tore his book to shreds.

Ultimately, for damning their religion—urging inner faith in lieu of form and ceremony—the degenerate people of Judah sought his life. Still Jeremiah did not desist in his labor for The Lord. When finally God commanded him to flee the faithful servant hired a scribe and dictated new sermons, to be read to the people in his absence.

Lehi hungered to hear those sermons; but the council of elders considered them too dangerous to be read. Now there was a new king. And believing that the young puppet ruler would not intimidate the old prophet Lehi expected to soon hear the words of fire again. But as he panted into the Marketplace Square, even before pushing through the crowd, he realized that it wouldn't be today. It wasn't Jeremiah; his ear had tricked him. But they were his words; someone must be quoting from his sermons. So today he might at least listen to legitimate words of prophecy. And then one of these days... For the faithful believer knew without a doubt that Jeremiah was destined to return to the holy city.

Concentrating on that thought, surging blindly past the first row of stalls, Lehi bumped into a bleating smelly lamb tethered to an unattended cubicle. His arm shot out like a tension spring, shoving the animal aside.

"Lehi. Dost thou rush to stand again with the peasants?"

He recognized the speaker, a regular seller in the next booth, but did not answer. Frowning, he hurried on, noting that most of the other sellers had deserted their stands. As he picked his way through scattered sun-heated dung and discarded over-ripe fruit (under canopies of flies) he held a rough brown sleeve to his nose, the other arm outstretched to facilitate pushing through the crowd. Thus the anxious patron finally joined the congestion of quasi listeners bunched around the low wooden platform.

Still, not being of great stature and facing the slanting sun, the late comer had to surge up on his toes and crane his neck for an unobstructed view of the speaker. And when he had confirmed what he already knew, emotional energy abandoned him. The all-consuming desire to see Jeremiah again, which had tricked his ear, had also strained his body. Nevertheless Lehi prepared to listen. Spreading his stocky legs he drew a deep breath, leaned on his staff, and settled down to endure.

Heat, elbows in the ribs, the pungent smell of dung, sweating unclean bodies... he considered not too great a price to pay for the words of God.

"... Or your beautiful city will be destroyed." Jeremiah's exact message.

The voice of the bearded figure in the billowing robe also seemed to burn with the same inner fire. Not the great prophet he wanted to hear, but Lehi sensed a deep sincerity. The man deserved his respect and attention.

Being a direct descendant of Joseph he held the conviction that it was his duty (for the blessing of his heritage) to always listen that he may learn to better serve. Years ago the good man had dedicated his life to learning God's will, and teaching it to his four sons. He felt blessed to have been born in the holy city, privileged to have lived within its walls his entire forty-seven years. He loved Jerusalem—from the holy temple to its teeming back streets—and firmly believed that eventually the prophets would get through to the people. The wayward ones were destined to repent, and keep God's commandments as they once did. For surely God would not destroy His city, His home on earth, the holy Jerusalem, where the majority of His servants lived.

Yet, circa 600 BC believers like Lehi and his peers were dwindling fast. Fewer and fewer served The Lord God of Israel. Painfully aware of his status in this minority, and his duty as a father, this man of means constantly prayed for personal guidance. Additionally, he listened to the words of whosoever claimed to be a messenger, despite aching legs and burning eyes, his ears remained fully attuned. By concerted effort Lehi managed to tune out the jabbering around him. But he could not ignore the tall well-dressed young man worming in before him, completely blocking his view of the speaker.

"All these old goats are just trying to scare us back to the ancient ways."

The stranger smirked as he said this. Neat and clean, a good cut above the slovenly majority, he had selected and sidled up to a man who might be a peer, a man who manifested the confidence of means and erudition even when wearing work clothes.

But Lehi did not feel honored. Rubbing his neatly trimmed salt-and-pepper beard, frowning, he studied the unfamiliar face wearing the superiority smile.

"Old goat? Why, young man, he may be a prophet. Certainly he speaks with concern for mankind. Therefore he deserves to be heard."

The younger man shrugged.

"Yea, there may be truth in thy words; but must he go about in that old ragged robe?"

While Lehi considered an answer that might possibly enlighten his questioner a sharp gust of wind peppered his face with malodorous sand. Some stuck to his brow in the perspiration. As he swiped at it, the stranger turned on his heel and left without further comment.

Smiling knowingly at the quick retreat Lehi licked the grit off his teeth, thinking of the cool spring water at home. His mind began blowing up pictures of shaded arches and padded chairs. But like an overworked youth starved for entertainment he couldn't leave until the stage was empty.

To many in the crowd the hairy old stranger *was* entertainment. From the time he wandered in off the desert to command a turn on the platform he'd been ridiculed, snubbed, and laughed at by ruffians. This Lehi knew; it was the usual. He also knew that his peers and the so-called pious ones sent their servants to report the messages of these itinerant preachers. Unlike them, he needed to listen personally, though the need often wearied him. And today he had arrived weary.

But hearing "heart" in the voice, he fixated on the preacher like the eyes of the beggar by the stalls had fixated on him. Only once did he briefly break attention—turning to the scuffling ruffians, and chattering shawl-draped women, with his ever unspoken censure.

If they didn't want to listen, why were they here?

Lehi hurt for the great majority wrapped in their various robes of complacency. But also, his patience sometimes weakened (with the progressive discomfort of their inattention, and inevitable uncouth remarks). This day he endured for almost an hour. He was about to abscond when the wind and the heat suddenly intensified. Thunder in the distance rumbled louder. The shifting mass of indifference began thinning. Now he could see the speaker without strain. And becoming grievously aware of his disbursing audience, opportunity ending, the man intensified his oration. Lifting wild eyes and hairy arms to the heavens, his voice shot to high wire tautness—as if entreating divine assistance.

"Oh wayward people of Jerusalem, repent…"

The scrawny figure, bent like a reed in the wind, paced the platform as if in some ceremonial dance. Raggedy robe flopping about him, one bony finger jabbing the air, raspy voice rushing on and on, he mercilessly chastised the remaining crowd. Having been wayward for centuries this "Basket of bad figs," (which Isaiah, the famous prophet aristocrat, labeled them) had forfeited God's promises of the past, and were now in dire danger. Accordingly, they threatened on the very brink of Jehovah's terrible curse.

When at last the would-be reformer paused for breath Lehi quickly looked away, to search the sparser circle of bobbing heads for the face of his kinsman, his one peer who would be there. But Ishmael was not to be seen.

The orator, now speaking slowly, and very distinctly, ended his gyration with a familiar warning.

"The Lord God sayeth: 'I will remove Judah from out of my sight!'"

Lo, the many times Lehi had heard that threatening prophesy. His breath caught. The ever-nagging fear struck again—and this time stronger than ever before, producing a clear mental picture. Despite his proclaimed good intentions, the new king Zedekiah would *not* lead the holy city to better days. Jerusalem would fall.

When Jeremiah returns to Jerusalem the king has him thrown down a cistern to die. He is rescued but again, imprisoned.

Nebuchadnezzar returns, and slaughters the king's sons before his eyes. The temple is destroyed, the city walls broken down, and the people carried off into captivity.

Now Lehi knew of a surety that all of the above would come to pass. But he was not yet burdened with the gruesome details—for heavy enough that which was yet to be given him on that fateful day.

CHAPTER II

When at last the fiery preacher relinquished the market square platform Lehi had hardly enough energy to make it home. Leaning heavily on his staff he shuffled through the familiar streets with half-closed eyes, oblivious to the wind and the heat and the primal blobs of rain.

Upon reaching the narrow lane that led to his garden gate the raindrops, decreasing in size and increasing in speed, had stirred up the fragrance of dampened earth. He loved the familiar smell. He paused and looked around contentedly—but the next moment seemed disoriented, as if he had lost his memory. Standing in front of his own gate he eyed it, as if this were not his home and entrance depended on someone inside. He stared around without comprehension. Then this erudite, always in control man suddenly turned child-like. Smiling up at the increasing rain he licked it from his lips. Having downed the last drop of water from the goat skin pouch back in the field, he thirsted greatly. Impulsively, he stuck out his tongue, eyes begging the stingy sky for refreshment.

Inside, a cool drink and a footbath awaited him, as did his loving wife. Lehi needed the comfort of both. He wanted to tell Sariah of the prophet that sounded like Jeremiah. And the aroma of her savory boiled-ox stew pulled strong. Still he hesitated to lift the leather thong latch. The man of the house remained outside his own gate, resisting the pull. Then he felt a stronger pull—too strong to deny.

Clamping work-worn hands to his chest, Lehi ceremoniously backed away from the gate and turned upon the slightly worn path that led through the bramble bushes into a small secluded clearing. There, safe from possible prying eyes, righting his robe, smoothing his hair and beard, he raised himself to full stature as if about to give a sermon. For some time he stood motionless, oblivious to the increasing rain. Then memory flooding in (the words of the fiery preacher back at the marketplace) he fell upon his knees. And begged.

"Oh, please, dear Lord God of Israel, forgive them. Save Jerusalem."

Gray eyes brimming with compassion for the wayward people, Lehi prayed vehemently, promising to do *anything,* if only God would not destroy The Holy City. He poured his heart out, unto exhaustion.

And with exhaustion came remorse for his weakness.

"Oh dear God, forgive me. Thy will be done. Thy will be done…"

Prostrate upon the wet earth, face down, he weakly concluded. "Oh great God forgive thy shallow servant. From debility the mortal mind doth fail Thee, but not the heart..."

A loud swishing sound. His head jerked up. There appeared a pillar of fire in the air before him, seemingly belching from the cold wet boulder below—an awesome crimson flame swirling, billowing, even swelling in the rain! And so close he could have touched it. Yet the mortal felt no heat.

Shaking uncontrollably Lehi clamped his eyes shut, dropped his head again to the ground, and lay as if lifeless.

Then the voice!

From the ground? From the flame? From above?

Strong and pervasive the words pierced his heart. And the last bit of strength went from him.

After the voice ceased, in the silver silence that followed, Lehi sensed the supernatural iron clamp upon his limbs dissolve; the rain became like balm from heaven; he felt strangely free. But he had never known such vulnerability, such an overwhelming feeling of lightness, combined with a profound weakness. B*ecause of the things which he saw and heard he did quake and tremble exceedingly.*

Born of good stock and godly parents, strong of mind and body, the feebleness frightened the good man more than what actually happened. For steeped in the learning of his people, and myriad stories of the miracles Lehi had never doubted these things. That prophets were periodically chosen and given a mission to reveal God's Word, he accepted without question. The story of Moses and the burning bush had long burned in his brain as fact. But that he, Lehi, should be chosen to witness such things was incomprehensible.

When at last the flame submitted to the rain naturally, the newly chosen servant of God felt wrapped in a cocoon of euphoria. Now completely relaxed, and assuaged by a soothing mist, he mentally floated. Time seemed suspended.

Then he heard the distant baying of a donkey, and gradually became fully aware. He felt his strength returning. Yet he did not move, or open his eyes—until he felt a hand on his shoulder.

His eyes flew open.

"Lehi! Lehi, what happened? Are you ill?"

With difficulty, Lehi focused on the beefy face of his kinsman, Ishmael already removing his cloak to warm his sopping-wet friend.

"Here, take off thy soaked robe and put this on."

Lehi flagged at the cloak attempting to get on his feet. His arms and legs seemed uncoordinated. Ishmael pulled his friend upright, steadied him. And picked up his staff.

"Did you fall?" He asked warily, handing it to him.

Frowning with concern at no answer Ishmael continued the questioning. "Lehi, are you all right? You are weak; you look flushed, different. What is it?"

Still Lehi did not answer, or look directly at him. And when at last he quietly said, "Thank you ," Ishmael stared, for his voice didn't sound natural.

"Lehi, look at me. It's as if ... Lehi, thou art strange, not thyself—even unto thy voice . . . Here, lean on me. What happened?"

"I, I cannot talk now," Lehi mumbled.

Sensing his kinsman's compassion, he knew in his heart that Ishmael was the one person he could talk to about the vision (besides Sariah); but it was too soon, too soon. He would need time to orient himself, and find words.

"When approaching your gate," Ishmael was saying, "something made me turn . . . I feared . . ."

Rambling now Ishmael attempted to pull Lehi through the shrubbery. When he let go of his arm and reached to part the bushes Lehi jerked back. Rooted to the ground, his ruddy face a white-whiskered map of consternation and question marks, Ishmael tried one more time.

"Lehi, you *must* let me help thee."

At this Lehi lifted his head. The eyes of the life-long friends met; but there was not the usual connection. The mind of God's newly chosen had not yet fully returned to reality. The rain now swirled about him in a gauzy mist. His face shone; even the matted wet hair seemed to be emitting light.

Ishmael could only continue to stare. For a long moment the two men stood like confronting warriors caught in a time warp. Finally the disconcerted friend dropped his eyes, stepped back, and stood waiting. Lehi leaned shakily on his staff, and began slowly pushing forward. Ishmael lagged behind. Not until they reached Lehi's gate did he speak again.

"Lehi, thou art sick; let me help thee to thy bed."

"No Ishmael, I am more steady now. And I have my staff." He turned abruptly, reaching for the leather thong latch, leaving his friend appalled, and unthanked. As his mind began clearing Lehi had suddenly felt concern for his wife. Sariah would be anxious, all his sons having reached home before him. By this time surely *all* would be home, and for the first time the father was late—he who had often chastised his oldest son for straying. Lehi constantly worried that Laman would influence Lemuel to follow in his paths of iniquity. Off to the city as soon as he dismissed them from the field, the two habitually came home late, sometimes not arriving until after Sariah had served the evening meal, even missing evening prayers... Surfaced the memory that lay particularly heavy on his heart.

"Go to bed and rest. You need..." Ishmael was saying.

"Yes, yes." Lehi' eyes were anchored on the house. Then quickly...

"Oh, my friend forgive me. You had business..."

"Not now. Now it is meet that you rest. I came only to tell of the speaker in the square. I did not see you there. We can talk of it tomorrow."

Lehi nodded. "Yes, tomorrow we will talk." And at long last he lifted the familiar leather thong latch.

Weary in mind and body the man of the house ached for the comforts of his home—and Sari. But the usually considerate husband still did not join his family waiting in the main area of the house. Just a brief hesitation and he turned off the entrance path and slipped around back, to the stock area. In the stillness of deepening shadows he could hear the burros breathing and the milk goats' contented chewing. He passed them without looking, eyeing the wet stone steps to the roof. Then drawing a deep breath (as if to conjure up strength, or courage) he began slowly climbing.

At the top of the stairs there was no further hesitation. Though exhausted he now moved swiftly toward the secluded latticed room, that part of the house where no one else came—where the man of the house came to talk with his Maker. He reached for the tapestry which covered the arched opening, clung to it a minute, then pulled himself inside and dropped to his straw-padded meditating couch.

Immediately, the spirit again overcame him. For the second time Lehi was carried away in a vision. *And it came to pass that he saw one descending out of the midst of heaven, and he beheld that His luster was that of the sun at noon-day ... he also saw twelve others following him and...*

After the Lord showed his newly called servant many great and marvelous things regarding the future, and the black cloud of destruction over Jerusalem, he was then given a mission. By holy commandment chosen, Lehi was to speak to his people for God.

This time upon awakening Lehi felt no fear. In the pre-dawn diffused light, suspended between heaven and earth, he floated in the pervading presence of pure love and perfect peace. But the ethereal bliss was brief. And until he completed the mission commanded by his Maker the good man would not know peace again.

With the emergence of earthly consciousness, and full mortal memory, he felt a lump arise in his throat. He cried out.

"Oh Sariah, Sari, my love..."

He hadn't even told her he was home.

CHAPTER III

The evening of Lehi's vision Sariah worried and walked the house. *Never has my husband been so late returning from the fields, even when he stopped at the marketplace.* Her mind raced; she began to feel dizzy, but she held to her duty.

With shaky hands she wrapped the just-baked bread in a burlap cloth to keep it warm, methodically stirred up the fire, stirred the contents of the clay pot for the umpteenth time... Then she hurried across the room to watch from the window box.

She'd heard her sons come home. They were out back now, all of them, washing up. Soon they would come inside, hungry, anxious, wondering why she had not called them to the evening meal. Growing sons had bottomless-pit stomachs; and they didn't know that their father was not yet home. Supper was served when the head of the household was ready. When the father appeared the mother would call her children—and not until. But this night maybe the tradition would be broken.

Time passed. The aroma of herbs and boiled ox meat permeated the sultry air. Thunder rolling in the distance became louder, cracking closer. The first over-sized drops of rain plip-plopped on the ledge outside the window. Sariah watched them unseeing, her mind racing, thoughts of the good man she had married alternating with worry. She bowed her head in prayer. Then raised her eyes once more to the lane, hopefully searching… Oh, so long the waiting.

But a middle-aged woman does not panic, or roam the house like a betrothed maiden waiting for her sailor's ship to crest the horizon. She must find things to do.

While Sariah busied herself her sons waited impatiently. Finally, as if sensing his mother's mental turmoil, Sam came in. He found her poking at the fire again, blindly staring at the flames.

"Where could father be?"

"Your father …"Sariah shook her head.

Sam took the poker from his mother and set it aside. He motioned that he would turn the heavy pot for her. Grinning at her over his shoulder he lifted the heavy black pot, turned it, and settled the handle firmly on its iron hook.

"I heard there was a preacher at the marketplace today," he said. "Maybe he was long-winded. You know father will stay and hear every word they have to say even if they're fakes."

Sariah gave her son a weak smile. "Yes Sam, I know, come rain or …" Her voice trailed off.

Sam put a comforting hand on his mother's shoulder and went out to rejoin his brothers roughhousing in the stalls. Nothing else to do. They had done their chores, all but milk the goats. And Nephi would do that after supper. As the youngest (though already the strongest and as tall as the oldest) it was his job to relieve his mother of this woman's chore.

The prosperous head of the house had assigned a number of traditional women's tasks to his growing sons—that his wife's burden not be so heavy, and his sons not develop pride. In the house of Lehi only pride of heritage was allowed.

Once again at the window, Sariah was thinking of these things, and the many other virtues of her husband. As it grew late her sons took turns coming in, hinting for offerings of bread or fruit to tide them over. Should she relent? She pushed back a tendril of hair, now damp with humidity, and reset a comb. Her soft brown eyes remained fixated on the empty lane.

Then suddenly, as if a flash from a crystal ball, she jumped up and rushed to the roof. *Could he possibly have come home and gone there without telling her?* She remembered that lately her husband had been spending more and more time in prayer and meditation.

Thus rationalizing, fully expecting to find him there, Sariah approached the small covered alcove on the roof. As she moved quietly toward the patriarch's personal retreat her sparsely lined face tightened. Like the tycoon's den, or the lion's sacred territory, the exclusive area for the master of the house should not be invaded. Such sanctioned traditions a good wife respected.

Since Lehi had taken her at fifteen Sariah had revered and respected her master. And at thirty-seven her smooth complexion, clear brown eyes and shiny dark hair reflected his care and consideration. While her slender body belied the approach of middle age. The hardships of the era and ever-prevalent hot dry winds would take their toll on her complexion. But whatever, however nature aged her, strong in faith, and the love of a good provider, Sariah counted her blessings. And she would no more bow to fate than she would question tradition.

But now…? Now justified an exception.

Her decision did not immediately allow her to brave the entrance however. Standing on tiptoe, slim form bending around the corner post, she peered through the vine-woven lattice. Her heart skipped a beat. The shadowy room was empty.

She ran to the parapet, lifting the ivory shawl over head and shoulders like an umbrella against the steadily increasing rain. Her eyes darted. Still nobody coming up the lane. She hesitated, turned to go, turned back… and at last carefully descended the slippery stone steps.

Inside, all four sons watched quizzically as their mother entered the eating area. Without speaking she proceeded to set out the meal. Methodically she unwrapped the over-warmed bread, set out the goat cheese, dished the stew, and motioned them to the table. As she handed Laman the serving dish to pass around she ignored his questioning looks—which Lemuel, with his devil-may-care charm and wily smile could be counted on to verbalize.

"Today, our father dallied . . .?"

"And in the rain!" Laman rolled his eyes.

Sariah shivered at the gesture. "Your father," she said quietly, "would not want his sons to be hungry any longer."

As they dived to their bowls her heart warmed at the mischievous sideways look of her second eldest son—Lemuel's hazel eyes so likes Lehi's. He was also built like Lehi. Not tall, but strong, and well proportioned. There the resemblance ended however. Lemuel found it hard to be serious about anything; while her husband, she thought, was inclined to take things too seriously.

In that way, Sam favored his father. But Sariah most appreciated her third son's sensitivity. Now she felt his questioning eyes on her face; they had looked up from the bowl after his first bite. She smiled weakly, wishing she could answer the unspoken question for all of them.

"I will wait for your father."

Sariah arose from the table and retired to another part of the house. Soon after, the rain stopped and the good wife again took up her watch on the roof.

At long last, in the cooled quiet of dusk, she heard voices at the gate.

Lehi! And that sounds like Ishmael. A puzzled frown possessed the woman's face. How had she not seen them come up the lane? And Ishmael was already leaving. She heard him saying, " . . . we'll talk of it tomorrow."

From her vantagepoint above Sariah clearly saw her approaching husband turn off the main path. He was coming to the roof. She waited at the top of the steps, on one foot, and then the other; it seemed an eternity until Lehi appeared around back. She stood silently, holding her breath as she watched him laboriously climb the steps. But at the top, without hesitation, he shuffled quickly toward the alcove.

One glimpse of her husband's illuminated face and Sariah had backed into the shadows—all the way to the parapet. She clung to it as if on a ship about to be swept overboard.

Incredulous that he hadn't seen her. Had she not stood plain before him?

Upon regaining her composure Sariah rationalized. Lehi had not mentally seen her. Even in the deepening dusk she could tell that he was not himself. So, like the best of helpmates that she was, the woman prepared to do her duty—to be available when her husband needed her. Out of sight but within hearing of his voice she would wait, all night if necessary.

In the first faint light of dawn Lehi called her name. She jumped; she must go quickly, but cold and cramped, she could hardly move. For countless hours she'd watched the stars and worried in agony, physical as well as mental. Now her body protested; but the sound of her husband's voice had buoyed her spirit. In the next instant she was at his side, all discomforts forgotten. The glow on his face confirmed that the temporary neglect had indeed been beyond his control.

"Sari, oh Sari, forgive me," Lehi cried.

So great was his joy in seeing her, his voice broke. He reached up for her. Sariah knelt down and held him.

"Lehi, Lehi, my husband." Nothing more; words were unnecessary. The heart in his voice had adequately conveyed his regret for causing her worry. Blinking back a tear of relief she waited expectantly.

After a short time of silence, and closeness, God's newly chosen messenger rose up and began to share….

"Oh Sari, The Lord God has spoken to me! He hath shown me many great and marvelous things. …"

Under a woman's tender touch, mortal man again, Lehi seemed almost his old self—but buoyed to the heights with enthusiasm. That spurt of strength, however, was temporary. More time would be required for coordinating revelation and reality. After the high of telling her, now devoid of anxiety for her feelings, Lehi closed his eyes, and slumped back down. Closing her out again.

In the stillness that followed there was no awkward silence. Sariah recognized the power of communication from heaven, and with this overwhelming knowledge needed no further words. Gently, she eased the comatose form of her loved one out of the confining still wet robe and began massaging the ridges it had grooved into his shoulders. She made her man as physically comfortable as possible. Then covering him with the tapestry she brought to the roof to cover herself, she sat back to await his strengthening by natural sleep.

Soon Lehi would return to normalcy. But for some time after, as Sariah expected, he would often have lapses. Sometime he would lie in reverie, like a child that was no longer sick but wanted to be.

Sariah wondered how else his revelation would change him, how it would change the lives of his family. She couldn't imagine the future. But for now she had done her part, and felt privileged to do so. As she sat there beside her sleeping husband his confession replayed in her tired mind like a silent interrogation. She ached to understand the full meaning of the message that had mysteriously transformed him. But it seemed that he would offer nothing further.

Repressing the long hard sigh that arose within her she finally closed her eyes, dropped her head, and dozed.

She felt a hand closing over hers. The familiar gray eyes were anchored on her face. Lehi looked like himself again. And Sariah knew he would now tell all.

Starting with the pillar of fire Lehi told his beloved companion everything about the two visions. And his soul rejoiced at the sharing. He related *all the great and marvelous things that he had seen, yea, which the Lord had shown unto him.*

"And I saw . . ." He went on and on reporting in detail. He told her everything. And at the end his voice broke. "Oh dear Sariah, it is true. Jerusalem will be destroyed."

With that Lehi clamped his hands on his wife's slim shoulders and announced that he must now tell his sons—and go tell the people.

"Yes my husband," Sariah whispered.

She could hear the animals moving about below, reminding her that dawn was breaking upon a new and different life.... Of that she was sure. But would it be a better life? She feared not. As the first energetic rays of sun pierced the lattice, lancing Lehi's face like miniature swords afire, her heart beat staccato. The new prophet, his mind soaring beyond mundane surroundings, did not even notice. And despite his announcement, he made no attempt to move.

The woman, however, could not but think of the mundane. Inherently conscious of her duties, Sariah would not neglect them. Her sons must now be awake and expecting their breakfast. Their appetites had not been shaken out of them with the knowing that had taken hers. Though she had not eaten before she *knew,* now she thought of food only in accordance with preparing it for others.

With another long look at her husband she arose, kissed his cheek, and slipped from his sanctuary.

Moving swiftly down the stone steps she reeled, and almost fell. It barely distracted her thinking. She must not only prepare food, but also prepare her sons for what their father would tell them. When, or if, he would come down to eat she didn't know, but she must prepare for him.

Then again it would be her lot to wait.

CHAPTER IV

Before entering the central cooking/eating area Sariah stopped at the pitcher stand. She poured water into the clay bowl and splashed her face, then quickly let down, brushed, and rewound her long brown hair. From there she moved mechanically, kindling a fire, wrapping bread to warm on the heating stones, preparing the gruel.

It wasn't necessary to decide what to serve. The meal that broke the fast was always the same: bowls of steaming gruel, milk, yesterday's bread (warmed), honey, and figs or grapes. When all was on the table she called her sons.

They entered warily. Having seen their mother descend from the roof they now knew that their father was home. And Sariah saw in their faces that they had been discussing the unusual situation.

"Mother?" Laman demanded, as if censoring her for not satisfying his curiosity.

Sariah did not acknowledge him. She stood at the end of the table while her sons noisily seated themselves on the side benches. Laman and Lemuel on the right, Sam and Nephi on the left, of the "head" place—the empty place.

Four pair of eyes stared at the unoccupied chair. Then they stared at their mother. The youngest dared to break the silence.

"Please mother," Nephi began, "if our father is so greatly troubled, inasmuch that he does not eat two meals, nor leave his sanctuary, wilt thou not tell us?"

Sariah tried to smile.

"My dear sons, your father..." she hesitated. And as she groped for the right words, lost her breath. Lehi had appeared at the doorway. Without speaking he shuffled through the tensioned atmosphere and ceremoniously seated himself in the vacant chair. Then clearing his throat he anchored his eyes on his helpmate, entreating assistance.

Face alight Sariah finished her sentence.

"Your father ... is feeling stronger this morning."

Lehi looked fondly at his wife. His face radiated. The deep-set eyes glinted like molten steel. But Laman saw only that they were bloodshot. Lemuel noted that that his father had not attended to his grooming—tangled beard, hair askew, clothes all wrinkled... Sam was studying his father's overly serious countenance with concern. While young Nephi appeared to be hypnotized.

Silence. From the head of the laden table it seemed to be commanded, as the patriarch studied the young faces, each in turn. When he caught the esoteric glint in the gold-flecked eyes of his youngest, the one with the great desire to understand, his heart swelled.

"Father r r ..." The whiny voice of the eldest. Daring a dagger look, jerking back the ever-unruly strand of hair, Laman unhesitatingly voiced his impatience.

"... say the blessing—we're hungry. We have waited, and waited, for . . ."

"We'll be late ..." Lemuel echoed.

The old man's face contorted, the piercing eyes again commanding silence. But in the next instant he dropped his shaggy head.

"Lord God forgive this firstborn son who has become a thorn in my side." His voice quavered. "Forgive the young; and grant strength to the old. Give thy servant the words to speak plainly that my family and friends, and all to whom I shall speak Thy words will understand. Oh dear God, help me to make them understand."

The voice dwindled to a husky whisper. Lehi now had his sons' attention. But his eyes sought the ones brimming over with love and concern. Sariah's expression fortified him to continue. Yet he would study his sons further before enlightening them. Laman, the eldest, tall, slim, fine-boned like his mother; but so unlike her in other ways. Mischievous Lemuel built square like him. Sam, the quiet, compassionate one. And Nephi, the youngest, a sensitive juvenile still pure and innocent, whose eyes were glinting as if he *knew.*

The father's face suddenly softened. Noting the spoons suspended over the bowls of porridge he raised his hand and blessed the food instead—that the hunger gnawing at young bodies might be gratified. It was understandable that as yet, young souls hungered less.

So the meal was consumed, Sariah, like Lehi, making a pretense of eating, while their progeny, bent to their bowls, each mentally worked on the mystery in his own way. When Lehi lay down his linen napkin and pushed back from the table they all looked up expectantly. Without waiting Nephi ventured a mundane question.

"Father, wilt thou go to the fields today?"

"Art thou well enough?" Sam wanted to know.

Laman and Lemuel, shooting sideways glances at each other, simultaneously stood up and bolted for the door. The action jolted their father back to his everyday problems. Some time ago Lehi had released his sons from the formality of being excused from the table. This day, however, he had expected ... He spun around and shouted an order.

"Go directly to the field."

"Yeah, yeah." And the elder sons were gone.

Lehi turned slowly back to the table and dropped his head in his hands. Sariah got up, patted his shoulder, and prepared to scour the pots. Nephi rose and moved toward Laman's place, on the right of his father. Sam slid closer on the left.

"Shall we go to the fields, father?"

"No, my son, not yet. Sit down Nephi."

Motioning his youngest to the empty bench he smiled at each of them in turn, then reached out and put his hands on their shoulders.

"Laman and Lemuel have forfeited the positions and the privileges of the elder sons, so I give them to the younger. Now you shall be the first to know that The Lord hath spoken to me. And I will tell you all."

Thus, Lehi gave his two younger sons a full account of his visions—all that God had revealed to him and what he had been commanded to do. And then for nearly an hour he answered their questions, as best he could. Sam and Nephi left inspired. By the time they reached the field the sun already burned hot on their backs; but they worked even harder than in the cool of morning. The unbelievers, who arrived earlier, did less. And less and less thereafter.

Laman and Lemuel not only did not believe but also resented the additional responsibilities that fell to them (since from that day their father did not work in the fields). Having missed the penetrating morning-after telling, the radiance of face and ring of voice that secured the hearts of Sam and Nephi, the elder sons were not convinced. It seemed inconceivable to them that their father had received visions. The younger two had no doubts. Nephi believed as a child. Sam gave full credence to the report because he trusted his father always told the truth. Both were secretly proud that he had been given a mission to speak for God. But they also hurt for him. anticipating that the suffering of "the chosen" would come upon him. They little imagined, however, the weight of the burden to come upon his family.

The sons not only had to work harder but were also sorely inconvenienced, and often embarrassed. Sariah worried about the future: Lehi, constantly in danger, the younger sons full of questions which could not yet be answered, Laman and Lemuel, harboring resentment … The mother saw her family being torn apart.

And instead of abating with time the problems and conflicts multiplied.

One hot day Laman's smoldering irritably exploded. Nearly an hour before quitting time he flopped down, mashing the stalks of barley he should have been cutting, and shouted to all that would listen.

"I'm sick, sick, sick and tired of our father's slacking. Fanatic old goat, all he ever does is pray."

Lemuel flung aside his scythe and sat down beside him. "Yea, what *does* father do all day, besides pray?"

Sam and Nephi continued working. They said nothing when their brothers put away their scythes in the field lean-to and took off for the city.

But Sam shouted after them. "He prays at night; he talks to people all day."

"And makes people mad all day," Laman retorted, without turning around.

Sam shrugged and said no more. He knew it was useless trying to convince his older brothers. He'd tried many times to tell them how earnestly their father labored in his mission for The Lord.

Nephi watched them go thinking of how seldom he saw his father these days. He missed being with him. And it troubled his young heart that a servant of The Lord must suffer hostility even from his own family.

"Oh God," he mumbled, "Thou hast called him. He is serving faithfully. Why dost thou allow it?"

The tender youth having not yet discerned the documented fact that God's messengers *always* suffer the anger of unbelievers, it seemed that his father was being unfairly punished. A hand on his arm interrupted the weighty thought. Sam tightened his grip, smiling, and nodded in the direction that Laman and Lemuel were hurrying. They hadn't turned toward the city as expected. The rebels were heading home. *This night, they might eat early!*

And when the four sons arrived early, almost together, their mother who had worried all day thought her cup runneth over. That morning, seeing the wire-like lines of suffering gouging her husband's face, the sag of his square shoulders, she had protested his going out. When Lehi arose from the breakfast table, nourished, and mentally armed, but ready in heart only, she had rushed to his side entreating.

"My dear husband thou art weary. Do not go out this day. God would not begrudge you this one day of rest."

His glance had been tender but fleeting, his voice warm but stern. "I must, good woman, thou knowest. For there is little time." And donning robe over tunic, the newly called prophet again girded up his loins preparing for the elements, and whatever the day would bring … wherever The Lord would lead him.

Watching him go Sariah tried to put down an inherent feeling of foreboding. She knew that her husband often trembled, facing his unknown tasks with untried abilities; but also, that feeling the invisible mantle upon his shoulders, he was ever determined. So she could only pray that God would give him strength for the day—and bring him back safely at night. Hopefully by dusk. Never did she expect to see him until almost dark. This day however he had surprised her. He came home early—and already had concluded his prayer and meditation time. She could hear him coming to her. Sariah thrilled at the sound of his sandals on the stairs. Then she saw her sons approaching, all four of them. Joy welled up within her.

The Lord God of Israel has blessed this day.

She served supper to her family with a lilt in her heart. When she sat down with them, and Lehi had asked God's blessing on what she prepared, her full warm smile circled the table.

"It is so good that . . ."

Crack!

A stone thrown through the open shutter broke the clay pot of porridge on the table. Nephi jumped up and ran to the window, just in time to see two scampering youths dive behind the gooseberry bushes. One he recognized. It was Josiah, son of Amos, a close neighbor.

"That's Josh!"

Lehi groaned, and staring at the oozing mess that Sariah was already attempting to contain, slowly shook his head back and forth.

"Oh Sari, I talked with Amos today. And I feared I made him angry; but I tried… I was trying …"

Laman's icy blue eyes sparked. The antagonistic son had come home early for a reason: to make a good impression and hopefully counter a reprimand he expected to receive for a guilty indiscretion that morning. But by this turn of events he may have been saved; his father might forget it. Laman could not resist stirring the fire.

"Yea," he quickly injected, "Our father makes people angry at all of us. Yesterday he called Jesse's father a sinner; and Jesse was so mad he wanted to fight." He turned to Lemuel for collaboration.

"Aye," Lemuel said," Jesse wouldn't come to the baths with us."

Lehi did not respond. Staring into the heaped pewter plate he lay his bread down beside it without taking the bite his stomach anticipated. He had no words to answer his sons' complaints. For perhaps they were justified. Because he spoke the words that God commanded he had trusted God to protect his family. The good man had clung to his faith in that trust. Now he faced the realization that help may not be forthcoming, not even protection from the pain of losing friends.

And that, he rationalized, must be the fault of the deliverer—the result of error in the delivery of God's message—his error.

In zealous obedience to his Maker Lehi had not always taken time for tact. Heated discourses often followed his "dictated" declarations, sometimes erupting into shouting matches, even blows. And each time it happened failure tore at his insides. He would rush in anguish to a solitary place to ask God's forgiveness.

Now at the supper table he prayed in the same manner before his family.

"Oh Lord God of Israel forgive thy unworthy servant. Help me to do thy will without causing further turmoil. Give me the right words. Show me the way…"

His pain-filled eyes anchored on the face of his beloved.

"Sari, oh Sari, most of my friends (and now Amos, I'm sure) will not talk to me any more. Few of them will even listen. I am failing, I am failing The Lord. Oh why hath He chosen one so unprepared and unworthy.?"

Earlier that day another friend and former supporter had hurt him personally. Bearing the humiliation like a leg of mutton tied to his neck, he had dragged home early, looking neither left nor right, lest he see someone who didn't want to see him. And he had quietly slipped up the back stairs to his sanctuary, to compose himself before seeing Sariah—having vowed not to burden her with another negative report.

Now, rocks as well as insults being thrown, her savory supper ruined, and his sons frightened …

Lehi eyed the oozing porridge as if it mirrored his abject failure. Except for the chattering birds outside the window, dead silence. The one responsible for the situation took a while to make a decision; and in the interim no one said anything.

When finally he spoke, again, it was to his wife only. And he talked as if his sons were not present.

"I grieve that my sons have witnessed their father's humiliation, that because of my blunders they too lose friends. Now we are all in danger. And, my dear wife, I have added to your burdens. Forgive ..."

"I have no burdens, my husband," Sariah said quietly.

Although her fine-boned face did not reveal her fear the incident had heightened her creeping terror that animosity was spreading beyond control. Lehi, in his fervent desire to do God's will, had unconsciously ignited a city of sifted chaff unto a dangerous fire. And even he did not know how dangerous.

But Sariah knew the good man felt compelled to right the situation for which he was responsible. She could read his thoughts across the table—that he *must* find a way to serve God without endangering his loved ones...

Finally he said, "I would not that my family should suffer because of me. I go to pray for guidance." And grabbing for his slipped dignity the father rose sedately from the table. Looking fondly at his sons, he added, "Other lives should not be burdened by my ineptitude and mistakes."

While climbing the stairs to the roof Lehi was thinking of the prophets of old who were cast out, stoned, slain by the people they tried to warn. *Should he go by the way of them, what would happen to his family?*

After a night of prayer however, he also remembered the tender mercies of the Lord over all those whom he hath chosen.

"*Blessed are they that serve the Lord.*"

Lehi repeated this to himself over and over. And thereafter, sensing more strongly that The Lord was with him, he began growing in confidence. There were fewer incidents. After one of his better days, upon reaching the sanctity of home, he paused at the gate to breathe a prayer of thanks. But when he raised his arm to unlatch it he was grabbed from behind, his arms were jerked back... Three men bound him with a rough hemp rope, then kicked his feet from under him.

Flat on his back Lehi frantically searched the twisted angry faces above him.

"No, no, please!" he shrieked.

Eyes averted, they ducked their heads, but not before he recognized them.

"Oh, dear God, wha . . ." One shoved a rag in his mouth. He was jerked up again, then dropped with a thud. Everything blurred. Excruciating pain. A red-blood geyser shot up from behind his left ear. He had hit his head on a stone.

"Look. I think we killed him!"

"No!"

The fellow landowners he used to call friends clutched at each other, their temporary masks of hate crumpling like cold ashes. Warily they looked toward the house, searched the lane, then frantically shook their victim.

"Lehi, Lehi, can you hear…?"

Lehi could not hear. They shook him, and shook him, and were attempting to lift him up to carry him someplace … any place to hide the body, when they heard running footsteps.

"C'mon, his sons are coming."

This time grown men dived for the bushes. When Sam and Nephi arrived on the scene they had disappeared.

"Mother!"

Nephi's shrill call brought Sariah instantly out the door. At the sight of her sons dragging her husband's unconscious form she swayed. She clung to the torch post waiting. From a further distance down the lane Laman and Lemuel (lagging) had witnessed the last of the struggle, and their brothers running to their father's rescue. They rushed to assist. All four of Sariah's sons carried her husband's lifeless form into the house.

"Lay him here, right here on the hearth." Sariah said huskily. "And put that cushion under his head. Gently!"

"Lehi, Lehi, can you hear me?"

As she poured water into a basin Sariah kept saying his name.

"Lehi, Lehi, oh Lehi." Clutching the pewter pitcher as if it had strength to sustain her, dipped cloth in hand, she hovered over the blood-splattered face afraid to trust herself to touch it.

"Oh my husband the slightest touch will hurt—but oh, you can't even feel it."

Her puzzled angry offspring, finally recovering from shock, all began talking at once.

"Who were those men?" cried Nephi.

"They just dropped him and ran," said Sam.

"They had murder in their hearts," Lemuel rasped. "They wanted to kill him."

Laman said nothing, his face a map of contradictions, as if he couldn't decide on which to express.

Sariah stopped the bleeding; but she continued bathing the bruised face, whispering repeatedly, "Oh my husband, my husband, open your eyes."

CHAPTER V

Lehi finally opened his eyes, and his head healed, but not his heart. In just a few days he returned to the streets, determined that he would find a way to fulfill the mission given him. He decided that it was not to be accomplished by expounding. Nor would he preach from the marketplace platform like the others who felt a calling. Lehi continued cornering small audiences, demanding full attention of a few at a time, but curbing his zeal. He tried to censure his fervor, replace it with tact, and curb his impatience. In this way, few by few, working tirelessly he would do what was commanded of him—to warn the people of the imminent destruction of Jerusalem. And he would succeed. He must succeed.

For God had spoken. God had spoken.

But few believed that God had spoken to Lehi, a common man, a neighbor of no particular credentials. And so gradually he began to speak more of his visions. "*...he began to prophesy and to declare unto them concerning the things which he had seen and heard.*" Now, as he talked of wickedness and abominations, he testified of the coming of a Messiah ... while repeating the warning. "Repent. Repent, or Jerusalem will be destroyed."

Such a hard thing God had asked of him, condemning friends and peers. And one after another they continued to turn against him.

"Is Lehi suddenly holy, completely without sin? Let him without sin… And now he's claiming to be a prophet?"

With this taunting from one he had known and studied with for years, the long repressed anger burning within surged out of control. Tact out the window. Lehi grabbed his denouncer and shook him.

When Laban, leader of The Elders, heard of the incident he felt compelled to counsel his kinsman.

"Lehi, hast thou lost all dignity?"

Sore in the spirit for another failure Lehi could not answer. He fled mid day to his alcove for prayer and meditation. Even kindred was against him now. And if Laban deemed him unworthy of association, then all those he had expected to work with him would follow. All but Ishmael, he thought, he hoped. Next morning he rushed to his best friend for assurance, and comfort.

He received neither. Ishmael added to his agony with news that Laban had already called a secret meeting of the elders to discuss him.

"My friend, try to understand. They were not only angry but embarrassed for thy lack of dignity. And, I'm sorry Lehi…but …" His voice broke.

Lehi looked up warily. Previously he'd always reclined on Ishmael's couch in comfort. Not this day. Suffering these menacing words from his best friend, was like wearing a hair shirt. He couldn't squirm out of it.

Ishmael continued, "…I have to tell you, it was voted last night that your actions are not befitting an elder."

Lehi drew a quick breath. He waited for further explanation. Ishmael arose from the seat facing his visitor and went to sit beside him.

"Lehi thou knowest I stood against it; I argued for thee, but I lost. Hereafter thou art to be excluded."

"Oh no. I must go to them; I *must* convince them." He grabbed Ishmael's arm. "You must go with me. Help me convince them.

You *know* that I had a vision, that it is truly God's words… You could …"

"Lehi, Lehi, contain thyself. Surely I do not doubt that God spoke to thee. But because thou art radical, yea, oftentimes offensive, their minds are set against thee, clamped shut—even with bands of iron."

Lehi dropped his head in his hands.

"But remember," Ishmael added, "The Lord can open minds. Dost thou not know that? Where is thy faith? We must believe The Lord will speak to their hearts. Let us wait upon the Lord."

At this Lehi calmed down, and sat quietly staring into space. Ishmael continued trying to comfort him with a vote of confidence.

"My friend, thou knowest The Lord better than I, and thou art blessed with wisdom, so how dost thou forget these things? You must believe God is with you, but He works in strange ways. Perhaps there is a plan."

Lehi nodded and leaned back on the straw padded couch. The aroma of barley broth and freshly baked bread wafting in from Anna's cooking area permeated the room. He looked up at Ishmael amiably, and tried to relax. He hadn't relaxed for a long time.

Looking at his friend Ishmael felt a constriction in his throat, remembering the day he found this troubled man lying in the rain. And the morning after, when he pulled back his window tapestry to see the one to whom God had spoken standing in shining confidence upon the stones of his entrance way—ready to tell him about it. Since then, the best friend of the "chosen" one had been expecting a personal, spiritual uplifting. Ishmael assumed he would be assigned a special role of support, if no other. But there had been no indication. From the time Lehi related his vision there had been no intimate, soul-stirring conversations between them. All this time, there had not been more sharing of confidences, but less.

And it seemed to Ishmael that Lehi's wisdom had not deepened and strengthened, but weakened. He never imagined that one of so great a faith would turn radical and negative. Traditionally, those blessed with visions preached holy expressions of love and peace. Lehi preached angry predictions of doom.

Ishmael spun around to face his visitor, and the words came out sharply. "Why Lehi, why dost thou continually unleash the dogs of doom?"

"Oh Ishmael have I not, lo these many times, told thee? It is to speak dire warnings that I am commanded."

The anguish in his friend's voice, the sadness in his face… Ishmael at last accepted the fact that Lehi had no choice. He had been distinctly commanded to chastise and condemn. That was his mission—the mission with which God had burdened him. A friend must offer sympathy, not criticism.

"Father?"

One of Ishmael's daughters peeking into the room wanted permission to enter. He managed a smile for her.

"Ruth, dear daughter, bring some herb tea for our visitor."

Then turning back to Lehi, "My friend, forgive me. I know of a surety that thou dost live and breathe The Lord's word; and I believe with certainty that God hath commanded thee. But do not forsake thy own wisdom in understanding people. Don't you know they cannot see clearly when they are angry?"

"But there is a reason for the pressure," Lehi cried. "There isn't time. For generations they've been blind. God hath many times spoken these things. Now time runneth out."

Fourteen-year-old Ruth returned with the tea and timidly handed Lehi a cup. Unconsciously twisting a strand of her long bronze hair she tarried beside him.

She seems to like this old man, Lehi mused.

Or was it one of his sons she liked?

Lehi had long been aware that Ishmael favorably considered his sons as future husbands for his daughters. He too had entertained the idea, for there would be no restriction. The two families were not "near" kin. And dowry was no problem. With the help of only two male offspring Ishmael had become prosperous. He'd never felt cheated because God sent him mostly daughters. Dutiful, attractive daughters were a blessing in disguise. Finding rich husbands for them would not be difficult. But finding good husbands? That gave the father some concern; and soon he must think seriously about the situation. He looked fondly at his young daughter.

Ruth gave Lehi another shy smile and retreated.

The visitor finished his tea. As he shook hands with the host a smile seemed about to break through. Despite the disheartening news given him upon arrival Lehi felt better than he had for some time. Fortified with tea and friendship, mellowed, he walked home mentally reviewing his friend's advice. As God's messenger he could not but speak the message intensely, however he could change his tactics. He decided to sometimes take the platform, and try a little showmanship copied from the polished speakers.

Thus the autumn of Lehi's frustration passed into a more comfortable winter. In the hot dry country of Palestine winter was welcomed. In the cooler weather he felt better physically. He found a few listeners, and some returned, boosting his confidence. Then came the day Ishmael had good news to report—possible reconsideration by the elders.

The following morning, in a surge of new faith, Lehi announced to his wife, "I go to Laban today. I think he will see me now."

"God go with you," Sariah whispered. But not since the day she prayed for her husband's return to consciousness had the good woman felt such apprehension. She thought Lehi's kinsman deceitful, had never considered him worthy of his position as leader of the faithful. And in addition to her distrust of Laban, she did not, could not, understand why God didn't open the eyes of the other elders. Why would He harden the hearts of those who professed to do His work, men of more worth, she thought, than the only living brother of Lehi's father. Sariah didn't imagine that sometimes Laban sought righteousness. She didn't suspect that he had prayed about the matter. But she did know it would be quite a leap from his primary concern. Mostly Laban worried about his position, and his reputation. Notwithstanding, when he excluded Lehi from the round-table meetings of the elders, the man had felt a tug of conscience. Still, not to be censured by those of lesser authority (who followed him like lambs) Laban had avoided his kinsman in public. Would he avoid him at home?

Sariah's heart told her that he would.

During the long walk across the city in the cool of morning, Lehi's flashback memory of Laban's character, and replay of recent humiliations, had somewhat unnerved him. His apprehension began returning. Upon approaching the impressive property, gained by stealth from others, he slowed. Flashed back a scene of his kinsman exploding on some of his followers…

For some time Lehi leaned against the intricately carved gatepost eyeing the house. And while ascending the path to the formidable door he began to sweat. He took the last few steps slower. Then over the twitter of sparrows conversing in the cedars that flagged the entrance he caught the sound of footsteps on the stone floor inside. The giveaway sound meant that he hadn't walked all the way in vein. He straightened up tall. At least the master of the house was there. A servant would not be in the front part of the house unless serving him. On the other hand, a servant would not open the door unless ordered.

Steeling himself against the negative possibility Lehi lifted the knocker.

He lifted it many times; but no servant admitted him. Lehi gave his kinsman the benefit of the doubt. Maybe Laban thought it best to avoid a confrontation. After all, could he (the offender) be trusted not to be argumentative? Probably not. Lehi could imagine Laban's side of it.

Yes, it might be easier for both to just let things slide.

It was only easier for Laban. With heavy heart and tired limbs Lehi retraced those many steps back across the city, bearing yet another heavy yoke of disappointment. Shuffling along deep in thought, looking neither left nor right (as had become his practice) made him easy game for two ruffians he had once attacked with angry words. Jumping him from behind they dragged him into a deserted stall and threw him down in the muck. Sneering faces, profanity, iron-like knuckles... and one on each side kicking him into a heap of pain. They ran away laughing.

No blood shed (no blood showing), so Lehi brushed the dried manure off his clothes, and did not tell his wife of the incident. Of his visit to the big house he said only that Laban was not at home. But reading his countenance Sariah didn't need details. She quickly pulled her shawl over her face, lest he read the map of sadness there. Her dear one had suffered another humiliation. And it had been months since he'd enjoyed the comradeship of his peers.

After the king tore Jeremiah's book of sermons to shreds the group had grown close. Taking it upon themselves to save the newly dictated sermons, and to insure the sacred writings of their people would be preserved for eternity, they were bound together by their faith, and the secrecy of the project. These devout determined men, working tirelessly, also translated and transferred all the ancient accounts on papyrus scrolls to brass plates. And once, after much discussion, they had voted another record worthy of being added.

So Lehi was adamant that his record be included. He had faithfully recorded the vision, the commandment given him, and the guidance he received by prayer. It was God's work that he'd been doing, God's words that he spoke. Therefore it must be included in the sacred history... His peers, and former friends, did not agree.

Sariah knew all this—just as she knew her husband would not give up trying, just as she knew their lives would remain in turmoil, just as she knew Laman and Lemuel would keep complaining. But somehow she must maintain faith. It mattered not that her friend Leah had begun avoiding her. Or that Miriam made excuses not to go to the market with her. She could weather these personal wounds; they were much less painful than her husband's. Whatever happened she would prevail.

But Lehi's helpmate couldn't imagine that a young, silver-tongued non-radical soon to appear in the holy city would be instrumental in bringing even more devastating changes in their lives.

Abler of Alexandria, master of rhetoric, manipulator of crowds, arrived just a week later. This professional crowd pleaser didn't prepare his articulate speeches for the rubble of the marketplace; he preached in the court of the temple. As paid runners had announced, he was an educated orator. With his expensive linen robes and neatly trimmed beard the high class Abler would draw the pious rich and the well connected—those who would not lower themselves to accommodate the marketplace regulars. Considering the seedy old prophets and local radicals not worthy of their time, it was their practice to send servants to listen and bring back a vocal report. But they flocked in person to hear Abler of Alexandria. And they hung on his every sugary word. Lehi among them,,

Although he felt guilty neglecting God's work to listen, knowing that the man spoke not for the good of the people, still Lehi would go to the temple court. For that's where most of the people were. Obviously, the handsome smiling Abner had studied and learned the tricks of the trade for his own gain and glory. The cultured compelling voice bewitched the listeners with what they wanted to hear. While the following band of sellers gathered on the outer edge of the crowd to enticed them with exciting wares. Everybody being charmed, one way or another. And the throng swelled day by day.

Nobody to speak to elsewhere Lehi continued listening to the opposition, but ever bristling at what he heard—until the day he reached the point of saturation.

"Good people, think," the silky voice entreated. "How many years have you been hearing threats and dire predictions? Yet your temple still stands, does it not? There will always be wars; there have always been wars . . ."

The man is inferring that the holy prophets deliberately try to frighten the people, to intimidate them into submission, that they not depart from the old ways.

"But good people, there is no sin in progress. You are not sinners because you do things differently than your forefathers. You have nothing to worry about."

Lehi's fists clenched. He ached to shake them in the face of the slick foreigner. He could hardly contain himself from shouting that they *did* have to worry, for the prophets' warnings were from God.

But who would hear him?

Frantically he searched the packed crowd, hoping to see a friend. He saw two former friends, Amos, and Matthew, entranced like the others, being reeled in by silken cords.

How could they not believe the wayward people's chances were running out? Since the time of Isaiah God's prophets had been warning the people, giving them another chance, and another, and another. How could they not doubt what this man was saying?

Overwhelmed with emotion Lehi exploded into action. Tearing his way through the pack, zeroing in on the enemy, he shouted.

"No, no! Do not listen to this man." He was only smirked at, or ignored.

Then all of a sudden flames of compassion welled up for the weak-of-faith listeners. Was it any wonder they listened to this man instead of him? While he flailed at them with ineffective nagging and irritating predictions, the charming Abner dispensed pretty-picture promises in silky language.

But Lehi's flash of wisdom came too late. At his "no, no" interruption the admired speaker had stopped mid-sentence, a frozen smile on his handsome face. And as if by a pre-arranged signal, myriad angry faces surrounded him; and a tight pack of sweaty bodies imprisoned him. Then fists to his stomach. The breath went out of him. He tried to defend himself with his staff. Someone wrenched it from him, and struck him with it.

"Fools!" he screamed, "The prophecies *will* come true. God has spo …"

Another fist in the stomach, then a blow on the head, and Lehi was down. The salt and pepper whiskers streaked red.

"Oh God forgive…" He groaned. Someone was clubbing his back.

"Stop, good people, stop." The mouth, temporarily frozen, slid into the practiced smile. The voice softened. "Let the man go. Are we not a civilized people? All the citizens of this great city must be allowed to voice their opinions."

The clubbing ceased. The menacing pack around him loosened, allowing him breathing space, and the inner circle spectators turned their attention back to the speaker. Lehi slowly, painfully, got to his feet. He righted his robe, and limped back through the throng. On the painful journey home his mind kept replaying the scene— not one person had showed compassion for the victim. And through this experience was manifest unto him the wickedness and hardness of hearts against which he had been commanded to testify.

At sundown Sariah found her husband sagged in the doorway half blind with pain. It shattered her composure—but did not entirely surprise her.

"Oh … oh, dear God of Israel, oh my husband, another attack. How much more? How much more?" The thought whirred in her head. *And he must have walked miles in this condition.*

Hardly enough strength to drag him inside Sariah could only eye the couch, and drop down beside him on the hard floor. Lehi lay comatose, eyes closed, barely breathing. Too weak from loss of blood and exertion to speak. And Sariah did not voice her fears. She cringed at the multiple wounds (more than before), and this time, his back). Was it broken? She felt the huge bump. Tears glistened on her lashes. For a long minute she just looked at him, went for a basin of water. As she tended to the bruises and gashes around his head her heart lightened a little. They were not serious. Nature would heal them in time. But the hard truth—that the herb poultice she would prepare for the camel-sized lump on his back would not be sufficient to its task—shook her.

When her sons came home, to hover over their father with concern and angry comments, Sariah retreated for a moment to regain her composure.

The patient, remaining behind closed lids listening to the young voices laced with concern, soon clamped them tighter—lest telltale drops of moisture escape. For the voice of his first born was missing. Laman did not ask his mother questions, as his brothers did. The father (mentally picturing the slim face with the familiar look of indifference) hurt as much for want of affection as from the wounds. In his vulnerable condition Laman's coldness was harder to bear than usual. So Lehi pretended sleep—until the pain lessened enough that he slipped into that blessed state naturally. He awoke early next morning, and while the others still slept, garnered enough strength to climb to his private place of prayer, where he remained all day.

And from that day forward all his days would be different. Nothing would ever be the same in the house of Lehi. For soon there would be no house.

But also there would be no more attacks. The Lord God spake again unto his servant Lehi in a dream. *"Blessed art thou Lehi ...because thou has been faithful and declared unto this people the things which I commanded thee ... they seek to take away thy life..."*

And it came to pass that God commanded Lehi that he should take his family and depart into the wilderness.

CHAPTER VI

Sariah handed the last package of dried fig cakes to Sam. He was helping her pack the food. She looked at him quizzically. "Where is Nephi?"

Sam ran a hand through his thick chestnut hair, slowly shaking his head. He looked at his father in the courtyard busying himself with the burros. Lehi did not hear Sariah's question. He was breathing heavily, concentrating on the problem. Sam too was reaching deep within for strength to face the mounting facts. It was sundown, almost time to leave, and Nephi had disappeared.

That his youngest son had disobeyed his orders the benevolent father found hard to believe. Mentally reviewing his own actions (what he had said and done after God's startling message) he'd been searching for the reason. The fault must be his.

Had he in his preoccupation with preparations somehow hurt the boy?

Ever obedient to the Lord, and fearing for the lives of his loved ones, as well as his own, Lehi had wasted no time in telling them of the commandment to leave Jerusalem, and depart into the wilderness. To their astonishment, the morning after the clubbing he had risen earlier than usual to tell them. And despite his condition, had been able to climb the stairs to his den. He spent the whole day in prayer, then re-appeared to command his household in complete control of his faculties. After the family conference, he gave each of his sons and Sariah specific jobs to do. Then he hurried to tell Ishmael and take care of business matters.

There would be no time to make out official papers at the city legal center, but Lehi trusted his friend implicitly.

"Thou may trust my word," Ishmael said. "I will oversee the selling of thy property exactly in the way you instruct me."

"No my friend, I *give* to thee my property," Lehi told him, "and also the authority to keep or sell my stock. We will take with us only beasts of burden, a few goats, and bare necessities."

"But surely, thou shalt return," Ishmael insisted, "when it's safe. A safer time will come…"

"If it be God's will. If it be His will."

Shaking his kinsman's hand after concluding the arrangements, Lehi found it hard to let go. For in his heart he felt it would be the last time.

Now, at twilight, sparse provisions and bare necessities loaded on the burros, gold, silver and jewelry in leather pouches (wrapped in burlap bags), ready to be buried, the time had come to leave.

And one of his sons was missing!

"Lemuel, come here."

Sharpened with worry and heavy responsibility, the father's voice rang out harsh. He put a gentler hand on his son's shoulder. And the pleading gray eyes belied the stern set of face.

"Lemuel, thou art quick and heedful. Go; run swiftly and find thy brother."

Laman, sulking in the stable, overheard, and rushed out. "I'll go with him."

"No. Only one …"

"I will," Laman retorted defiantly.

Lehi's face turned red. With wide-legged stance he planted himself before his sullen son like a cedar of Lebanon. But a lump arose in his throat. Well aware of their resentment for not having allowed them a farewell trip to city hangouts, or even to tell their friends, he had watched the two eldest all day. They had deliberately not done their fair share with the preparations. And he'd been expecting Laman, especially, to run off—but never Nephi.

The father's heart hurt for what he must do. His bent shoulders ached with responsibility. After forbidding any of his sons to go he quaked at the risk of sending one now. But the situation had become desperate. The sun was sinking, dusk creeping upon them—and God had commanded they leave at dusk.

"Lemuel, go!"

As Lemuel sprinted toward the gate Laman's icy blue eyes slitted. He threw his head, turned his back on his father, and glancing sideways at his mother and Sam retreated to the stable with swift exaggerated steps.

Sariah stood agape, her face a map of conflicting emotions. Then as if finally finding her voice she shouted after Lemuel. "Find thy brother; find thy brother. But do be watchful. Take care for thyself." Without acknowledging her husband's look she rushed back into the house.

Lehi cringed. That "something-must-have-happened-to-my-child" expression had hardened his wife's face. For a long minute he stood mute, as if trying to swallow his Adam's apple, Then slowly turned back to the loading.

Inside, Sariah clasped her hands to her breast and tried to slow her racing heart. She wiped her eyes with the edge of her shawl. Now two of her sons might be lost. They could not be back by sundown. She fell upon knees in supplication. But prayer didn't stop her mind from churning. A mother will forever worry for her children. Nephi's disappearance still baffled her. The son most recently receiving the spark of manhood was yet to be magnetized by women, nor did the excitement and sins of the city sparkle for him. Of all her sons Nephi was least likely to have gone. She couldn't imagine that he would leave without his father's permission. Sariah's slim shoulders shook. Something *must* have happened to him. Wrapping her arms around herself, she slumped to the chipped stone hearth, staring at the cold ashes. They seemed symbolic of her life.

"Oh, Nephi, Nephi."

As she repeated his name a flashing mental picture of glossy hair, finely chiseled nose, clear gray eyes with golden glints, stirred her mother-pride. Although the youngest he was already stronger than his brothers, and ahead of them in study of the scriptures, also the one who believed without doubt. They could not leave him.

God would not let his father leave him behind.

Sam watched his mother from the doorway. He heard her prayer, and a rare masculine tear slipped out. For he felt certain there would be no deviation from the plan; there could not be. The Lord had spoken. They must abandon their home and the land of their inheritance this very night, at the time of the evening meal when everyone would be indoors—as soon as the creeping dusk deepened.

Shaking off the thought, remembering there was one last thing to do, he hurried to the tree and began digging the hole. Under the old olive tree in the middle of the courtyard they would bury their most precious possessions. For a trek in the wilderness there'd be no need for valuables so they must not be burdened with carrying them. They were to carry only serviceable clothing and personal necessities in their individual packs. And on the beasts of burden: their food, tents, tools, and weapons (for hunting only). The Lord God would protect them.

Sariah stared after Sam as if she were about to lose him too. Frozen by the thought she jumped when one of the loaded burros bayed. And the unexpected interruption jolted her out of her reverie of self-pity. She gathered her skirts, and her ebbing strength, and walked outside.

Laman had come out of his pout. He'd joined his father and Sam in preparing to bury the valuables. This surprised her.

Unexpected cooperation from the rebel son, and her family working together lifted the mother's spirits. She calmed her breathing as she came up behind them. Concentrating on the job and talking together they didn't notice her. After a brief hesitation, she reached down and selected the smallest sack from the waiting pile beside Sam—the sack that contained her personal jewelry. Stealthily, she slipped her hand inside and withdrew a gold bracelet. Her hand shook. She dropped the "forbidden" back in the sack as if it had burned her.

"Leave thy gold and thy silver."

The etchings of nature on the woman's forehead deepened. She studied her husband's back. Then clutched up the bag again. As he appeared to turn she turned white. But no danger. Lehi gave complete concentration to the job at hand. None of them noticed her. Sariah dared to slip her hand into the bag again.

She retrieved another item (a smaller delicately carved ivory bracelet) and retreated to her empty kitchen, wrapping the purloined jewelry in a linen cloth, and concealing it in the folds of her mantle. Then for the third time the woman of the house mentally took inventory of her deserted furniture and familiar objects. Her eyes fell upon the four abandoned cooking pots hanging on pegs on the adobe wall. Of the set of six, each for a specific purpose, Lehi had allowed that she take only two. Her husband had said, "You *must* make do with two."

Impulsively she reached for another, and was wrapping it in burlap when Sam came back in.

Mother and son tip top, their eyes met on equal level. But clutching the pot as if it were her most valuable possession Sariah seemed the child. Without a word Sam took it from her, tied up the burlap package and went out with it. Her eyes followed him—and watched him put her pot in his personal pack. Only then did she breathe easily. Her husband had not seen. He was leading out the burros.

As Lehi busied himself, taking more time than necessary to re-check the packs on the animals, Sariah watched him. In the almost dark she found it difficult to read his face; but noting the determined stance she knew what he was about to say.

"We must go now."

"But, my husband…" Running to him, she put a would be restraining hand on his arm, her soft brown eyes pleading. The lines in Lehi's face softened. He patted his wife's shoulder.

"Dear Sari," he said quietly. "Thy sons know the place where we will spend this night. If the Lord wills, they will both be there before morning." His eyes were kind, but his voice weary. "Get thy pack."

Sariah obediently shuffled away and brought her pack from where she had concealed it. Lehi lifted it to her back and helped her tie the thongs. Sam and Laman retrieved their packs (and Lemuel's) from where they had hidden them. Nephi's pack was gone. Finally the leader strapped on his pack—a too heavy load for an injured back— and raised his arms. All heads bowed for the prayer of departure.

"Oh, Lord God of Israel go with us; and be thou with those not here. If it be thy will, bring the missing sons to us safely, that all my family may be together to serve thee, and keep this commandment thou has given…"

At the final syllable of Lehi's prayer Laman charged ahead. Sam led the tethered-together goats. Lehi led the burros. Sariah lagged behind, looking longingly back at the house, and worriedly down the lane. Those who sought to take her husband's life may have abducted her youngest son. And yet another was sent to risk his life. She let out a long sigh. Her heart felt as heavy as her pack.

Lehi's too. He knew that he lifted the latch on his garden gate for the last time. By commandment he would lead his fractured family stealthily, by short cut, to a secluded ravine outside the city walls, where they would spend the night. And once there he could do nothing but wait—and pray.

Seemingly ages later, safe in seclusion, the deep of night upon them, the sleepless father heard approaching footsteps.

He rushed out in the open without thinking. And relief broke out in a raspy whisper.

"Thank you Lord, thank you."

Silhouetted against the autumn moon were two figures. One tall, built like a gladiator, the other of average form, built like him. A weary man on shaky legs ran to meet his sons.

"My brother went to the house of Ishmael," Lemuel blurted out breathlessly. He brushed past his father to Laman, who was just exiting the hiding place. "And for no good reason," he slung back over his shoulder.

Nephi stopped before his father and bowed his head like a laborer expecting the whip. "Father, forgive, I, I . . ." He slowly shook his head. "We grew up with them, and I feared … I thought we might never see them again."

Sam and Sariah emerging from the hideout rushed forward, straining to hear what Nephi was saying—Sariah praying that her husband would not deal too harshly with the first offender. But her prayer was not needed. The verbal whip did not fall, nor did Lehi lift his staff to his son. He leaned on it. Head down, holding his robe about him, the father left the boy suffering in anticipation while his mind flashed back to his own youth. Recalling a similar transgression long ago, before *his* maturing. He understood the pull; and he shared the sentimentality. For what the youth said could be true. They might never see Ishmael and his family again.

Lehi looked up at his tall son with wet eyes. But he spoke gruffly, "Get thy pack, and come on; we must get out of sight."

The voice of command had spoken. The boy relaxed. He just stood there, shivering in his short tunic.

"And put on thy cloak."

"Yes, father."

As patriarch, Lehi would not drop the stance of authority, but he could not reprimand a youth for doing what he might have done. He had entreated the Lord to allow a visit with the family of Ishmael—to give Sariah time with Anna, and the children who had grown up together time to reminisce. That it had been denied was hard on all of them, and only the youngest had weakened. Surely the Lord would forgive… *The Lord will forgive.* Sighing with relief the leader followed his charges into the cave behind thick vegetation, confident that they would be safe temporarily.

Safe and ready to commence their journey, humble and thankful, everybody quieted for the night. All were reasonably comfortable. But sleep wouldn't come. Anticipating the suffering and sacrifices that would be required of his family, Lehi knew that sometimes they might sleep in their cloaks under God's sky. He hoped they would learn to sleep soundly anywhere. This first night, however …

At first light they quit trying—and were well on their way by sun up.

After another hour, coming upon a fitting place, Lehi allowed a stop for rest and nourishment. Back off the dusty path behind a boulder Sariah prepared her first meal in the wilderness. Initially, she brought forth her surprise treat of pomegranates. Then while her family rested and enjoyed the fruit she prepared the porridge, in the smuggled pot. Supper seemed long ago, so it took only minutes to consume the sparse meal. Growing boys waste no time filling their stomachs. And like most men Lehi ate what was set before him, giving no thought to the preparing.

But during the re-packing he was more observant. He noted that the burlap bag containing Sariah's cooking pots had not been removed. Yet they had porridge. Sariah turned in her husband's direction just in time to see realization spread over his face. She quickly surmised, and dropped her head.

But once again Lehi demanded no reckoning for a transgression. And when he didn't say anything about it Sariah understood. The dear man hurt for the hardships his family would be required to endure. He would not censure such a misdemeanor. Love lighted her face. But her husband had bowed his head. Remembering the sight of his wife seated like a Bedouin on the hard ground, cooking on a campfire… he was thanking his Maker for an uncomplaining woman. And after the evening meal, worries lessened by distance (and the fact that they had seen no one since the outskirts of Jerusalem) he went apart to formally thank God for bringing them out safely.

Although the majority of people in the city he loved had turned against him, Lehi kept in mind that The Lord was with him. As they traveled south through the rocky hills of Judah and the barren desert wilderness they saw only an occasional camel caravan at a distance. Their guided route skirted the few scattered villages. Circa 600 BC the cradle of civilization had not spread far south. In three days they were in complete isolation.

Ahead of them only barren wilderness as far as they could see.

CHAPTER VII

After three days of traveling in hot rough terrain Lehi and his family sighted a greening … bordering on a river—a river that emptied into the Red Sea.

Shouts of joy. Dirty, bone-weary, they all thanked God in unison.

Lehi stood in reverence taking in the view. His sons ran to the river and boisterously jumped into the water. His wife shed tears of relief. She washed her face and hands—but could not immediately treat her body to the luxury. Sariah had her duty. Her loved ones were hungry. The head of the family hesitated on the bank. Bearing the strain of responsibility and the pain of yet unhealed wounds, Lehi ached to join his sons. The soothing comfort of cool water would feel like heaven. But he wouldn't give in to personal desire until he had ceremoniously thanked his Maker.

No one would follow them this far, he reasoned. He *knew* they were safe. The Lord had saved him from persecution, and hereafter would protect him and his family. Heart swelling with gratitude, the humble prophet rested but a few minutes, then shouted to his sons.

"Come, my sons, first we must give thanks to God for bringing us out of danger unto this beautiful place. We have been exceedingly blessed. Let us build an altar and make an offering unto The Lord."

The dripping wet youths reluctantly crawled out of the river. They were famished; but protest was futile. And they knew they could not eat until their mother cooked. Thus, as usual, Laman and Lemuel lagged after their father, while Sam got water from the river for his mother's pot and Nephi gathered sticks for her fire. Then the younger two quickly caught up with their father and brothers.

Left alone, Sariah luxuriated, gazing at the green around her, and the river. At first sight of this verdant valley with it's sprinkling of rare trees, her countenance had brightened. After days of dry desert and hot rocky hills, coming upon a span of green had seemed like a dream. And now she feasted her eyes on flowing water….

She washed her hands again, for good measure, and dutifully began preparing the meal. Unwrapping the dusty food packs she thought of her clean kitchen and the convenience of a cistern in their own courtyard. More than anything else the fastidious woman missed the comfort of cleanliness

All of a sudden she rushed back to the river.

Only a few minutes later, refreshed and invigorated, she pulled clean clothes on her still wet body. The balmy air would dry her. A warm feeling of thankfulness washed over her like a second bath. Yet the city wife of a man of means still felt a tug for the missing… She longed for the feel of fine linen. Excepting her best blue mantle, the wardrobe pack she must hereafter choose from contained only old, sturdy garments, No finery—or jewelry. She dropped her head.

Later that night, her family all deep in sleep from weariness, Sariah again immersed herself in the purifying water. She succeeded in washing away all the grit, but not the guilt. Lying beside her companion in their tent she looked over at him, and suffered the memory of her deceit. As she would many nights thereafter. In the long days to follow Sariah would often slip a sunburned hand through the folds of her inner garments to touch the culprit of her torment—the intricately carved bracelet that she wished wasn't there.

Her tumbling thoughts zeroed in on the future. *What would it bring? What exactly was her husband's mission now? What kind of life could she expect for her sons? Isolated from civilization how could they reach fulfillment, raise a family, reach their destiny?*

Sleep continued to evade her. She rose up and looked out the open tent flap across the ashes of the dying campfire to the still forms of her sons. They had chosen to sleep upon the coveted green of nature instead of in their tents. And they seemed to be sleeping as soundly as their father. The mother would do the worrying for the whole family, and additionally, for the children not with her. For the hundredth time Sariah wondered what the two infants she lost would have been like. Lehi had fathered six sons, but two she had failed to give him. However, she never forgot to thank God for the four uncomplicated births, and for the greatest of blessings—that all four sons were healthy.

As she looked upon them now in sound sleep she also felt a tinge of pride that they were not afraid. But perhaps they should have been. She shuddered, remembering that before they left the city it had become no less dangerous for those of Lehi's blood, than for him. She turned and looked again upon the face of her sleeping husband, who had been given such a heavy burden, and whispered a prayer.

"Lord God I thank thee for the love and protection of this man that thou hast made a prophet. Make me a worthy helpmate. Give me strength for future adversities. Help me support him in the mission which thou has given him."

After his bath in the river, relaxed for the first time since leaving Jerusalem, Lehi had instantly fallen asleep. This verdant campsite on a riverbank had lightened his heart, and also his responsibility. Water enough for everything, and pure enough to drink. The river also offered reeds from which to weave sleeping mats. It contained food, fish and otter… And after counting all these blessings, Lehi thought of another: rest. He sensed they would tarry long in this place..

In the morning, awakening to a familiar odor, he smiled at his wife. Sariah had built a fire, and improvised a steamer to warm the bread. Upon a makeshift reed cover, over the largest pot filled with steaming water, two flat loaves scenting the air.

"My good woman I did not even hear thee leave the bed." He looked at her fondly. "God has blessed me in so many ways… besides leading us to safety." Sariah smiled over her shoulder. "Thy morning meal is soon ready,"

She glanced beyond the fire to where her tousled sons lay watching her, and motioned them up. "Quickly, wash thyselves. And bring water for your father."

Life in the wilderness had begun. And all was well. They were wholly without conveniences or friends; but hard traveling and immediate danger were behind them The worry, that perhaps those who sought their lives would follow, gradually diminished. Compared to what they'd been through, they believed they could cope with whatever the future, and nature dealt them. And certainly they would not face hunger. According to the signs there would be plenty of game. Minds as well as bodies were at rest.

After the meal Lehi left camp to survey the area. For a long time he had not known such a feeling of well being. Contentment crawled over him like a warm blanket. And when he discovered that Nephi had followed him his heart swelled.

"Come, my son, and pray with me."

Lehi knew that his youngest son believed without reservation. And that Sam truly believed also. Even while traveling his quiet son had often sat apart in meditation, or contentedly playing his lute. So the benevolent father had only to worry about his older sons.

Laman and Lemuel, still skeptical about his mission, grumbled constantly, whispered together, and soon began leaving camp, staying longer and longer. Lehi secretly feared that they were conspiring to sneak away and return to the city. But he kept his suspicions to himself. He wouldn't worry their mother with his imaginings. He tried to keep his mind off the wayward sons and their restlessness—and on the faith of the other two.

But as time passed Sam and Nephi began questioning…

"Father what is going to happen? How long will we stay here? Where are we going to go?" They wanted to know many things for which he had no answers.

Nephi's questions were more spiritual, but also practical. "What is the Lord's will for us? If we are to dwell here should we not prepare the soil and plant?"

Possessing a great desire to know the Lord's will, Nephi had already asked these questions of God. He only asked his father when he did not receive answers. The youth assumed that Lehi still received communication from The Lord—but not since they arrived at the river. Lehi had nothing to tell his sons, nor his companion.

Sariah would ask, "What doth the Lord require of me before we leave this place? And how long will it be before we go?

That God was granting them a long rest in this comfortable place, Lehi realized. But "long" not given in the context of earthly time, could not be translated into days. Also each member of the family valued the count of days differently.

For Sariah they stretched endlessly. And she knew her duties would not change though they continue without end. There was also the fact that they had become more difficult. No hook to hang the pot over the fire; she must balance it on stones. No oven in which to bake bread; no kegs to store milk; she must process cheese in goatskin bags… And what began to be more important—as the ribbon of days stretched into a year—when her chores were done there was no padded chair by the hearth (no hearth). Also, Sariah desperately yearned for a feather bed to cradle her tired bones when all was done.

Sam sensed his mother was losing her spirit. He understood how hard the situation was on her, and tried to make things easier. In addition to carrying water from the river he scoured the cooking pots, sometimes even helped her wash the clothes. And when her work was done he treated her soul to music.

Nephi also helped his mother while in camp, but he was seldom there. He did most of the hunting, and frequently prayed with his father—but more and more often alone. For while the family of Lehi sojourned in the valley near the mouth of the Red Sea, the youngest son had begun to develop wisdom. Lehi confided this to Sariah.

"Nephi is maturing beyond his years," he told her. "He knows things before I tell him. And his faith grows like unto a mustard seed."

Sariah smiled wanly. She was thinking *nothing else grows. The heat of the summer sun is wasted. Nothing has been planted, though the food supply keeps dwindling.* She'd just checked the barley and found less than half a sack left. Soon they'd have only meat—if the hunting stayed lucky. This of course her husband knew, so she would not speak of it. But the plague of worry wore her down. Just a few days later she broke her silence.

In the cool of evening, as the couple sat together in closeness, Sariah dared to question her master Leaning into the slight breeze barely rippling the water, breathing in the freshness… She sighed, and brushed back her hair before speaking. Best to talk about something else first.

"Nephi follows exactly in thy footsteps, my dear husband," she began.

"Oh, that Laman would." Lehi almost wailed. "Sari, I worry greatly that our firstborn still does not serve The Lord.

Sariah put a gentle hand on his arm. "If I may have license to say it, my husband, thy eldest son needs firmer discipline."

Lehi frowned at her; but she bravely continued.

"When faith and example fail must thou not try being firmer? Has a father any choice?"

Lehi hesitated, "I think …" Then he gravely nodded. "I shall speak firmer to him, to both of them."

After discussing their children they talked about the food situation. Lehi again asked her to have faith, assuring her that The Lord would not let them starve. But the next day, immediately after the sparse morning meal, he left camp to petition God for guidance about all the woman had said. Perhaps he had been too lenient with Laman; perhaps they could plant some barley…?

Faulting himself for weakness, and another failure, praying and meditating, Lehi remained in solitude most of the day—and upon his return, went immediately to talk again with his wife.

She was nowhere to be found.

"Sari? Sari?" He called. No response. There was nobody in camp. The lines in his face deepened. Then he saw Sam approaching in the distance. He waved, raised his voice and shouted,

"Where is thy mother?"

Sam pointed over his shoulder. Charging in that direction the distraught husband found his helpmate resting under a scrubby terebinth tree, farther from camp than she had ever been, farther than she was allowed to go. Red in the face from exertion he panted up to her.

"Sariah this is too far! Much too far. There may be danger. You know you shouldn't … Oh my dear wife, what is it?"

Sariah didn't respond.

Lehi surmised what her silence and her bowed head meant. A lump arose in his throat. His good wife had resigned her hopes. Last night, after they talked about the disappointment with Laman, and Nephi's surprising maturity, when she again pressed the trying question for which he had no answer, he should have realized …

He clenched his staff groping for words. He had long sympathized. The woman had no comforts, and no company; but he had not ascertained the deeper implications of their isolation. Since the day he took his wife away from her home, she had talked with no other women. Several times he had found her talking to herself, her way of coping … But this, this running away… His heart hurt. *Oh dear Sari, dost thou not know it is out of my power? We wait upon the Lord*

Of course Sariah knew that ending the waiting was not in her husband's power; she knew that he would have built a house for her and planted all their seed had it been allowed. She also knew that he would tell her *when* … when it was given unto him.

But she had weakened.

Breathing heavily Lehi dropped down beside his distraught companion. At the gentle look of resignation on her tear stained face the harsh words building up inside him subsided. And he had no new words to give her. He tried to soothe her with the old ones.

"My good woman. Would that I could build thee a home in this lovely place. But it is not to be. This site is not for sojourning. In His time, in accordance with His plan, God will lead us to another land."

She smiled wanly.

Lehi patted her shoulder, then took her hand and led her back to camp, to their tent. He talked quietly to her, trying to soothe her mind. When she seemed comfortable he went again to the river (which had become his natural therapy). For a long time he stood on the bank leaning on his staff, staring at the soothing water.

CHAPTER VIII

The days dragged by. The Lord had not communicated with His servant since giving the sign to tarry at this place—a much longer silence than usual. Lehi began feeling unworthy. Nagging thoughts going round and round in his head, beginning to believe that God was displeased because he had not brought all his family into service, he was again at the river for therapy. The conscientious father had talked to the wayward sons, strongly, as he'd promised his wife, but with meager results…

"Oh, dear Lord show me how to reach their hearts."

Suddenly loud voices, bickering, coming from behind their tent.

"Laman, Lemuel, come here."

Laman jerked his head in his father's direction. "The old man wants to lecture us again." Lemuel shrugged, a look of irritation on his face. "I guess we must listen to yet another sermon …"

They dawdled.

Lehi shouted again. "Come here!"

They sauntered toward the river and flopped down on the grassy bank before their irate father. Laman frowned up at him through unruly strands of black hair, but he said nothing. Lemuel picked at the grass, the same sullen silence and get-it-over-with attitude. Staring down at his insolent sons Lehi was about to be consumed by anger—but surprisingly held his tongue. For compassion arose within him. *If the sons knew not their creator—and they knew not love—their father had failed them.*

Suddenly humbled, and filled with The Spirit Lehi began to speak of love.

"Laman," he quaked," thou art my first-born; and my heart cries out that you might believe and be like unto this river, continually running unto the fountain of righteousness, For this cause I have named the river Laman."

"And Lemuel, that thou might be like unto this good earth, firm and steadfast, I call this place the valley of Lemuel."

Lehi now spoke charitably—for surely their irreverence must be due to lack of understanding. He did not rightly teach them. Resolving to speak more unto their comprehension, vowing to be a better teacher, he went on and on.... Laman and Lemuel remained stoically unresponsive. Ultimately it came to Lehi, without a doubt, that Sariah was right. He *must* deal more sternly with them; they were his responsibility before God. He exploded.

"On thy feet!"

Laman and Lemuel scrambled to their feet. Their father seemed to have grown in stature. His eyes reflected fire like they'd never before seen. He had their attention at last, and he took advantage of it. He reamed them up one side and down the other, finally dismissing them with a dire warning.

"The Lord God of Heaven is not mocked."

Then as if to soften the blow he added, "But also remember, God is ever merciful unto those who do His will. Follow His commandments and He will forgive you, and shower His blessings upon us all. Know in your hearts that He doth lead us to a promised land—a land of plenty, where we will be prosperous, and safe."

They were truly shaken, but when out of hearing, Laman could not resist whispering to Lemuel, "Now he thinks he's Moses."

When they disappeared behind their tent Lehi dropped to the grassy bank as if he couldn't stand another minute. He sat there until Sariah called him to supper.

Had his words made a dint this time?

It seemed they might have. Laman and Lemuel didn't entirely slip out of their old skins; but their behavior and attitude showed signs of improvement. Whether from fear or the beginning of belief Lehi didn't know. He could only pray.

Sariah noted the change in her elder sons, and her strength returned on wings of hope. She began to believe that the uneasy truce would one day develop into harmony. For it must be. Surely God would reward a faithful servant who tried so hard to bring all his family into the fold. Sariah suffered no doubts that her husband was deserving. Or that he had been given a mission—that night on the roof of their home in Jerusalem, when he first told her of his vision, was burned into her memory.

Conflicting with that memory however was the proven fact that God's intervention in the lives of His "chosen" did not traditionally bring harmony.

And it proved out again. Just when an amiable relationship between Lehi and his wayward sons seemed possible, more friction developed between the brothers. The personality conflict between Laman and Nephi increased.

Nephi now prayed incessantly. With the zealousness of youth, fascinated, almost consumed, by his father's visions he suffered a burning desire to understand God's mysteries. Since leaving Jerusalem he had ceased to be a boy, and fast approaching manhood, was growing in wisdom beyond his years. Sam marveled at this, and listened intently to anything Nephi told him. But to Laman and Lemuel their younger brother was a radical. Nephi's developing spirituality became a never-ending subject of their conversations.

"His holier than thou attitude turneth my stomach," Lemuel confided. "And it worsens every day."

"Yeah. Now he thinks he knows more than I do," Laman retorted.

Since their father's explosive speech on the riverbank Laman had done some serious thinking. And these days he refrained from criticizing his father. Something about the fire in the old man's eyes ... But in no way did he hold his youngest brother in awe. So when Nephi began preaching, and then claimed he had a vision...

A mundane war broke out between them.

The father was unaware of this. But as a prophet, waiting for Nephi to return to camp one day, he knew before he saw him that his son's countenance would shine—that his eyes would glint gold with revelation. For it had been given him to know. That day the silence was broken. The Lord God had finally spoken to his good servant Lehi—and the same was given to his son. Rushing to meet him Lehi clasped his tall strong son in his arms, and held on until he caught his breath—and felt composed enough to speak.

"The Lord has spoken unto thee!"

Nephi nodded. He repeated the full message given his father, the new commandment they had both been given—that God would make Nephi, the youngest son, a ruler and a teacher of his brethren, in the Promised Land *"...the land which I have prepared for you ...choice above all other lands. And there shall be no kings upon the land of promise. "*

Just a few days later the old prophet received a commandment, given only to him, and not what he had been expecting.... Lehi's sons were to return to Jerusalem, to the house of Laban, to seek the records of their people "... *and bring them down hither unto the wilderness."*

"It is the Lord's will," Lehi confided to his youngest, "that you obtain the plates of brass, that we may take with us the genealogy of our forefathers and the words which have been spoken by the holy prophets."

"But," Nephi stammered, "Laban is against us. His big house is well guarded, and ..." Abruptly, he stopped protesting, ashamed to have slipped back into his own reasoning. Squaring his shoulders, bursting with commitment, he said, *"I will go and do the things which the Lord hath commanded, for I know that the Lord giveth no commandments unto the children of men, save He shall prepare a way for them, that they may accomplish the thing which He commandeth them."*

Lehi beamed with pride. "Come, we must tell thy mother, and thy brothers."

When the old prophet related the commandment to his family, Sariah and Sam gasped in unison. Laman and Lemuel didn't know whether to smile or not. They secretly rejoiced to be *commanded* to go back to the city). But... what they were commanded to do! And Nephi to be the leader, favor and power again given to the youngest! Looking daggers at his father, Laman loudly protested.

"Yea," Lemuel added, "And if we do go on an expedition without our father the oldest son should be in charge."

"It's only right," Laman retorted, "except that I shall not be going just to come back." He stomped away, slinging back over his shoulder, "If I go I'll stay."

Lemuel spurted to catch up with him. They walked a while in brooding silence, until the heat of Laman's anger began to subside. When he slowed to a normal pace Lemuel queried him. "What are we going to do?"

In a cool calculating voice Laman reiterated, "If ever I make that long hard trek again, you may know of a surety that I *will* stay."

And that was the risk that most worried Lehi. While merely the talk of sending all four sons on such a dangerous mission almost incapacitated Sariah. Strong was her faith, but mother love beat stronger. That evening, against her better judgment, Sariah pleaded her case.

"Oh Lehi could not one of them stay? Could Sam stay?"

At that moment Sam happening by their tent, overheard. He hurried past, not to eavesdrop, but his stomach churned, not knowing what to hope …

Did he want to go or not?

It didn't matter. For the firm voice of authority rang out. "Dear wife, hold thy tongue. They all must go. God has spoken."

Nevertheless, at the family conference the following morning (with Laman and Lemuel absconding) Sariah pleaded again for one of her sons to stay.

Nephi gently reminded his mother, "The commandment was *all* the sons …"

Lehi looked at her compassionately. It was a hard thing The Lord required of her, of them all. He spoke softly. "Sari, hold strong thy faith. We must all hold strong, for we have no choice." Then in a firmer voice, "How could thou imagine that I have authority to alter God's commandment?"

And when later he cornered the wayward two who refused to come to the family meeting, he emphatically told them the same thing. The Lord had spoken—no response allowed.

The following morning, after the family ate a substantial meal together, Sariah prepared each of her sons a food pack: mostly dried dates (the most nourishment for the least weight) and a small pouch of goat's milk. One precious goatskin of water they would share. Shakily, she handed them their bundles, then kissed and clung to each in turn. For the farewell moment she kept her composure, but her heart pounded so she could hardly breathe. *What if they could not find their way back? What if robbers waylaid them? What if they did not succeed in obtaining the records? Or worse, her deepest fear, Laban (who had become their father's enemy) might order his servants to kill them!*

The distraught mother strained after the distancing forms of her sons, and then at the blank horizon, for so long her husband was forced to turn her around. Lehi gently took her arm, and slowly walked her back to the tent. Attempting to console her, he could only think of what he'd said many times before.

"Faith, my good woman, have faith. We must have faith that God will protect them. Remember, they go on His mission."

"I know, I know," she said weakly.

Back in camp Lehi held his wife close for a moment, then tried to distract her mind with duty. "Come, prepare thy husband some nourishing soup for evening. We still have barley. And do we not also have a few beans left?"

"Very few," she said. "We are nearing the bottom of everything."

Lehi managed a smile, and as he turned to go once more reassured her that God would be with her children.

"And God will provide," he reiterated. "Good woman, dost thou not know in thy heart that The Lord will not let us starve?"

Sariah turned away without answering.

As Lehi left camp he wondered if God would make Sariah's meal sack bottomless, like the barrel of the widow who sheltered the prophet Elijah.

If not… Game was plentiful; there were edible plants around the river… With concerted effort Lehi put mundane worries behind him. More pressing at the moment were his wife's unhappiness, and his sons' safety. Both would remain paramount in his mind for a long time.

CHAPTER IX

The four sons reached Jerusalem without misadventure. But not in the shortest time. The trek from the tent in the valley, back through the barren wilderness to the clover-scented fields surrounding the city, took much longer without the leading and leveling control of their father.

With two claiming leadership (Laman by tradition, Nephi by commandment) much valuable time was wasted, even squandered. They continually argued over which route, even what direction to take. And sometimes neither of them felt sure. For on the way down, being followers, there had been no reason for them to take note of landmarks.

And inevitably, in every contest Sam and Lemuel took sides, Sam with Nephi, Lemuel with Laman. The sides being equal, in this verbal civil war within a family, created a stalemate—which was often broken by blows. Several times the "seconds" necessarily interceded to prevent bloodshed. Other times, when they managed to contain their anger they would settle the matter by casting lots, or throwing marked stones. Thus, after much wandering and backtracking, the inexperienced travelers were unduly weary when at dusk the fourth day they reached the city. Nevertheless, they advanced upon it like musketeers, caution to the winds.

But barely inside, uneasy, remembering… they were soon arguing again. This time about where to sleep.

Contention halted abruptly when a stone bounced off Nephi's shoulder.

"Ha, ha, ha, the sons of Lehi are back."

"Where is your crazy old man?"

Looking around they saw no one. The dusky street was deserted. It seemed the voices had come from behind a crumpling wall, from whence they now heard taunting laughter. It trailed away with retreating footsteps.

Silenced by the incident the divided brothers now looked at each other more charitably, and automatically linked arms.

Sam broke the silence.

"We are tired; we must rest. And since all the traveler shelters at the gate are occupied, let us retrace our steps and find a place without the walls to sleep."

"Yea," Lemuel quickly agreed, for the third time looking over his shoulder. "I would find more comfort on soft earth anyway. Wouldn't you, Laman?"

"Yea, How much rest can we get cramped together in a cold stone cubicle?"

" Nephi's voice rang out. "We'll go straight to the house of Laban. We can rest later."

Laman stopped abruptly, breaking the arm in arm chain. "I'm going to the baths before anything."

"No," Nephi cried. "We can't risk it."

As Laman and Nephi glared at each other Sam moved between them. "Perhaps," he suggested, "we could go to Ishmael's house to rest, and wash ourselves. We will in truth be safe there."

"I agree," said Lemuel, cocking his head at Laman. "So is it settled?"

"No! No," Nephi repeated. As the words rushed out his eyes darted; he had spoken louder than he intended. He reconsidered the situation. "My brothers, we must not dally, but perhaps we should be rested, to have our wits about us."

Sam smiled. "Yes, let's go to Ishmael's house. Our kinsman will want news of us anyway."

Laman stubbornly held to his vote for the baths, Lemuel siding with him. "Well, you two go where you want; we're going to the baths. We can meet ..."

Nephi interrupted in a loud whisper. "We will *not* separate. Our father commanded that we stay together."

"Yes," said Sam, "we must stay together." Then he motioned. "Look"

Two robed figures had appeared on the street, and were walking toward them. The brothers quickly formed a huddle, backs to the approaching men. And after the men had past they cast lots to make the decision.

It was decided to risk a quick trip to the baths. Then they would go outside the wall for the night. But on the way, still inside, they discovered an abandoned stall—a secluded relatively safe place to rest, and plan.

Finally, they all agreed. They *would* separate, temporarily, three to tarry there while one went to case the great house. Then they cast lots to see who would go.

And it came to pass that the lot fell upon Laman.

Laman left very reluctantly, the streets now dark, and few doors boasted torches. Yet when he reached the tall torch burning at Laban's gate he wished it wasn't there. On the flint-paved path leading up to the house, eyeing the torch at the door, he walked slower and slower. Long limbs of huge trees overhanging the indented parapets resembled giant arms. Strategically placed closely planted shrubs on both sides, seemed like a silent army guarding the sanctuary. At last he faced the heavy mahogany door.

He jerked his head nervously. The dark hair did not flip off his forehead; it stuck there, in perspiration. The click of his sandals on the hard slate rang in his ears. Standing exposed by the light of the torch he almost bolted—but finally recruiting enough courage, he reached out to raise the knocker...

The door creaked open. A swarthy little man in servant attire motioned to him. Laban was ordering him in.

With his heart in his throat, the first born son of Lehi followed the servant through a long dark corridor to the ornate inner courtyard of the enemy.

As was his practice on hot summer evenings the master of the house had been lounging on the roof. Startled to see someone approaching his domicile at such a late hour he got up from the cushions, crept over to the parapet and looked down. Upon recognizing the tall slim form with the hair flipping habit, his curiosity flamed.

Laban ordered the servant in attendance to bring the visitor to him. Then he descended by inner stairs to his elaborately furnished center room, and stood waiting to receive the son of Lehi like a spider that had spun a web and was waiting for a fly.

"Well, well, if it isn't Laman, the first-born of Lehi. He brings me a message from his father, I'm sure."

The visitor swayed; his knees were about to give way.

"Seat thyself."

Laman dropped down on the leather lounging pad, eyes darting. There was no one else present but the servant.

The syrupy voice continued. "Son of Lehi, where *is* my kinsman? I'm anxious to know his whereabouts. And what could it be that he would send his son to beg of me?"

"Ah, my father…" Laman stammered, cautiously searching the room again.

" My father sent me, sent us, for…"

"Speak up. For what?"

"For, for the records of our people. He said The Lord has commanded…"

All pretense of civility vanished. Like a threatened warrior the big man sprang to his feet and drew his sword. "Lehi shall not have the records!"

"But my father says it has been revealed that they are unsafe, for Jerusalem is soon to be destroyed. And ..."

"I know the scriptures. I am the elder of highest standing in this city. For generations my family has been blessed with the responsibility to keep the records. When and if the time comes that such a prophecy is fulfilled, I shall protect them."

"But, if it be commanded... If..."

"There is no such commandment. If there were I would know it. Now, get out. Get out!" Laban screamed. His sword crashed down on the stone table between them air-shaving the side of the offender's face, now alabaster white. Laban's face boiled red. He raised the sword and crashed it down again, then aimed it heart-level at his tormentor.

"Leave my house. Or thy deluded father will be minus his first-born."

Laman sprang up running, and never looked back. When he reached the stall where his brothers waited, carrying nothing, and gasping like a fleeing fugitive, they all chorused, "What happened? What happened?"

Laman dropped down on the smelly straw and quickly peeked between the cracks in the dung-splattered wall before attempting to answer.

"I nearly got killed, that's what."

"Oh what are we going to do?" Lemuel wailed.

"We've gotta get out of the city," Sam cried.

Nephi spoke sternly. "Sam, you know we can't go. We all know that. We must get the records. Now let's sit down and think, and figure out a way."

Thus the dawning day found the sons of Lehi huddled like homeless waifs on a pile of malodorous straw, tersely whispering together. With fear drawn faces, first one and then another kept repeating, "There's no way. There's no way."

"What are we going to do?" Sam wailed.

Laman got to his feet, moving warily, as if the rustling of straw rang bells.

"Well I know what I'm going to do. I'm getting out of here,"

Lemuel jumped up. "Yea, let's go while we can."

"But," cried Sam, "we can't return; we…"

Nephi's voice rang out. "My brothers," he said sternly, "we cannot return to our father and tell him that we failed him, that we failed God." He stood straighter, and squared his shoulders. "The Lord has commanded that we bring the records out of this doomed city. It is of utmost importance to the future of our people. And it is our duty. So we will find a way to do it."

The fire of Nephi's faith may have begun to waver, but it was far from being extinguished, and now it surged stronger. He stationed himself at the stable entrance and continued.

"It is God's commandment; it is His will that we succeed. So we must have faith that He will protect us, and reveal to us the solution."

The strong young voice rang with authority; and not quietly, as if being heard by passers-by was no longer of any consequence.

"I *know* that God will guide us and prepare the way."

His brothers looked up from their prone positions like lost frightened children. Nephi stood over them, a tower of strength. Their apprehension lessened. The budding leader grabbed the opportunity to preach.

"The brass plates contain the words of the holy prophets, delivered unto them by the Spirit and power of God since the world began, even down unto this present time. They contain the genealogy of our forefathers, which must not be lost. Our father told us, and as The Lord liveth, we have been commanded to do this…"

As the three listened, the tension on their faces ebbed. Then they all prayed together. And soon the solution came. It was clear. Why hadn't they thought of it before? Nephi presented it with confidence.

"Jerusalem will be destroyed. We know not when; but we know of a surety. Therefore should our father return to dwell in his homeland, the land from which he hath been commanded to flee, he surely would perish. So he will not return. And therefore will not have further need of riches."

The brothers understood. They remembered the gold and silver and all their precious possessions left hidden under the olive tree in the courtyard. The plan might work. Their wealthy kinsman of position and notoriety would not *give*, but for enough, his kind would sell. And when Nephi reminded them of the commandment given to their father, "*...leave all manner of riches...*" there were no further doubts. Now had come to light the reason thereof—that they might accomplish this mission,

Thus on their second day in Jerusalem the four sons of Lehi left their hiding place, and stealthily slipping through the back streets of the city, came to their home on the outskirts—the home of their inheritance. As they approached the gate, anger spread over their faces. The latch was broken, as were the window shutters. Forgetting to be furtive they rushed as one through the overgrown garden around to the inner courtyard, to the big olive tree in the center. The large stone at the base had not been disturbed.

"Thank God!" They exclaimed in unison. And like a trained team they fell on their knees before the huge stone, hands reaching greedily to grab hold of it.

"Don't touch it!"

At Nephi's intense whisper Laman's eyes shot daggers. Lemuel looked as if he had never possessed a mischievous grin. It appeared they had no intentions of following another order from their junior brother. But his eyes pleaded; he leaned closer to them, and this time whispered quietly.

"Please. Would it not behoove us to wait until dark?"

"Of course it would," echoed Sam. He looked back toward the gate. "Nephi is right. Think. What if we had it taken from us?"

Laman and Lemuel hadn't thought of that. They quickly conceded. So once more the four sought a hiding place. Crouched in the weed-thickened grape arbor, working together, they fleshed out Nephi's skeleton plan. Then they settled down reflectively, to await the cover of darkness.

When the last purple shadows deepened into night the four of them removed the boulder from the base of the guardian tree, and digging with their hands, retrieved the family treasure—all the gold, silver and precious things their father had acquired in all his years. Without quarreling they divided the sanctified loot evenly, and hid it in their clothing. Nephi asked for the Lord's blessing upon the deed. Then standing together, rallying their courage, the sons of Lehi stealthily creeping through the darkness, made their way back across the city to the big house.

When within sight of the familiar dwelling they hid near the entrance gatepost for a final conference, and to wait for full daylight. Then, as the sun peeped over the horizon, when they were sure that Laban would be awake, they proceeded up the pathway.

Decked out like gilded legionaries awaiting accolades—money and jewels in evidence—they did not expect to be refused entrance. And they were not, though their revved up courage definitely ebbed at the sight of the man who received them.

Laban had not yet attended to his morning grooming. They had never seen him that way. He looked like he'd been drinking instead of sleeping: bloodshot eyes, hair awry, heavy beard in need of trimming… He resembled a hungry wolf. And he was licking his chops. But Nephi boldly stepped forward.

"We proffer to buy the records of the Jews."

And he brought forth from his garments all the gold and silver he carried, laying it out on the long low table before Laban's couch. Sam hesitated, as did Lemuel; but as Laman began to do likewise, they followed suite. The sticky smile on Laban's face spread wider, and wider. His deep-set eyes glinted like wet diamonds. While the silent servant stared as if hypnotized.

After the brothers had displayed all their property (that Laban could see how exceedingly great it was) Nephi restated the proposition.

"For God's purposes we give you all our father's riches in exchange for the plates of brass."

Laban's bloodshot eyes riveted on the display, the corners of his mouth began to curve. Then suddenly his countenance changed. His red face darkened—a dark thought overpowered the facial façade. The greedy man had suddenly realized that with a revised strategy he could keep the records and the riches too. He jerked a silken cord. As if from out of the walls myriad servants appeared, all armed with swords. And simultaneously the lofty Laban, as tall as Nephi, swished his sword back and forth over his head—the signal for battle.

"These rogues have insulted an elder of Israel," he barked. "Woe unto them; I want them out. Out of my presence forever."

At the points of a dozen swords, the sons of Lehi were forcibly obliged to leave the family riches and flee for their lives. Laban also commissioned soldiers to follow them and slay them. However, burdened with swords and armor, the pursuers could not run as swiftly as the unencumbered fugitives. The sons of Lehi escaped.

Half a mile outside the city walls they finally dared stop running, and in the rugged countryside soon found a cave for refuge. They were safe. But there was no security from each other. As soon as Laman ascertained that they had truly escaped, he pounced upon Nephi in a frenzy of repercussion. Sam and Lemuel both tried to pull him off. He fought like a lion being robbed of its prey, but they managed to contain him. They could not contain the harangue, however. Slim face all screwed up, eyes shooting bullets, Laman spat out the words.

"Now what, oh perfect one? You didn't hold out anything. Not even a mite of silver to buy food and sandals for the return journey?"

"Yea," echoed Lemuel, siding again with Laman, "Doth our holier than thou brother think he can pray, and things we need will miraculously appear? We could starve, before we get back."

"We're not going back," Nephi shouted.

"Oh yea," Laman screamed. "I wasn't going back; but now after two attempts on my life, I am, If I have to kill you!"

He spied an old rusty rod on the cave floor, and snatched it up.

Lemuel hesitated only a second before grabbing Sam, who was moving to intervene on Nephi's behalf. Pinning Sam's arms he hissed out, "Don't forget, brother, that God-inspired plan did nearly get us all killed."

While Lemuel wrestled with Sam the wiry Laman slithered around Nephi like a panther, repeatedly striking with the rod, landing strategic blows to the head.

Nephi reeled and fell.

Suddenly a blinding light. The dingy cave illuminated like magic. And before them appeared an entity in glowing white, standing in air.

"Why do ye smite your brother with a rod?"

Laman froze. The rod fell from his hands. Sam and Lemuel fell apart, dropping wide-eyed to the dirt.

"Know ye not that the Lord hath chosen him to be a ruler over you, and this because of your iniquities..." And after the chastising, the angel said, *"Behold ye shall go up to Jerusalem again, and The Lord will deliver Laban into your hands."*

The brilliant light dissipated back to the natural semi-darkness of the cave. Nephi rose up, bloody and dirty. He limped out into the sunlight. Sam got to his feet and shakily followed. Laman and Lemuel stared after them, too weak to move. But after a moment they could talk.

"Go to the house of Laban again?"

"Yea, the man commands, and fifty will be slain; then why not us?"

"Hold thy tongues. An angel hath spoken to you."

Nephi's voice echoed off the cave walls. His tall form silhouetted in the opening appeared unsoiled. All the blood and damage from the rod had disappeared. His face showed no pain. With three giant strides he towered over his brothers on the cave floor, his voice ringing with conviction.

"We will do as The Lord commanded. For behold He is mightier than all the earth, then why not mightier than Laban and his fifty, yea, than even tens of thousands? And lo, He hath sent an angel. Wherefore can you doubt?"

"We have seen an angel!" Sam echoed.

"Oh my brothers of little faith," Nephi continued. "When will you know in your hearts the power of God? The Lord God is able to deliver us, even as He delivered our forefathers. And He will destroy Laban, even as he destroyed the armies of Pharaoh."

And it came to pass that Laman and Lemuel were humbled... Shaking in their sandals they followed Nephi back to the city, but only as far as the wall. It was decided they should hide outside, and wait. Sam prepared to go, his faith in Nephi unshaken, but Nephi insisted that he too wait. Led by the Spirit, the budding prophet knew that he must go alone. Nephi must confront the powerful Laban as David confronted Goliath. And he would complete the mission.

But he knew not how. It had not yet been given him to know the terrible, fearful deed that would be required of him.

CHAPTER X

Nephi pushed his way through the throng of vagrants and stray animals in the narrow dusty alley, holding a hand to his mouth, and watching where he stepped. Here, the permeating odor of human dung, as well as the ever present burro and dog droppings. A pack of scavenger dogs sniffed at his heels. All this, a trade-off for safety. He had opted to enter through the dog gate, because in that part of the city he would least likely be recognized.

He walked swiftly to put it all behind him.

Upon reaching the cobblestone streets he drew a deep breath of the cleaner air, and relaxed his pace. But still in the grip of tension, his mind raced. Proceeding on blind faith, stomach churning, at last he approached the landscaped rise that afforded Laban's commanding view. The youth stared up at the big house apprehensively. He had received no guidance.

"Oh Lord God of Israel, I know thou art with me; but give me guidance. I know not how… I know not what to do."

At Laban's gate, the memory of sword-swiping servants and that greedy angry face sapped his renewed faith. Imagining eyes upon him, he retreated to a nearby grove, fell to his knees and prayed. Then slowly approaching the house, about half way, Nephi weakened again. Reeling off the path, seeking the cover of closely planted cedar trees, he once more fell to his knees in supplication.

Nephi raised his head. He had gradually become aware of the permeating odor of strong wine. He looked around warily. Not twenty feet away, a body, lying face down beneath a tree. A large body, wearing headdress, boots, and costly garments. The golden hilt of a fine sword projected from under the cloak.

Staring, Nephi edged toward the body. There was no movement. He reached down and slowly, carefully withdrew the sword from its sheath. Then, weapon at ready, rolled the man over with his foot. The breath went out of him.

"Laban!"

As the angel promised, The Lord had delivered Laban into his hands.

Veritably bursting with renewed faith the strapping young believer stood over the one who had slighted his father, stolen the family savings, sought to take their lives, thwarted God's holy purposes… Passed out in a drunken stupor the man of power could be bound without a struggle. Then it would be possible to enter the house, where he would find what he came for.

By this unearthly turn of events Nephi now *knew* that he would soon possess the brass plates. He shook off the ethereal and turned his mind to the practical. Where could he find something to bind him?

But in the next instant he became paralyzed with fear—fear for his very soul. The Spirit was telling him to kill Laban. With this sure knowing from within the youth began to tremble. He swayed, and dropped the sword. Never at any time had he shed the blood of man. He could not slay even this dangerous enemy; his heart would not allow him to kill. Yet, the Spirit insisted.

"Slay him!"

Sweat beaded his brow. He began mumbling in delirium: "Thou shalt not kill; thou shalt not kill." Trembling to his toes in confusion, disillusion—and the blackness thereof—it seemed to the youth that the sun of his world had dropped from the sky.

The traditional commandments of God, received through Moses and taught by his father, he had *always* kept. Thou shalt not kill, primary among them.

Nephi spread his strong legs to triangle stance, to keep his balance, and tried not to look at the body. But his eyes remained riveted on the puffy distorted face with its loose hanging mouth. This repulsive person, he kept telling himself, had ridiculed him and his brothers, stolen from them, and attempted to kill them. While claiming to serve God, the man had deliberately thwarted His purposes. He had sinned against heaven….

As the youth struggled with these conflicting thoughts the voice interrupted. The spirit said again, *"Slay him, for the Lord hath delivered him into thy hands."*

The words pounding in his head were clear and undeniable; but still Nephi could not. Exceedingly young, and pure of soul, he hated not enough. Yet, how could he disobey? An angel of the Lord sent him… He had been commanded to obtain the holy records…

The confused youth stared at the still form as if in a trance. The voice continued, *"Behold, the Lord slayeth the wicked to bring forth His righteous purposes."*

Nephi now remembered the words of the Lord that had come to him in the wilderness… that his father, Lehi, would lead his descendants to a Promised Land; and that he, Nephi, had been chosen… *"Inasmuch as thou shalt keep my commandments, thou shalt be made a ruler and a teacher over thy brethren."* That revelation, while he still straddled the fence of adolescence, tipping alternately between adulthood and childhood had lifted him, beyond measure. The present battle of decision, tradition versus revelation, was tearing him apart. How could the Spirit be commanding him to do that which was against God's formerly given law?

The mortal mind fighting the light of higher wisdom then brought forth a question: How could he teach the descendants of Lehi to keep the Lord's commandments according to the Law of Moses unless they had the law—the law engraved upon the brass plates hidden somewhere in the house of Laban.

Strangling with the contradiction, Nephi raised his eyes to heaven, "Oh Lord God of Israel, give me a sign! That I may know of a surety it is thy will."

The sun brightened with extreme intensity, and shot it's rays between the trees, as if spotlighting the young servant for the act he had been commanded to perform. Simultaneously, a powerful gust of wind bent the boughs of the trees around him all the way down to the ground, and held them there.

Dead silence…

Like a puppet controlled from above Nephi grabbed the besotted Laban by the hair, and smote off his head with his own sword. Staring at the severed head bleeding in his hands, he froze rigid. Then with a convulsive shudder he slung it through the trees. And with trembling hands began removing clothing from the body.

A short time later, dressed in Laban's garments (every piece, even unto the rare and coveted seal skin boots) and wearing the gleaming sword, the obedient servant, by Spirit direction, entered the house of Laban to complete the mission.

Laban's most trusted servant, the keeper of the keys (and all God's commandments) met him at the door.

"Master," the servant said, bowing, eyes cast down, "thou has been long in returning. Thy servant feared the king's spies had searched out thy secret meeting place, and harm had befallen thee."

"Take me to the treasury room," Nephi commanded. And the servant heard the words in Laban's voice.

"Yes, master."

Without hesitation he opened the locked door, and left the man he thought was his master alone with the treasure. Nephi immediately recognized the bags he and his brothers had brought from under the olive tree. They were all piled together in one place. But as he was about to appropriate the family property, reason intervened; there was no way he could possibly carry them and the plates too.

Where were the brass plates? Expecting to find the sacred records in the locked room with the treasure Nephi began a frantic search—soon forgetting about the gold and silver and precious possessions of the family. For him, the plates of brass held more riches.

"Oh, Lord God, where? Where are they hidden?"

Then a flash of insight; surely the most trusted servant would know. He rushed out into the corridor, and without benefit of knowing the servant's name, or how he was called by Laban, commanded in a loud voice, "Come!" The servant materialized instantly. As was the custom, ordered by Laban, the little man had waited just outside the door, on guard. And it would be his duty to re-lock the door.

"I require the plates of brass," Nephi said gruffly. Then he added an explanation. "We take them this day to another hiding place; it was decided at last night's meeting."

The son of Lehi (a man of means who had no captive help) failed to remember that propriety between master and slave did not require justifying an order. But the words he was saying without any thought on his part did not arouse suspicion. All seemed to be going smoothly. His escort led him through the house to a secret niche far from the entrance, where the plates had been sealed up in the wall. The most trusted servant, who had done the mortar work, pulled aside a damask curtain and stood back waiting. Nephi stared at the blank wall. Only a slight variance in color indicated a re-plastering.

"Get a tool, and get them out," he heard himself bark. "And mind no one follows you. Let no one enter this area of the house."

In this way, without concentrating on what to say, Nephi would subsequently give appropriate orders (in Laban's voice) to accomplish the mission.

While the domestic went for the tool, Nephi prayed his humble thanks. God was directing the obedience of the servant, as well as *his* every action. However, during the chiseling out of the opening, he writhed in sweat. And when at last his eyes fell upon the plates his body reacted with chills of excitement. While the servant of Laban stood respectfully aside looking at the floor, he studied the pile of gleaming brass. Engraved on those plates were the words of God, and all the sacred records of His people. For them, he and his brothers had forfeited the family riches, and almost lost their lives. *For them, he had killed!*

His heart beat staccato. He hesitated to touch them. Not until he sensed the servant shuffling near, did he reached out and carefully lift one off the pile. He handed it to the servant. He loaded them all on the servant's outstretched arms.

Only then did he notice the two sealed pottery jars marked with a familiar emblem. Son of a devout follower steeped in the traditions of his forefathers, Nephi knew what such storage jars contained—the original scrolls. And he thought it was the custom to bury disintegrating scrolls after they were copied to brass.

Why had these not been buried?

Did his father's kinsman perhaps believe the predictions after all? Did Laban and the elders plan to escape? Were they going to take the original scriptures, as well as the plates? Thereby doubly insuring that God's word would be saved?

Juggling these imaginings, Nephi stalled. The domestic waited, subserviently holding the treasure. Finally, with a deep breath, straightening to full height he took the plates from his humble helper and commanded that he close up and re-seal the opening. Then trying to stay in character, he barked another order.

"Bring a burlap bag; bring two." With the second bag he would doubly protect the precious records.

Ultimately, Laban's servant following, carrying the holy plates, Nephi departed the big house, and the city. About to burst with thankfulness, he kept repeating to himself. Mission completed. Mission completed.

But when he continued without the walls, toward the place in which his brothers were hiding, the servant stopped. Nephi noted a change in his demeanor. The little man was looking at him curiously, apprehensively. He appeared about bolt.

"Hurry," he said gruffly, "the elders await the records, in this special hiding place we've prepared for them."

He strode bravely ahead feigning a confidence he did not feel, restraining the urge to peek back to insure his order was carried out. Surely it would be. Servants were not given to expect explanations for unreasonable orders. But for good measure, the inexperienced master continued....

"It was decided that the Words of God are no longer safe within the city."

Gripping the heavy burlap covered treasure closer to his chest, Laban's servant continued following the man that he believed to be his master.

Soon they approached the place where the other sons of Lehi waited. The brothers ran out of hiding. Ever watching for Nephi, and seeing a tall figure in the distance, they couldn't run fast enough. But then they stopped, and shrunk back. There were two figures coming. And the one of great stature wore a longer, fuller robe, with head covering held by a golden band. A sword glinted in the sunlight.

"It's Laban!" They turned to flee.

Nephi shouted, "No my brothers, it is I, Nephi."

They ran to embrace him.

Upon hearing the natural voice of Nephi the servant of Laban dropped the plates, and attempted to flee. But the brothers surrounded him. Quaking with terror the little man fell on his face. Nephi grabbed him by the back of his garments and lifted him up off the ground.

"Servant of Laban, what is thy name?"

The black eyes bugged; and when the frightened domestic found his voice it cracked. "Z, Z, Zoram."

Nephi set him back on his feet. "Take courage Zoram, and listen." He spoke quietly. But Zoram crumpled to the ground again, prostrating himself before the appropriated seal skin boots, as if waiting for the lashes.

No lashes fell upon his back. And as the brothers crowded in around him, he heard a kind voice in low tone, speaking unbelievable words.

"My good man, because of thee our mission for the Lord has been accomplished. Hearken unto my words. As the Lord liveth I am going to reward you, not punish you."

The servant slowly raised his head from the ground and stared up, from the boots to the hem of the robe, to the glinting sword, and all the way to the speaker's face—no longer appearing as the face of Laban.

"Zoram, sit up," Nephi said.

He didn't move. Nephi reached down and again raised the little man, this time setting him on his feet, as one would do an infant learning to walk. And Zoram reacted like a baby; he began to blubber. The brothers attempted to comfort him.

"Fear not, fear not; we will not hurt you."

Nephi spoke again. "Zoram believe, we will not harm you. If you come with us into the wilderness, unto our father's tent, and try to follow his teachings, he will make you a free man."

"What sayest thou, Zoram?" Lemuel put the question to him like an equal, punctuating it with a grin.

The swarthy face broke into a quarter-moon smile. The head bobbed up and down. Nephi picked up the burlap bag, brushed it off and handed it back to him. He reached for it eagerly, still nodding, and smiling. And finally he regained his voice. The words gushed out.

"By the most merciful God I will follow thee anywhere. From this time forth I will stay with thee." He clutched the heavy bag close to his pounding heart, and stood as tall as he could. "I shall protect the holy records with my life."

Thankfully, that did not prove necessary.

While it had been imperative to keep the servant with them (they couldn't risk letting him return to Jerusalem to tell of the purloined plates) converting him to the cause was a bonus—and a blessing for all.

Faith and confidence restored all around, Nephi led his little party into the rocky hills south of Jerusalem without incident. They were not pursued. No one else in the city knew he had taken the plates. They had succeeded in the mission, and gained a convert. Under God's protection they would journey safely back to his father's tent. And on the return trip he would not be plagued with worry over the right route. His older brothers no longer bickered about new sandals, or how little they had to eat. And it appeared Laman would no longer contend with him…

The young leader, elated by the turn of events, set a faster pace (it being well past the time for them to have returned). And no one complained about that either.

At the end of that adventurous day, resting in the protected spot Nephi selected, they all relaxed, even Zoram. The brothers having talked with him congenially, as an equal, the little man fell asleep with a smile of incredibility upon his face—and the weight of his charge upon his stomach. At first Sam had been apprehensive; he'd kept a watchful eye on this new member of their party all day. But come night he went to sleep beside him. All were soon asleep, except Nephi.

Before submitting to the blessing of safety and rest, the young leader went apart to once again thank God for delivering the holy records unto their hands. The great weight of responsibility (for completion of the mission) had lifted from his shoulders. And soon he would see his father.

Nephi wrapped himself in the luxury of Laban's long cloak, and settled down in comfort, body and soul. All was well.

But all was not well in the tent of his father.

CHAPTER XI

In the tent by the river Sariah sat alone. Staring unseeing out the opening, her long brown hair devoid of it's sheen and hanging loose, she hardly resembled herself. Since she last saw her sons time had taken expensive tolls. And recently her soft brown eyes, tinged with red, were often brimming over—this morning, steadily.

Since dawn she'd been wailing, "Oh Lord God of Israel forgive, forgive, I have sinned against my husband; I am not worthy of the good man thou hast given me. I am not worthy; I am not worthy."

She kept repeating these words, torturing herself with the memory of her out of character performance. She had never done anything like it before. When the estimated time for her sons to return had passed—and more time, and more time, the distraught mother had died inside. And the previous night, hurting and bereft of hope, she had lost control. She raised her voice to her husband and accused and berated him for the loss of her sons—for sending *all* her children on such a dangerous mission....

And Lehi, suffering a similar condition, had reacted like a wounded wolf. Not only grieving, but bearing the burden of guilt for what he now thought might be the death of his offspring (it didn't seem possible that they still lived), he hurt the same.

Additionally, he feared he had lost favor with The Lord. At the breaking point also, when accused by his wife the righteous husband had reacted violently. For the first time, he struck her. And Sariah's response left him no chance to apologize. She wrapped herself in silence.

By morning she still had not spoken.

When Lehi left the tent she pretended sleep. When the sun sparkled high, still she did not get up. Now, sitting cross-legged on the sleeping mat, rocking back and forth, she rubbed the place on her shoulder where her husband struck her, wishing that it hurt. As if it were recorded in her brain Sariah kept hearing that strange shrewish voice which she had to admit was hers. And all the while memory replaying the picture of her dear husband's face flushed with anger—and those deep grooved lines of suffering over the high-bridged nose that bore out his bloodline.

She shook with sobs. Had she seen more clearly last night, she could not have continued that hateful harangue.... *How could she have so thoughtlessly blamed the good man for what God commanded him to do?*

"Thou hast led us forth from the comfort of home in the land of our inheritance, unto utter desperation," she accused. "Now my sons are no more. And there is no reason to believe that we too shall not perish in this wilderness!"

Choking on the thought of having screamed those words at her loved one, she couldn't even pray.

U*ntil a wife makes the journey back to her husband's side, and begs his forgiveness, how could she ask for God's?*

At last rational, and knowing her lifelong companion so well, Sariah sensed that Lehi walked the riverbank, not fifty yards away. But there were unseen miles between them—miles for her to walk. She pushed herself up, drew a deep breath. and dragged around the tent. The one she had wronged stood knee-deep in color, staring down into the swift running water. And she knew that he was standing there asking God's forgiveness for striking her.

"Oh my dear husband," she breathed, slowly moving toward him. She smoothed her hair, and dried her puffy wet face with her shawl. A few steps closer— and then she waited.

When Lehi raised his graying head and turned toward the tent his wife held out her arms. Belying their years, they rushed together.

"Oh, Sari, Sari."

"Lehi, my husband, forgive me. Forgive…"

"Dear wife, forgive *me*. I know that I am a visionary man. I forget…"

His voice broke. For a few minutes they clung to each other, comforting and consoling in silence. Then Lehi continued.

"My dear Sari we must have faith that our sons will return, even after so long a time. For it was on God's mission that they departed." He gently removed her arms from his neck, and looking deep into her eyes repeated, "Have faith. Have faith a little longer. My heart tells me that God will soon bring them home."

"I know, I know …" Sariah sobbed, "But when?"

"Soon, soon." Lehi again repeated his assurance. "By command of God they departed. They are on His mission. He will deliver them from the hands of Laban, and bring them back to us."

Caring fortified, faith bolstered, Lehi and Sariah prepared to face another long, lonesome day. They busied themselves as best they could. She dared to use the last of the meal in the last barrel to make the honey-wheat cakes him. He decided to get meat for her pot.

The prophet had not hunted for ages (no man with four sons needed to). But now he grabbed the best bow of steel, belonging to Nephi, and took off across the valley like an adolescent in search of adventure. He was gone a long time. Returning in late afternoon, tired and without game, he heard,

"Lehi! Lehi!" The once warm voice, that became temporarily shrill, calling his name with hysterical intensity.

Sariah was fleeing from the tent like a mad woman set free. She kept screaming his name; while looking and running in the opposite direction. Lehi dropped the bow, threw off his cloak, and charged after her. But his aging legs soon balked. For more than a score of years speed had not been required of them. One cramped so severely it brought him down. *Oh dear God. Had the heartache and hardships, which had taken their toll on her body and soul, affected also her mind?*

"Sari, Sari, stop. Come back."

Frantically rubbing his leg, he got to his feet and again began hobbling over the rough ground. Eyes on his wife, instead of his footing, he stumbled and fell flat. It was then, as he looked up from ground level, that he understood.

Emerging over a distant rise were four figures. His heart surged into his throat. Instantly, he bowed his head.

"Oh dear God, merciful God, thank you; thank you."

But when he looked again there were five figures. Lehi strained his eyes at the unrecognizable form, the small form following the four. Watching them, and Sariah, he regained his feet and began walking as fast as he could. Sariah had ceased calling him, but she was still running toward her children.

Not until the father reached the knot of mother and sons hugging each other did he recognize the fifth man. As Lehi stretched out his arms to embrace all his family together he looked beyond them. And gasped.

"It is Zoram, servant of Laban!"

Standing apart from the intimate reunion Zoram had not noticed Lehi's approach. He started at the sudden loud voice which rasped out his name, and warily backed away, holding the burlap bag before him like a makeshift shield of armor.

"Yes, father," said Nephi. "It was with Zoram's help that we succeeded in our mission. We have obtained the sacred records of our people. And Zoram carries them; he carried them all the way."

Nephi reached out to Zoram and brought him to stand before his father, saying "The Lord delivered Laban unto my hands; and by Zoram, delivered unto us the brass plates."

He gripped the little man's shoulders, easing him toward the patriarch.

"Father I gave this man my word that if he would follow us into the wilderness, and tarry with us, we would spare his life. And I promised him that when we returned to thy tent, if he would follow thee and hearken unto thy words, that henceforth he would be free."

Nephi kicked a small stone from between them, and pushed Zoram closer.

"Wilt thou honor my word father? It was by act of God that he was given unto my hands. And I know of a surety that he doth serve God."

The trembling slave with bowed head awaiting his fate did not see the emotion in Lehi's face as he reached out and embraced his son. But he heard it in the booming voice.

"My son, I will gladly honor thy word."

The head shot up as if on a spring. The black eyes sparked. And at the following words the swarthy face glowed.

"Zoram, as the Lord liveth, from this day forward thou art a free man."

That evening in the camp of Lehi there was joy overflowing. While the weary travelers refreshed themselves in the river Sariah and Lehi celebrated the blessing of their presence. Far into the night the parents talked, and over and over prayed their thanks for the joyous turn of events since morning. Sariah sleepily mumbled prayers until she lost consciousness. God had protected her sons, delivered them out of the hands of Laban, and returned them to her. Never again would she doubt.

She was overwhelmed with relief, and overtired, having hardly slept the night before, so Lehi did not expect his wife to arise as usual. But the following morning at sunup—when he offered the traditional sacrifice and burnt offerings to The Lord, she was at his side. And thereafter whenever he took the plates of brass and searched the records graven upon them the good woman desired that they be read to her. She would listen intently to the holy words, committing special accounts to memory.

...an account of the creation of the world, and of Adam and Eve, and also a record of the Jews from the beginning, even down to the commencement of the reign of Zedekiah ...and many of the prophecies of the holy prophets ...and many spoken by the mouth of Jeremiah ...

Upon the return of her sons with the records, and Zoram, Sariah's soul soared. Her energy, her beauty, and her disposition were fully restored—and her faith, tenfold.

While Lehi, filled anew with the spirit, exalted that he found upon the plates of brass the genealogy of his forefathers—proof positive that he descended from Joseph, son of Jacob (who was sold into Egypt and preserved by the hand of the Lord). Inspired beyond measure, he began preaching to his family about the future.

"These plates of brass shall never perish. They are of exceedingly great worth unto us, and our children, and our children's children. It is the Lord's will that we should preserve them, and carry them with us as we journey to the land of promise."

Sariah frowned at the words, "land of promise." To her the beautiful broad expanse of grass, the wild flowers, and the river, had become the land of promise. Hoping and praying that God would not require them to leave it, she began experimenting to make more palatable meals from plants that grew in the area. And from the seeds they brought, with Zoram's help, she planted a garden.

"This soil is fertile;" Zoram told her, "lots of things will grow here."

In dawn's first light the air held a definite chill; but Sariah was up and out tending her garden before preparing the morning meal. Smiling at her eager helper she took the crock of water from Zoram and finished pouring it in the little ditches he had made between the rows.

"I can hardly wait to see what comes up," she said.

Zoram's quarter moon smile curved to the limit. He reached for the crock, and ran back to the river for more water. The former slave could not do enough for the lady who talked to him as a friend. He remembered her long ago visiting Laban's house with her husband. But she hadn't remembered him. The young woman of regal carriage, wife of his master's relative, had paid no notice to the house servant. But now in the wilderness she treated him as one of the family. For the first time in his life Zoram was happy.

It was a time of relative contentment for all. Lehi and Sariah, basking in their renewed faith, felt blessed beyond measure. Laman and Lemuel seemed to be conforming. Sam was content helping his mother and relaxing with his music. Nephi, bolstered in confidence by his success in obtaining the plates, gloried in his father's unreserved approval—and reveled in the resultant responsibility. After charging him with the safety of the holy records which he had obtained, Lehi directed him to compose and scribe the account of obtaining them.

"Write also, all of God's commandments since thou has been chosen. Do not write much of the commandments given to thy father, for there will not be room. The records must contain a fullness of God's word in accordance with thy mission to teach my seed." And Lehi solemnly emphasized, "Write only His commandments, not what is pleasing to the world."

"I will write only that which is pleasing to God," Nephi vowed. "And I shall command my ancestry, that after my time they not occupy these plates with things which are not of worth unto the children of men."

At this declaration Lehi's heart swelled. When alone he threw himself upon the winter-turned grass and thanked God for giving him a son of such caliber to follow in his footsteps. So wrapped up in the wonder of Nephi's parallel mission, the father paid little attention to his other sons. Thus he was unaware when Laman and Lemuel became restless. And not long after they were again whispering and plotting. "This time we'll know the way," said Lemuel, "so it won't take so long."

"Yea," Laman retorted. "And I think the danger is over. By now the people may have forgotten our father and his threatening words. And Laban is no more."

"I can hardly wait," Lemuel whispered. He peeked through the bushes to be sure no one was near.

Laman's icy eyes lighted with excitement. He took a quick peak in all directions—double insurance that they would not be overheard.

"Now is the time," he said confidently. "The old man is so wound up searching scripture if he thinks God says go, he'll go whenever, wherever. He'd not delay an instant for looking after us."

As they left their hideout they simultaneously turned and looked in a northerly direction.

"You know brother," Laman said, "we *could* be on our way."

"Yea…" Lemuel cocked his head, and with a grin suggested that they just keep going now. "Why not? The girls are waiting."

Laman thought a minute. "Yea, why not? If we …" He hesitated, picking a burr from the sleeve of his tunic. "But we have no packs. What dost thou say we make it tomorrow? Early, real early."

Lemuel's grin spread wider. He nodded. They linked arms and went high stepping in a mock march back to camp, discussing details on the way.

"… and tonight we'll watch where our mother puts the bread, so we can add it to our packs. Let the old man want when there's none in the morning."

They stopped just out of hearing and shook hands. There was little more to say, little whispering left to do. And arriving obviously happy they did not worry their mother. Their father in conference with Nephi, as usual, Sam off somewhere playing his lute, no one noticed the glow on their faces. No one paid them any attention. It was going to be easy.

It would have been easy…

At the evening meal the head of the family announced that The Lord had again spoken. And the new commandment displaced their plan; yet they would go, and automatically benefit. It was too good to be true. They beamed at each other.

Lehi beamed at the circle of faces leaning forward, hungry for details. Everybody listened intently.

"It is the Lord's will," he said, "that I should not take my family into the wilderness alone. In His great wisdom God hath spoken for posterity. *"...thy sons should take daughters to wife, that they might rise up seed unto the Lord in the land of promise."*

"And for this purpose, my sons, you are to go up again to the city and bring down my kinsman, Ishmael, and his family."

The plotters looked at each other incredulously. What they wanted to do had been commanded. They could now go with their father's blessing. That all of the brothers were to go, was no problem. Two of them simply would not be returning.

CHAPTER XII

Ishmael awakened with a start. Had someone called his name? He cocked his head. He heard the voice again.

Throwing back the patchwork coverlet Ishmael pulled his bulk from the comfort of the featherbed shared with his wife and padded toward the front of the house. He cautiously drew aside the tapestry, unlatched the window shutter and peeked out. Shadowy figures at the gate. Three or four men. In the pre-dawn half darkness he did not recognize them. *Who would seek admittance at this hour?*

"Who goes there?" he called

"Ishmael, we regret to awaken you; but our father…"

"It is the sons of Lehi!"

Ishmael's loud response brought his wife and daughters running. By the time the travelers reached the door they faced a full reception committee, all beaming. Wide-eyed and wreathed in smiles Ruth stared at the visitors unselfconsciously. Her face radiated. Little Eve, like the half-child she still was, jumped up and down. Abigail, Hannah and Josepha, the daughters of an age to be conscious of their appearance, lifted their shawls over unwashed faces and unbrushed hair. While stocky, motherly Anna, her colorless hair awry, rushed forward unabashed to embrace the sons of her dearest friend.

"Seat thyselves," she said, edging them toward the long leather couch. "And remove your sandals. I will heat water that you may wash your tired feet."

The woman's eyes were full of questions, especially about their mother, but she would wait to ask them. The comfort of guests in her home was paramount. Ascertaining the business of their surprising visit was the privilege of her husband. Already Ishmael had rasped out the question most crucial to all.

"Lehi, your father, how is he? I pray no harm has come to him."

"Our father is safe," Nephi assured him.

"Thank God," Ishmael mumbled, "Thank God. But, where *is* Lehi? How is he? And why have his sons, all four of them, come to me?" The genial host paced back and forth before his visitors with a continuing barrage of questions, leaving little time for answers.

Anna tarried long enough to hear that Lehi still lived, and Sariah, then immediately went about her duties. Laman, Lemuel and Sam leaned back and luxuriated in the comfort of padded seating, leaving Nephi to answer their friendly white-haired interrogator. While five pair of eyes peeked from the shadows. But before Nephi could answer their father's questions, and fully satisfy their curiosity, Anna called her distracted daughters to duty.

"Josepha, check the oil, that the lamp is full, and carry it to your father. Hannah, bring us candles. We will prepare the morning meal immediately. We do not wait for sunlight when we have hungry guests."

Anna briefly returned to the guests, taking their dusty cloaks to clean. She lay the garments in a pile near the back door, and continued instructing her daughters.

"Ruth, fetch more water from the cistern. Eve, you know your duty; set bowls and implements for five. Your father will take nourishment with them while they discuss business."

"But they are kinsmen," Hanna injected. "Times before, we..."

"Hannah! First your father must confer with them. We will know their business when he tells us. Now don't dawdle. The sons of Lehi have walked a long way; they are hungry. Take another candle and go help Abigail."

Abigail had gone without instruction to the fire pit. Already she had kindled a cooking fire, and was patting out wheat cakes. Having held a wife's responsibility the eldest daughter no longer required a mother's direction.

She did, however, require a mother's comfort. When her charioteer husband was killed Abigail had begged to return to the house of her father, lest the next of kin take the widow to wife. And using his considerable influence as a righteous man of means, Ishmael had arranged this breach of tradition. For the first-born was her father's joy. Reminding him of Anna as a bride, Lehi favored his eldest daughter. She was his first born, and almost like a sister to her mother. With two sons (next younger) Ishmael broke tradition by favoring a daughter.

After he and his guests had eaten it was normal that Abigail was first to enter. As she started clearing the table Anna joined her. The head of the house smiled at them, indicating that anything he said was for their hearing.

" ... Blessed is the Lord God of Israel," he concluded. Then under his breath quietly, "I am much shaken. I must think, and pray, that I make the right decision for all of my family."

He smiled at his guests in dismissal and motioned toward Anna.

"My good wife will show you where you may retire, and rest. I go to get my sons and their wives. After I have conferred with God, and with all my family, we will talk again."

As the sons of Lehi passed from the room Ishmael shook each of their hands traditionally, from eldest to youngest, holding on to the last a bit longer. He looked deep into Nephi's eyes before letting go.

When the young men had departed Abigail went to her father. She noticed that his hands were shaking.

"Father what is it? What is it that Lehi has sent his sons to tell thee?"

Ishmael absently patted his daughter's hand.

"Patience, patience, my dear. It is too much to say quickly. I must go and bring my sons. That which Lehi requires of me concerns all of my family."

When Ishmael told his family about the words of the Lord to Lehi, it disrupted his household like an earthquake. They all stared at him like statues, mute and immobile. The eldest son broke the spell.

"Leave the house I have just built! Take my wife and children to live in the wilderness!" Heleman looked at his father as if he were daft.

Newly married Hiram could only shake his head at the idea. His delicate young wife had lived a sheltered life of luxury. He couldn't even consider it. At first mention of leaving the city she had begun crying.

Anna's reaction did not reveal her conflicting emotions. She longed to see her dear friend Sariah, but she wanted the best for her family. As she listened to the responses of her sons and grown daughters, the maturity lines in her face deepened with compassion for the one who must make the decision.

And what would her sons do if Ishmael decided against their beliefs?

Anna knew that they had trouble believing Lehi was called of God. She also knew they didn't believe that God's holy city would ever be destroyed. At the family conference these were the main subjects of dissertation. Heleman voiced his beliefs stronger than anyone.

"Jerusalem will never fall; it's all a ruse. I think those fanatical prophets enjoy trying to scare us. And also … Father, forgive me, but I seriously doubt that God doth ask this sacrifice of us. Or, that he talks to Lehi. Yea, this I doubt more than the prophets."

Ishmael's initial doubts about his friend's mission had long ago vanished. He *knew* Lehi had received commandments from The Lord. Could he therefore not believe in another? A mandate for his family. The heart of the easy-going father rebelled at the thought. He could not order grown sons to act against their beliefs. Especially with frightened, unhappy wives contending against them.

He made a mental inventory of the feelings of those assembled. Two of his daughters, Josepha and Hannah, and his daughters-in-law, might need serious persuading. The juveniles, Ruth and Eve, were no problem (they had listened wide-eyed, imagining a great adventure). Abigail, like Anna, would be quietly obedient. And of course whatever he decided, his faithful partner would convince the women. He had only to convince his sons.

Finally, after much prayer, and considering every detail of the commandment as related to him and his family, Ishmael felt sure what he must do. But he could not yet say. Again he called them all together, and told them to pray and think about it for a while. Then it was time for Anna to talk with her daughters, and daughters-in-law … She counseled them in the garden, listened to all their questions, answering them as best she could. And upon dismissing them she said,

"You all know that your father would not of his own volition subject his family to the hardships of an unknown wilderness. And he will not make this decision hastily. He spends many hours in prayer. Since God spoke his name … Yes, The Lord spoke your father's name, so he must personally seek God's will."

Although Anna had faith in Ishmael's wisdom, and fairness; she secretly wished that he would sometimes seek her will, or opinion in solving their mutual problems. But her partner's needs of a helpmate did not include help in making decisions.

No matter how earth shattering, or how much they concerned the wife, tradition dictated that the husband could go only to God for guidance. It was man's responsibility. And no head of a household took this responsibility more seriously than Ishmael. He prayed constantly for three days.

And it came to pass that the Lord did soften the heart of Ishmael, and also his household.

As they began making preparations for a journey into the wilderness the sons of Lehi worked together with the sons and daughters of Ishmael—as the one family they were destined to be.

The entire clan now at peace with his decision Ishmael organized the venture with confidence. Exuberant but humble, he inspired the young men by working along side them, addressing them as equals, and sharing responsibility with them. Lehi's sons also. To Laman and Lemuel he said, "Come with me to attend to the selling of thy father's property." To Sam and Nephi, he gave money to buy supplies. "In this pouch is enough to purchase all manner of seed, and the special requirements for such a journey. We shall hold back nothing for the fulfilling of Lehi's mission."

Truly, God had given Ishmael conviction. His ruddy round face beamed, as if he had never doubted. Faith-guided, he made the decision—and God convinced his family. His sons soothed their wives fears. They sold their houses, and all their stock—except for the necessary pack animals, and three recently freshened milk goats, to augment Lehi's herd for the enlarged family.

Ishmael always considered the practical side of a venture. For whatever hardships they might encounter on this journey he would be prepared. the traveling would not be too hard on his family. And he anticipated contentment at the end of it. His dear Anna would have the companionship of her best friend; he would be with Lehi. And the children would be together. The father also did not overlook the possibility that fate may have blessed him with worthy husbands for his daughters.

The strong young sons of Lehi had long found favor in his eyes—and shortly after their arrival he'd seen indications that his daughters might agree.

Ruth continually blushed in Nephi's presence. Her heart was in her face for all to see. Once, in the bustle of preparations, they bumped into each other. The touch of the youth's muscular bare arm against the back of her hand could have been a tongue of fire; Ruth dropped her bundle. When Nephi stooped to retrieve it her eyes caressed the back of his neck. When he put the bundle in her hands she swayed like a nymph in water….

Hannah (who had eyed the son of a neighbor) now melted under Lemuel's grin. His practiced glances at her alabaster skin, and bouncing black curls were reciprocated. It appeared that Hannah had obliterated the memory of the city women for which Lemuel had almost deserted.

Josepha, who enjoyed admiring glances from all young men, discovered she had much in common with Laman. Both were adventurous, slim, active, and ever ready to reject tradition. After a few days of reminiscing their escapades as children, they had become *openly* close.

Ishmael was pleased with these indications—but he told Anna to watch them.

As patriarch of a large family about to commence a journey from familiarity and comfort to the fearful unknown, he prayed for wisdom to counsel and guide his loved ones. Having taken note of the budding changes in his feminine offspring, and anticipating the daily discomforts of their new and different life in the wilderness, Ishmael implored God's blessing that his daughters would not suffer unduly.

At last came the morning of departure. After pronouncing a benediction on their old life, and asking God's blessing on the new, Ishmael also prayed for guidance in assisting and supporting Lehi in his mission.

The apprehensive group set out in high spirits, expecting the heat, prepared to look for shade in a hot dry wilderness. But they were wet and weary by evening. The gray drizzle that began about noon and continued until dusk had definitely dampened the high of adventure—but not yet their spirits. Everybody seemed happy—each with an individual dream of the exciting future.

Imaginings of the unknown future fully occupied their minds. Particularly Ishmael's sons. Hiram and Heleman hoped to find farming country, their own fertile land somewhere beyond the hot rocky hills of south Judah.

I know father believes it is God's will that he support Lehi," Heleman whispered, "but doing what? Will he have time to help us plant and harvest?"

"I kept wondering," Hiram said guardedly. "It was as if to ask a question meant dissension. So I don't know what he wants to do. But I found out how much he wants us with him.."

"Perhaps he thought if we didn't come he might not ever see us again."

"Yea, it is good that we're all together."

By the end of the second day, however, Ishmael's sons had joined Laman and Lemuel, talking apart. The four of them conversed out of the old man's hearing. When Ishmael went to kick out the fire, and check to insure the women were all in their tents, he looked curiously at the four seated together on the ground, heads bent as if whispering. He called out.

"My sons, which of you will stand first watch? I think we should still have a watch tonight."

No response.

"We must assure the safety of our women," Ishmael continued. "We might yet be within the region of robbers."

After an awkward silence Lemuel ventured, "What about Sam and Nephi.?"

"They're still helping the women."

"I will, then," said Heleman.

"And I'll keep him company," Laman volunteered. He arose mumbling to himself, something about sleep would evade him anyway.

Laman still couldn't understand why he had agreed to return to his father's camp. The first evening he and Lemuel just looked at each other like "What happened to our plan?" The second day they began whispering. Then Hiram and Heleman exchanged knowing looks. And finally the four of them together.

Just two days out from the city, and already rumblings of a conspiracy.

Ishmael sensed the virus of insurrection; but since he hadn't forced them (everyone had consented to come) he put it down to nervousness. A man of much experience he understood that the uninhabited wilderness could be very daunting to city dwellers. Not only women were ill at ease, and exhausted by day-long treks. His own lack of energy surprised him. And Anna noted that his beefy face seemed redder than usual.

Abigail had noticed it earlier.

"Mother, why does Father push himself so? He has only to order Lehi's sons to go slower. They are young, and they know the way so they walk at a run."

"Your father is wont to get to the tent of Lehi even more than his own flesh and blood," Anna told her. "He is driven. That he hurts is not important; he…" She paused. "Ishmael is anxious to see Lehi; but mostly he needs to know what The Lord requires of him, as one chosen to serve in support of Lehi's mission."

"I guess it's like being in labor," Abigail mused, "the harder it hurts, the sooner it will be accomplished."

Anna looked at her daughter quizzically. That Abigail still yearned for a baby her mother knew; but she had no idea how desperately. Practical Anna would not have lost sleep over it anyway. When her aging bones ached for sleep, she did not conjure up worries to prevent it. The first night in an uncomfortable bed on the ground she had managed six hours, and awakened without complaint—as she would tomorrow. And tomorrow… Anna flushed with anticipation. If all went well she would soon see her dear friend Sariah again.

Ishmael's thoughts of the morrow, when he came in from checking the camp, concerned the strain of distance. Nephi told him there would be yet one more full day of travel. He wondered if his aching bones would be up to it. The aging body couldn't compete with the energy of the mind. Everything hurt, like when he first got up in the mornings. But when he settled in Anna made him quite comfortable. He decided that he had been mentally manufacturing problems; he was just tired. Remembering the blessing of God softening the hearts of his family, he relaxed. With a sigh Ishmael pulled up the feather lined coverlet that Anna made for him (especially for the journey) and put worry out of his mind.

Soon he was sleeping soundly—never imagining that in the morning his quasi-cooperative family would explode into open battle.

CHAPTER XIII

Nephi awoke with a jerk, unwound himself from the rough robe he'd slept in, and was immediately on his feet. Shivering in the dampish gray dawn, he fumbled with the thongs of his sandals. The intense whispering which had awakened him came again. And now he recognized Laman's voice, then Lemuel's.

"We can *not* go to the women's tent."

"Well, would you have me call them?"

"Forget them," Lemuel hissed. "If they're not ready we'll go without them." Hefting his pack he attempted to stalk away. His brother's long arm jerked him back.

"No. We planned to take the women, and I'm not going without Josepha."

"I want Hannah, too, but, not at risk of the whole operation. There are women in Jerusalem." Forgetting to whisper, Lemuel spat out these words. " Come on; it's almost daylight."

"Sh, shush," Laman's eyes darted. "Ishmael might hear you. Or worse, our holier-than-thou brother."

"I already heard you."

Nephi loomed up before them silhouetted in warrior stance against the red-tinged horizon. His face contorted. His voice rang out harshly.

"May God forgive you. To leave would be a sin against God's commandment. We are to stay together. And, my brothers, think. Ye have seen an angel, Your lives have been saved from Laban's men; you have been delivered from the evil destruction of Jerusalem. *Still*, you would go against commandments?"

Moving toward them, a tower of determination, Nephi continued. But his voice had softened.

"My brothers, how is it that after all you've seen and heard, still you do not hearken unto the word of the Lord?"

The would be deserters eyed their younger brother in angry silence. Laman's thin lips pulled to a wire, Lemuel's eyes shooting daggers. Nephi reached out to them imploring with his eyes and his hands, as well as his words.

"You must not do this thing. You must not break up the family. Our father is waiting for us. And it is God's commandment that all the sons return, with all the household of Ishmael."

"That is what you want; we want no more wilderness living," Lemuel pronounced each word emphatically. "We want a chance to live before we die."

"Yea," Laman retorted, "in a civilized city, where there's something to do. I'm not a gypsy; I've had enough of this bohemian life."

Nephi's anger flared. "Behold, how is it that ye are so hard in your hearts and so blind in your minds, that ye have need that I, your younger brother, should speak unto you, yea, and set an example for you? The Lord will..."

Laman's eyes sparked ice.

"Shut thy mouth! We are weary unto death of your infernal preaching."

But Nephi kept preaching, and moving forward, reaching out to put his hands on his brothers' shoulders.

A look flashed between them; in an instant they were upon him. Advantaged by the element of surprise, they were able to bind Nephi's arms to his sides; but the two of them were not strong enough to hold him. As they attempted to tie his wrists he broke loose.

Lemuel sprang upon his back. Simultaneously, a long leg swung out and tripped him—and Laman jumped on his head, shoving his face into the dirt. they bound his arms again.

"Stop! Oh, Lord God of Israel, stop them."

The quaking voice of Ishmael. Short legs propelling him across the rocky terrain, he kept shouting "Stop, stop. Fighting is not for the sons of Lehi."

The only son of Lehi who heard him was Sam. With a painful look of helplessness on his face Nephi's would-be rescuer was restraining, and attempting to calm Ruth and Eve. Abigail and Anna were shadowing Ishmael. While his other daughters Hannah and Josepha, fully dressed and carrying packs, peeked from behind their tent, looking nervously toward a small grove of terebinth trees (where Hiram and Heleman hid with their wives and children).

"Heleman, Hiram, come quick. Come quick."

The distraught father kept pleading for help from his sons, while jerking his head back and forth looking for them. Pleading for obedience from another man's sons had proved futile. So Ishmael could only try with the strength of the old. Upon reaching the struggle he grabbed at flaying arms. But his best efforts amounted to little more than irritating interference. And the cloud of dirt stirred up by the fighting started him coughing. They flung him aside like rubble.

His wife and eldest daughter picked him up.

And as Anna and Abigail held Ishmael upright between them, their eyes still on the fighting, both women screamed. Blood was spurting from Nephi's temple. His head lolled. Laman and Lemuel ceased their pummeling. A knowing look passed between them. They had succeeded in subduing the opposition to their plan. And if Ishmael had been a minor obstacle he was no longer. Their eyes turned from the still form on the ground to the man sagging like an empty sack between his wife and daughter, to the grove of trees on the edge of camp.

Ishmael's sons came out of hiding.

Then Hannah and Josepha came out from behind their tent. And upon revealing themselves each looked at Laman and Lemuel as if expecting them to stand up in triumph and announce that they could now leave. But the perpetrators seemed to have lost their voices. A red-gold sun arching over the horizon was so unnaturally bright it seemed as if the air was on fire. Starring blindly at the exaggerated spectacle of nature, then down at their bleeding brother, they froze in position. Like Lot's wife, dead as a statue—lifeless as the form at their feet.

But the spectacle shot Sam into action. Forgetting his honorable intentions to protect the young he let go of them, and rushed forward screaming.

"You killed him. You've killed him."

Suddenly the co-conspirators (conscious stricken too late) were also rushing forth. As would be rescuers Hiram and Heleman couldn't run fast enough. Hannah and Josepha also had a change of heart. Young Eve, clinging to her sister, began sobbing. Ruth appeared to have died upright—but in the next instant she screamed.

"Nephi, Oh, Nephi. Thank God!"

Nephi was on his feet, the double-knotted cords dangling from his muscled arms like worms. Belying a bloody countenance his voice rang out strong.

"The Lord God hath given me strength …"

When their victim started to speak Laman and Lemuel came alive. They flew at him in a double fit of fear and anger, without hearing what he was saying.

"No! No." shrieked Heleman, "Look, look at him."

"Stop; we're afraid," Hannah and Josepha blurted out in unison.

Anna, who had been watching the scene in horror, made a decision. Leaving her husband to Abigail, she usurped his position. As matriarch, the woman would do what had to be done. In a stern controlled voice she commanded.

"Young men, do not touch your brother again."

A woman speaking firmly, with an air of authority, caught everyone's attention. Even Nephi's. He ceased speaking and listened to Anna.

"For thy own sakes," Anna said to the fighting brothers, "cool the anger within you, and think! Could anyone else but God have loosed the cords?"

As if those words ordered the action, the blazing sun now free of the horizon, turned full power on the group. And the blood on Nephi's face turned to gold—and while they all starred the gold dissipated, disappearing entirely.

Laman and Lemuel, now in-hand by the sons of Ishmael, felt their hearts slam into their throats. Shaking in mutual recollection of another time, an interceding angel in a cave outside Jerusalem, they fell to their knees begging forgiveness.

And once again Nephi forgave all that they had done.

For the remainder of the trip harmony reigned. In fact the last day of travel resembled a game of follow-the-leader. Every one followed Nephi, watching him in awe. They watched his every move, whispering to each other. But no one spoke to him, unless he spoke first.

Just before sundown they reached the valley by the river. The combined family entered the camp of Lehi in silence; and the old prophet knew by their countenance that there had been an incident of renewed faith. His heart swelled with gratitude. Thanks to God his sons had returned safely, bringing all the house of Ishmael. They had succeeded in their mission, and now the evident blessing of a blanket faith renewal…

With soaring spirit Lehi welcomed his combined family and called them all together on the river bank for prayer. *"... they did give thanks unto the Lord their God; and they did offer sacrifice and burnt offerings unto Him."*

For years thereafter the wayward sons conformed, respected and listened to their father—and made a concerted effort not to resent their younger brother. The incident on the trek from Jerusalem burnt into their memory, and the fact that Nephi again forgave them, had finally brought conviction. But jealousy that he was chosen to lead instead of the elder brother still smoldered.

"Truly I believe Nephi is called of God," the humbled Lemuel said to Hannah. "for an ordinary man would not be able to forgive all that we did."

The two were walking along the river, alone together. It had been allowed. Since their return with Ishmael's household the repentant sons enjoyed a new measure of freedom. Throughout the membership of both the soon to be joined families a growing measure of happiness prevailed. Tension was rare—until there arose a subject of discord in regard to the imminent joining.

Everyone believed that marriage between the sons of Lehi and the daughters of Ishmael had been ordained; but how would it be accomplished? Devout families of Judah did not deviate from the traditions of their fathers. And tradition, in some instances, would seem to go against God's will. As the family marriage authority Lehi prayed constantly for a solution—while the subjects of the controversy worried. In more than one case, if he strictly followed tradition, hearts would hurt. Additionally, Abigail already hurt. And Anna hurt for her widowed daughter. There was no son of Lehi for a widow.

One day Anna found her dutiful daughter still at the river long after the washing was done. She was staring at the running water as if it were her life rolling away. The mother reached out to hold her. Abigail smiled weakly and leaned her head on her mother's shoulder.

"Oh Mother, I dreamed ..." Her voice broke. "I've dreamed all my life of having a baby. And when my husband died I prayed with strong faith that someday the Lord would give me another partner. But now in this wilderness, how? There is no one. There will be no one . . ."

"My dear daughter. It is unfortunate that Lehi has but four sons; and of course they must have thy virgin sisters. But don't lose faith. Wherever God leads us, I truly feel that there will be..."

"But I will be too old." Abigail wailed. "My father sayeth this wilderness is vast. And we, ... there is even yet no talk of going further. So there is no chance."

Anna soothed her daughter as best she could without offering false hope. Then back to her duties. As she bent to the river to fill her cask with water Zoram, who had followed to carry it (as he carried Sariah's) came forward from the discrete distance where he had waited. Keeping his eyes averted from the woman's daughter, he took the filled cask from her. Abigail didn't even know the little man was there. Wrapped in the suffering fear of being childless, completely oblivious, she had been seriously considering ending her empty life in the river.

"Come on daughter," Anna said, "Come back with me to Sariah's tent. Help us prepare the meal."

Blessed with a big family Anna felt no woman should have to suffer the tragedy of being childless. And back in the city, she would find ways to remedy the situation. But in this wilderness, the mother had no answer. There was no way of helping. Abigail would even welcome an unhappy marriage, if necessary, that she might be fulfilled. But they could not even hope for that. Finding a respectable man of similar social background (one who would accept a widow) was hard enough in a city, impossible in an uninhabited wilderness.

Oh, that she could do something... But what could anybody do?

When they entered the cooking tent Sariah exclaimed.

"Oh Anna, this tent, and all the food you brought: leeks, garlic, figs, grapes—and you to talk to! I'll be forever thankful that you came. That day I saw you and your family, and my sons approaching was the happiest day of my life."

Anna smiled, and hugged her friend.

"How about the day your sons returned from their first trip," she teased. "You told me you thought they were lost for ever. What about that day?"

Sariah flushed, and brushed some flour from her sleeve before answering.

"That day, Anna," she began slowly, "I hurt too much with relief and shame to be happy. All I could do was cry." She muffled a sob. "Oh, Anna, often I want to cry because I am lacking in strength. I am not worthy to be the helpmate of Lehi. He is so good, and being God's chosen …"

"Shush," said Anna. "You're a strong, good woman, who learned to accept the finer things of life which her husband provided. And you bear the present hardships without complaining. Lehi is blessed to have thee."

"But," said Sariah; "I have managed without comforts here only because I did not expect them. And now it's better than before. I deserve no credit."

"Yes you do," said Anna. "Here let me knead the bread, while you prepare the cheese. You make it tastier. What is your seasoning secret?"

Sariah straightened and smiled. "No secret, nothing special. I bless your Ishmael. It is thanks to the goats he brought that we now have cheese, and plenty of milk. Our goats were all dry."

Glancing out the tent opening to the tethered goats grazing on the riverbank, Anna said, " I see you now have one about to freshen."

"Yes." Sariah smiled over at Abigail, and back to Anna. "Thanks to God, and Ishmael, our families will not go hungry. We have much to be thankful for."

Abigail looked up from her preparations. Pleased that her mother had a close friend with whom she could exchange confidences, she smiled fondly at Sariah. The three women worked in harmony. The nutritional meal was soon ready.

All assembled for the blessing of the food, Sariah was dishing it up… Her heart skipped. Sam was missing. In the pre-prayer silence (before Lehi bowed his head to say the blessing) she motioned toward the vacant place near the end of the rough-hewn table. It was rectangular in shape to accommodate traditional seating: one family on each side, oldest to youngest, with the parents at each end. The vacant space was across from Ruth, second to youngest.

As they all shuffled into their places Eve also noticed the vacancy.

"Sam isn't here," she exclaimed, as if an absence at the table was a tragedy.

In wilderness life, with little to keep young girls occupied, the evening meal was the event of the day. And in the innocence of youth, Eve could not imagine anyone missing it. Ever since she'd come to this camp no one ever had. Nobody had even been late.

Everybody looked at Lehi, waiting for his response. Would the patriarch offer the prayer and allow them to eat? Or would they have to wait for Sam? In that moment of silence, the faint strains of music wafting across the valley became audible. Sam's lute.

"My husband," said Sariah, quickly, "Wouldst thou allow me to set a portion aside for him, that the others may be nourished?"

Lehi cleared his throat. "Sam plays no more for us in camp. Why doth he…"

Misty eyes told him that the mother knew her son was troubled. And he, the protector of the family, had not seen it. Lehi contemplated only a minute before nodding his consent around the table. Sariah gave him a warm smile. She set portions aside for Sam, and appeared to relax. But by the time they had all finished eating her face had tightened again. Sam still had not returned to camp.

Nephi looked plaintively at his Mother.

"I will go get him."

Lemuel jumped up running. "No, I will."

No music now to lead him in the right direction. But Lemuel finally found the fugitive from food sprawled beneath a straggly tree. Sam did not acknowledge his brother. His lute lay in the stubble beside him.

"Sam, what are you doing here?" Lemuel questioned. "What in the world is it; why didn't you come to eat?"

Sam didn't respond.

"Well, it's almost dark. Dost thou expect to worry thy mother all night?"

"Leave me alone. Just leave me alone."

The unnatural response from congenial Sam was startling. Lemuel waited for the words that would explain it.

"Sam?"

"I said leave me alone."

Lemuel shrugged his shoulders and did as asked. Back at camp he said to his mother, "He's not hurt; but he wouldn't come. He wouldn't even talk to me."

"Thank you, Lemuel."

Sariah released a long sigh, and took up her watch outside the tent, facing the direction from whence Lemuel came. And when at last in the deepening twilight she saw her troubled son coming, she went to meet him. Sam smiled weakly. He did not withdraw from her physically, but brushed off her concern, making no attempt at an explanation.

Sariah swallowed the lump in her throat and told him she had saved some food for him. He said he wasn't hungry. He went to bed. She went to Lehi.

"My husband he is not himself; something weighs on his mind. I can't imagine what it could be. And he is not ready to tell me."

Lehi didn't seem too disturbed, advising his wife only that "maturing requires times of insecurity, even temporary depression."

So as they made ready to retire she said no more. But a mother cannot rest when one of her children hurts. *My son is sorely disturbed; my son is troubled; and I don't know how to help him.* Her worried mind kept sleep at bay for hours.

At breakfast Sariah looked haggard. She tried again to talk to Sam. He was still not ready; he came to the table but left without finishing his meal. Later, however, after the young women had cleared the table and taken the vessels to the river to wash, he came to her. Sariah looked up from her mending with a warm smile. The chestnut hair and beard had been groomed. But his eyes were red. She held out her hand.

"Come sit beside thy mother."

After a moment of silence Sam unburdened his heart to his mother. But Sariah could not solve the problem. Immediately she took it to the head of the family. But Lehi would have to confer with Ishmael. He took his wife's hands and pressed them together in position of prayer.

"Faith, dear Sari, have faith. With God's help we will work this out. We will find a way, the best way for all."

For hours Lehi and Ishmael conferred, in a spirit of cooperation, for the good of both families. But the solution evaded them. Tradition could not be broken—but for honorable purposes, maybe slightly adjusted. At long last, the fathers decided. In their hearts they believed their decision on the pairing of their progeny would be to the mutual gratification of all.

And a few days later arrangements were finalized for the formal betrothal and marriage of Lehi's sons and Ishmael's daughters.

CHAPTER XIV

The morning sun caressed the valley, and the two men walking across it. Heads bent together, they were walking slowly, talking earnestly, but their faces showed no tension.

"My friend," Lehi said, "The day approaches. And I feel warm in the wisdom of our decision." He put an arm on Ishmael's beefy shoulder, and slowed him as they approached the tents. The camp was buzzing, everyone working on last minute preparations, all in a sunshine mood.

"I know," Lehi concluded, "that our decision is right; I know in my heart it's as God meant it to be."

Ishmael beamed a smile that resurrected the ghost of his youth, and walked ahead. Over his shoulder he added. "I know my daughters will be happy. All my daughters are going to be happy."

Both men seemed energized with the rightness of their final decision. But Lehi had more to say. He grasped Ishmael's arm.

"When I came to thy tent at dawn and required of thee a conferring in private, my heart fretted for Sam and thy young daughters. But now I know the slight deviation from tradition is wholly acceptable to The Lord. I *know* God will bless the unions, and both couples will be happy."

"And I am blessed further," Ishmael said humbly, "I am blessed beyond measure in the matter. That in God's great wisdom my dear Abigail shall also have a husband fills this old heart to overflowing. Anna too will be happy. For soon, she'll be relieved of her worry and watching.

Lehi had also considered how the news in regard to Zoram and Abigail would please his Sari. When the lifelong dream of Anna's eldest daughter comes true, his wife would not only rejoice with her friend, for Abigail, she would be pleased to see Zoram happy. She had become fond of the kind little man.

"The heart of Zoram is good," Lehi said aloud. "Your widowed daughter will become a mother, and she is blessed with a gentle …

Ishmael interrupted. "Thanks be to heaven that she is not yet beyond the bearing years. My Abigail shall have her child; she will have her baby. And he who will be the father is no more a servant than we. Are we not all servants of the Lord?"

"We are, my friend."

"But..." Ishmael's face clouded. Lehi looked at him quizzically. "About the younger ones … I want nothing changed. I do believe that Ruth is meant to be the companion of thy chosen son; she is the strongest of all my daughters. But..."

"She does not care for Nephi?"

"Care for him…" Ishmael's oversized hands raised to the sky and dropped. "The maiden has been wont to die if the betrothal should be in the usual order. Oh, not that Sam was unacceptable, but…"

Lehi interrupted, "then why? I have seen the love in her eyes for Nephi; which only confirms the wisdom of God. So why dost thou worry?"

"My worry … forgive me," said Ishmael, "is for Eve. Our choices are right, but she is yet so tender and young. She is not ready for a man, any man."

The prophet had held to his word that *all* must marry at this time. And Ishmael had agreed. But now he pleaded again for assurance, one father to another, that his pubescent daughter not be deflowered too soon.

Although Lehi appreciated the gravity of Ishmael's concern, he could not grant an exception. It was expedient that all marriages take place. And Eve had reached the age of the law.

"Ishmael, thou knowest that soon we must leave this safe valley to travel in an unknown wilderness. Wherever The Lord doth lead us your daughters, all, will have need of protectors on the journey."

"But, I, her father, can protect her."

"My friend," Lehi said gently, "think thee that I have not seen the weakness come upon you? The time cometh when a man must be relieved of a father's burdens."

Ishmael attempted to square his rounding shoulders.

"I am still able to provide a father's protection."

Lehi let it pass, allowing him to think about the situation, continuing only when a long sigh revealed that Ishmael was at last ready to trust in his promise.

"You must not fear for your tender daughter," Lehi reiterated. "For herein again the wisdom of The Lord is revealed."

"What art thou saying?"

"I am saying, my kinsman, that of all my sons, Sam is the most gentle, and patient. Sam can wait. And as I told you, I shall require it of him. I shall require that he wait at least a year."

Ishmael stopped and turned to face Lehi squarely. "I do not question thy good intentions. And I doubt not thy word. But the urges of youth are strong …"

"Ishmael, Ishmael, where is thy faith? Dost thou not fully trust that God has sanctioned the unions? And have we not witnessed Sam's special protectiveness toward Eve? Dost thou forget how he became overwrought with concern that one barely budding would be given to wife the same as her sisters?"

As Lehi was saying this, Eve came running out of the cooking tent, shouting back over her shoulder, "Mother, they're here." Skipping up to her father, honey colored curls bouncing like brass springs, she took hold of Ishmael's hand and smiled up at him.

"I'm glad you're here father. I'm hungry; my stomach growls. And I can't become a lady if my stomach makes noises, can I?"

She flashed a mischievous grin at Lehi. Then as quickly as she took her father's hand she let go of it again. "C'mon, father, hurry." she said, and scampered back to the eating tent.

The two men followed a bit slower, Lehi again assuring Ishmael that his tender daughter would not be robbed of her innocence prematurely.

That concluded the prenuptial duties of the fathers.

The mothers had much more to do. Sariah and Anna outdid themselves preparing special food, and improvising wedding finery out of a scarcity of better garments, backed by colorless materials.

After mending her sons' least worn tunics Sariah stitched to each an accessory of gold-beaded material from the costly cloak of Laban that Nephi had appropriated. For their headdress bands, and Zoram's, she braided chains of spring flowers. She fashioned a special tunic for Zoram from the bright silk lining of the garment formerly worn by his affluent master.

The prosperity of the brides' father was much in evidence in the gowns Anna fashioned for her daughters. And they would wear fragrant garlands of variegated color to secure their head shawls. Nature generously cooperated with the plan. The latter rains of April had produced abundant flowers. Jonquil, primrose, and flowering ash all donated their beauty for the auspicious occasion.

The mothers planned their own outfits befitting their personality. Sariah would stand regal in her best blue mantle (the purloined ivory bracelet still hidden in the folds). While the pleasantly plump Anna, decked out in the finery of her professional embroidery, would display an intricately carved gold pendant. This beauty of dress, and happiness in their faces, they would only see vaguely—reflected in the river. For neither had brought her polished metal mirror.

At last came the day, and the hour (the sun smiling down center sky). All organized and ready the participants stood nervously awaiting their leader. And Lehi didn't keep them waiting a minute beyond the time. The soon-to-be-brides and grooms, honoring ancient custom, had abstained from the morning meal. All was in accordance with tradition, except the location. They were gathered together beneath a *temporary* canopy in the great chapel of nature.

As the spiritual leader began the ceremony he marveled at the beauty of youth and health before him. Radiant faces reflected the glory of the occasion. Though far from a synagogue, outdoors in the wilderness, the spiritual leader for this isolated segment of God's chosen people would carry out his responsibility with but one deviation, and one exception .

Under the makeshift "required" canopy Lehi lined up the couples in proper formation. Then he positioned the spectators in a semi-circle around them: the other father, the mothers, the already married sons of Ishmael and their wives and children.

The fair sons and daughters turned to face their partners: Laman and Josepha; Lemuel and Hannah; Nephi and Ruth; Sam and Eve (Abigail and Zoram waiting apart). Their ceremony would follow.

A serene silence prevailed. It seemed that all God's creatures quieted in reverence, even the birds and insects. The domesticated animals, the goats and burros tethered on the riverbank lay down to listen. All in readiness, surrounded in beauty and the perfume of nature, Lehi commenced the sacred ceremony.

For the officiator, as well as the participants, it was a time and a feeling that would long be remembered.

Lehi felt The Lord's presence, and he thought perhaps there were angels in attendance. Strong in faith, and treasuring the sacred rituals, he performed the liturgy of love with joy and confidence. By this celebration the tradition of their forefathers his progeny and the offspring of Ishmael would be lifelong partners, helpmates and companions. And from this day forward, they would all serve The Lord. Of this Lehi felt confident. And it was with equal confidence in the virginity of Ishmael's daughters that he made the exception. He would not require exhibition of the bloodstained sheet. Those whom he this day joined together were allowed to commence their conjugal lives without challenge.

In conclusion the patriarch smiled at his enlarged family and bowed his head. All heads bowed solemnly for the benediction. Then, formalities over, he talked to them as a father.

"Now my children, I ask that you live joyfully, with love. Marriage is not a concession to man's weakness. It is a sacrament for God's purpose. If it were not for the natural inclination man would not beget children. And it is commanded that we rise up children to follow after us." He paused, and sought their eyes, each in turn, before continuing. "It is not good that man should be alone. Therefore be thou good wives and husbands; love one another; comfort one another, help one another… Be fruitful; multiply and replenish the earth. For that is the holy commandment."

The couples then pledged their promises by sipping from the sacred cup.

When all had partaken of the ceremonial wine Lehi directed the wedded pairs to sit and be spectators while he performed the separate ceremony for Abigail and Zoram—the special rites for marriage of a widow.

Upon conclusion of all the ceremonies the officiator sought the eyes of *his* companion. Sariah smiled at him, her eyes brimming, remembering the day she had sipped the sacred cup with him. After their moment Lehi turned back to his children.

"Bless you my sons and daughters. By sanction of the Lord God of Israel, He who created joy and gladness, ye have been wed. By His love may your love grow. My sons rejoice with your brides. And when you taketh her, be thou gentle. Always be kind. Daughters, perform your wifely duties willingly. All of you remember that ye are consecrated unto each other according to the Law of Moses. And forget not the sacred covenant of wedlock, "*If the husband and wife be worthy God shall dwell in their tent…*"

"Now may the Lord go with you, and keep you; may His blessings be ever upon you…" And the blessed couples departed to their individual abodes to prepare for the subsequent feasting and merrymaking.

Basking in the warmth of Zoram's worshipping attention Abigail fairly glowed. Sam, now calm and contented, treasured the responsibility of his precious charge, while Eve trusted and adored him. As a legal foursome Laman and Josepha, Lemuel, and Hannah were free to laugh and frolic without parental restraint. Every soul rejoiced. And all the couples came comfortably together in their respective degrees of intimacy—except one.

That first evening, upon entering the tent of her husband, Ruth froze. Mature beyond her years, she had long dreamed of the love of Nephi. However, facing intimacy with the benevolent giant to whom God had spoken suddenly overwhelmed her. With the full realization that she was not only blessed to be his chosen, but also his possession, came panic. She trembled exceedingly.

"Ruth, what is it!"

Nephi gently took her in his arms, searching for the love he had seen in her face. But his bride dropped her head, cringed, and pulled away. Anticipating her shyness he reached out and raised her chin. She kept her eyes downcast—lest he see the fear in them. But he sensed it.

"My dear Ruth, my wife, thou must not fear me. I would never take you against your will. I have great love..."

Tears trickled from under her lashes.

The young husband's handsome face lost its glow; a puzzled expression replaced it. He tried again to hold her; she pulled away. He tried talking firmly to her. She did not respond. Sorely disappointed that his bride did not warm to him the inexperienced groom lost his confidence. The joy went out of him. Hurt and disoriented he moved to the far side of the tent.

For a long time he sat in silent agony, watching, waiting. Darkness deepened. The camp became quiet. Still Ruth did not move. Out of his reach, shawl over her head, she lay curled like a fetus unmoving as stone.

Finally accepting his fate Nephi slipped out of the tent.

The new bride heard her love walk away; and the dam broke. Tears gushed beyond control. She cried herself to exhaustion, but not to sleep. Hour after hour she tossed and turned, *What of the morrow? Oh what of the morrow!*

It was almost sunup before sleep overtook her.

CHAPTER XV

Ruth awoke with a start, sensing a strangeness of place. The feel of the grass mat under her was the same—Zoram had braided sleeping mats for everyone—but nothing else seemed familiar.

Then memory returned. With a lump in her throat she remembered yesterday's beautiful ceremony, and the warm feeling walking hand in hand with her husband to his tent... And then ... "Ohhhhh... " she groaned.

Yesterday's bride was alone today. Despite the coolness of early dawn sweat beaded her brow. She touched her face, still puffy from crying. Nephi must not see her this way. And worse, she could not bear to think of what she might see in his face. But when would she see it?

When would she see him? Where was he?

"Oh Lord God of Israel do not let my beloved cast me aside. Let him find it in his heart to forgive me. Please Lord, let it be, let it be..." She wrapped her arms around herself and sat upright in the center of the mat rocking back and forth, back and forth whispering, "Come back my love, come back to me. Oh Nephi..."

At long last she quieted, and sat staring into space.

Footsteps! Her heart skipped a beat. She grabbed her shawl and shakily rose to her feet just as Nephi pushed through the tent opening. His white teeth flashed. Cradled in his arms was a shiny black newborn goat. She swayed, and almost lost her balance. With one hand Nephi reached out and balanced her. With the other he held out the soft, warm bundle of life. And as he did, it bleated. She jumped. He laughed—that musical laugh she loved. Like ice encountering a roaring fire the tension instantly dissolved. Nephi eased the tiny animal into her arms.

"The mother died last night giving him birth," he said. "I give him to you."

Ruth could not speak. Her heart had come up in her throat to choke her. The furry life squirmed in her arms. Shakily, she began stroking it. And the feel of that warm body refueled the fire that smoldered within.

"Wilt thou, my wife, feed and care for…"

At the words, "my wife," her heart dropped into place like a dislodged boulder. And so strong was the pounding Nephi could see it pulsing at her temples. Gently, so gently, as if he feared it would break through the translucent skin, he touched the throbbing blue vein. A strand of bronze hair fell across his hand. He fingered it back, speaking huskily.

"Peace, dear one. Do not ever have fear of me; I have great love for thee. Dust thou not know this in thy heart?"

He kissed her on the forehead.

"Always remember, The Lord hath chosen you to be my helpmate. And I want you to be my companion forever."

Ruth's blue eyes flooded. She shifted the drowsy weight to one arm, and thrust the other around his neck. They fell back on the mat together, the black ball of fur between them. And then they were laughing.

When, not long after, Ruth's insecurity surfaced again—her imagination working overtime conjuring up inadequacies, versus all that a "special" helpmate must be—Nephi interrupted her thoughts.

"My love thou art strong and pure, as well as fair. Were I a king, I would want no other wife."

Ruth clung to her husband. *How could she be worthy of such a blessing? The love of the strongest, handsomest son, the chosen one; and in addition, she would never have to fear a thrashing.*

Inevitably, traditionally, this physical form of man's discipline (control of the woman) took place. After the waning of desire, and the elements took their toll on a woman's beauty, it was commonplace, an accepted custom. Ruth's sisters would expect it. Gentle Sam would be kinder with Eve, she thought. But she *knew*—her heart soared with the surety—that she would be altogether spared.

"Oh, Nephi, I will serve thee always; I will work hard to be a worthy wife for thee. Thy will shall be my will all the days of my life."

Nephi pulled her closer. "And my dear Ruth I will cherish thee always. We will share everything; we will serve God together."

And ever after when God's young servant scribed on the leather scrolls, his record of their journey, and all that God revealed to him, he would read to her what he had written. When he talked with Sam, entreated Laman and Lemuel, or her brothers to listen, he would tell her what he said to them. The days of Nephi and Ruth were filled with service to The Lord, and each other.

But in other tents there was not that contentment. As the long days of inactivity grew into months other members of Lehi's extended family searched for diversion. Laman and Josepha, Lemuel and Hannah, ever quarreling, seemed to forget the words that they heard on the day of their wedding. Yea, even the commandment to love one another. Ishmael and Anna continued faithful; but suffering advancing age and the effects of a comfortless existence, they too, sometimes lashed out at each other. While their sons wrangled, and suffered continual nagging by their wives. Hiram's wife, now heavy with child, and Heleman's, worrying about her growing children, became like pebbles in their husbands' sandals, grinding away on their good intentions. Regret for upholding their father's support of Lehi's venture grew.

And the good intentions of Laman and Lemuel weakened.

It seemed that time had dimmed their memory of the angel in the cave, and Nephi's miraculous release from the thrice-knotted cords. Those marvelous truths, so hard for the rebels to swallow, now seemed at times explainable. They had humbled themselves and asked for forgiveness out of fear. Professed to believe pursuant to advantage… And ever since, had been living in limbo, waiting for they didn't know what. Where was the advantage?

Lehi sensed this discontent. His wayward sons were again about to slide off the path of righteousness. So he fired up his speeches, and once more peppered them with dire warnings. He felt it was his duty.

"Hearken …hearken… hearken "*… he did exhort them with all the feeling of a tender parent, lest they be cast off from the presence of The Lord."*

The young prophet also preached to them. Nephi told his brothers, "Only the guilty taketh the truth to be hard."

All to no avail. So the old prophet softened again. Considering the circumstances, and the fact that for a long time they had been conforming, Lehi wanted to believe that they would have kept the faith and settled down in the verdant valley had they been allowed to build houses and plant crops. Soon it would be the time of barley harvest; and lo, again they hadn't planted. Restlessness spread like the plague. Everyone began to fear going hungry.

One day Laman surprised himself and went to his father for advice. But the eldest son was about to develop responsibility only to see his father seemingly disregard it. When he strongly presented his case for building, and planting, that the families could settle down and live normally, Lehi only said that he must be patient.

This quasi-answer from his father re-ignited Laman's anger He swallowed his pride and went to Nephi.

Laman coming to him, Lemuel in tow, actually asking for his advice… Nephi felt a surge of hope. As his brothers seated themselves in his tent (for the first time in ages) he turned his back and breathed a prayer that God would give him words sufficient to their needs. Then he called his wife.

"Bring refreshments for thy husband's brothers."

And not to waste a minute of the opportunity, he began talking before they asked a question.

"Oh, my brothers, if it be thy desire … if desire is now in thy hearts…"

Nephi picked his words carefully—and when they asked, he listened and tried to answer specifically instead of preaching. When they talked against their father he didn't berate them. He tried to explain.

"My brothers, our father is one of many chosen to make manifest God's word among men. And being commanded to make warnings, that the people of Israel repent, can you not see how it hurts him that his own sons do not repent? Contend no further against him, for his sake, and for your own, for all our sakes. Know the reason our father doth persistently bid thee to keep the commandments. It is because he fears in his heart for his sons, *lest they be cast off from the presence of The Lord."*

In this way Nephi counseled his older brothers.

"And they gave heed to my words!" he reported to Ruth. "Inasmuch as it is in their nature, they humbled themselves before me, and before God. I have great hope that at last they will turn upon the path of righteousness." He hugged her, tightly.

"Now I must go and give humble thanks to The Lord."

"But it is now near darkness."

Ruth cut off her own words, and dropped her eyes. Nephi kissed her on the forehead; his hand sliding down the burnished braid of hair. Then he was off to the cave on the mountain, where he habitually sought the word of God.

And that night the word was given,

The long awaited word was given to Nephi, and to his father. They were to depart the green valley by the river.

That same night on the mountain Nephi was also given a vision.

"... Blessed art thou Nephi; because thou believest thou shalt behold...Look. And Nephi looked and beheld the Redeemer of the world, and also the prophet that should prepare the way before him, and the twelve others following him, and angels descending upon the children of men..." Also a dire prediction about the future of the land of promise, and the multitude of gentiles who would build up a great nation.

After the vision, overcome with great weakness, Nephi slept. It was nearly midday when he returned to his wife.

Ruth rushed to greet her husband. While yet at a distance she ascertained that he was much changed. His face glowed; and he seemed to have grown in stature. But as he came closer she did not see joy emanating from beneath the radiance.

"My husband, what is it? What hast thou seen?"

Nephi looked kindly at his wife. He put his arm around her as they walked to their tent, but he told her nothing. First he must go to his father.

So, as it was with Sariah after Lehi's first vision, Ruth could only wait. The fate of a helpmate, to serve, and wait.

CHAPTER XVI

The waiting was over!

As Nephi approached the tent of his father, mentally recounting the vision he had been given, his heart beat staccato. *How to tell the prophet that the son had been given the word?* But he found Lehi awaiting him.

"Father, thou knowest."

Lehi nodded, holding out his arms. He patted the strong shoulder he could barely see over and clung to his son past propriety. At last he looked up to meet the steady, gold-flecked eyes of a peer. It had been given Lehi to know that his son had also received the long awaited message—that they were to continue the journey—and also the same revelation. Together they left the tent, and walked and talked for more than an hour. Then Lehi called a conference.

As his people assembled on the riverbank (surprisingly, or perhaps by unseen hand, all were in camp) the patriarch stood waiting, counting them as they came like a king counting his money. For his richness was in family. Elated over the dual vision he could hardly wait to share it with them. As a father and as a leader he expected the news would end, or surely curb, the rumbling in the ranks. But as they assembled he read fear and apprehension in their faces. So when all were seated in the traditional sermon-semi-circle he curbed his zeal to preach the vision and quietly related only what immediately concerned them.

"God bless us all. The Lord has spoken; we wait no longer. On the morrow we begin our journey to the land He hath promised us."

The response was not what he anticipated. They looked at their shepherd as if he were about to drive his flock through wolf country. But bursting with faith after the vision Lehi felt confident he could allay their fears. With divine guidance, he would bring his fold together in harmony. With Nephi's help he would lead them safely to the new land.

He looked over at Nephi and Ruth standing together, emanating faith, strength, and optimism (the very picture of what he wished for everybody). He reached out and pulled his exemplary son forward.

"My loved ones," he boomed, "fear not. The Lord is ever with us. In His great wisdom He hath revealed the word, and great things also unto Nephi—thus supplementing the weakness of age with the strength of youth. So have peace in your hearts for the future. If we walk in the paths of righteousness and keep God's commandments no harm will befall us."

"Which way are we going?" someone shouted.

"I know not yet in which direction; I go now to pray for this guidance. And I would that all of you pray too, while you are making preparations. Nephi will advise whatsoever things ye should carry."

Noting the apprehension in their faces, Lehi favored them with one of his rare smiles, then held up his arms. All heads bowed for the benediction.... "Go now and make ready, then early to thy beds."

When the stars twinkled over the darkened valley all were packed and ready. And most were ready in their hearts. The leader, however, still walked and prayed. "Oh, Lord God of Israel, when wilt thou give me direction; whither shall I lead them?" An hour later he went to Nephi's tent, whispering at the opening.

"My son, art thou asleep?"

Nephi came out immediately. His father grabbed his arm and pulled him out of hearing distance. "Has the word of direction been given thee?"

Nephi shook his head. He had been pacing, waiting for his father to bring the word to him. Now his father had come—not to tell him, but to ask him. The heavy weight of responsibility was already being transferred to stronger younger shoulders.

Nephi accepted the load. His voice was steady. "Father, let not thy faith weaken. God will not leave thee standing mute before thy family."

Lehi looked sheepish. "My son," he said, "I may sometimes worry but never will I doubt the wisdom of God in selecting you to lead my descendants. When my time cometh I shall go to my maker in peace."

The enlightened leader went back to his tent and slept.

And with the first light of dawn *"...went forth to the tent door... to his great astonishment he beheld upon the ground a round ball of curious workmanship; and it was of fine brass. And within the ball were two spindles...one pointed the way."*

"Sari!" "Nephi, Nephi!"

The tremulous voice that split the early morning silence brought everybody running. Curious faces crowded around their leader. He held up a strange looking object unlike anything any of them had ever seen. They all began talking at once.

"What is it?"

"Where did it come from?"

"Is it gold?"

"No, it's brass," said Nephi. He came close, and Lehi pushed the ball into his hands as if it were hot.

"It lay on the ground in front of my tent," he said excitedly. "I beheld it immediately when I arose."

Nephi studied the strange instrument, tipping and turning it. Then he held it high for all to see. "This is what will guide us to the Promised Land. The Lord gives us guidance in our hands, as he gave Moses the cloud by day and the fire by night. God is with us; the Lord God of Israel is ever with us. Let no one doubt."

When he handed the ball shaped object back to his father the old man took it reverently. He held the instrument cupped in both hands and studied it further. Then his gray head jerked up; his voice rang out.

"Women, prepare a good, substantial meal. And my sons, when you have eaten help the women take down their tents. Waste no time in assembling your families with their packs. Prepare them to cross the river."

And it came to pass that Lehi and his descendants crossed the river that he called Laman, departing at last from the valley that he called Lemuel. And they commenced their journey, traveling in a south-southeast direction.

Energized by the "magical" ball ever in his hand, Lehi led his people like a general, directing their every move night and day. On the afternoon of the fourth day he allowed they could pitch their tents and camp. The small glen selected for their much-needed rest boasted a bit of shade and a sparkling spring. Lehi called it Shazer. The weary travelers called it heaven.

While the others were setting up the camp Lehi went to comfort Ishmael. Several times that day he had noted his friend lagging behind. He found the older man sprawled out under a carob tree. Ishmael was panting; he smiled weakly. Lehi dropped down beside him, then turned and called over his shoulder.

"My sons, before it gets dark take your bows and arrows and hunt over near yonder mountain. We need a supply of meat that the women can prepare for our continuing journey."

"Let the great hunter go," said Lemuel, flopping down by the stream."

"Yea," echoed Laman, with a flip of his long hair. "Nephi has the fine steel bow. He can slay…"

"Go," Lehi ordered, "all of you but Sam; you stay and help your mother."

"Heleman, Hiram," Ishmael echoed, "You too."

Nephi took off in an opposite direction from the others, and soon returned with the carcass of a wild boar on his shoulders. The rest of them returned empty handed.

"Well, did I not say the steel bow would provide for us all?" Laman sneered.

"It isn't the bow," Sam countered. "Nephi doth practice shooting; he..."

"It is not the bow," Ruth beamed. "It's because The Lord doth lead my husband in all he does." She stepped forward smiling at her sisters as if Nephi providing the meat put her in charge of preparing it for cooking. Sariah and Anna helped, while the other women brought forth provisions from their packs, to make it a full satisfying meal. And when they had eaten they slept soundly.

They enjoyed a good rest at that place. Lehi allowed them a few days. Then the little band went forth again, traveling in the same direction, *unto the more fertile parts of the wilderness, which were in the borders near the Red Sea.*

For the space of many days they traveled, experiencing only minimal hardships. They were blessed with pleasant weather. Setting up camp became routine, and each time easier. The city sojourners were adjusting to a gypsy life. Even those plagued by the inhibitions of age and pregnancy did not find the traveling too uncomfortable. And game continued plentiful. Since Nephi enjoyed solitary hikes with nature, and communing with his Maker, he would go out whenever they stopped—and usually returned with meat, ample for all. So it became routine. The other men went out less and less often.

Then came the fateful day that Nephi returned bruised, bleeding, and carrying nothing but a broken weapon.

First to see his idol limping into camp, Zoram flew on rubbery legs to meet him. Sam right behind him.

"What happened?"

"Were you attacked?"

Laman and Lemuel, resting in the shade, were not so solicitous. When Nephi reported that he merely missed his footing and had fallen down a rocky ravine, they criticized instead—as if the provider had shirked his duty. As if fate had afflicted their brother's wounds upon them.

"So you fell down a cliff," Laman taunted. "What are you, a strong, cunning hunter, or just big and clumsy?"

"Yea, a man of courage would not protect his fall with a fine bow—the only bow that's any good," Lemuel complained.

Hiram supported the complainers.

"It is true. All our bows have lost their spring."

As those who would now have to make stronger bows and hunt in earnest, murmured against him, Nephi dropped his head. Zoram stood like a silent buffer between him and his accusers. Sam reached out for the broken bow.

"It can't be fixed, Sam," Nephi said. "We have no facilities to bond steel."

His voice was weary; he swayed, a Goliath about to fall. Sam and Zoram braced him up, mentally as well as physically.

He smiled his thanks for the support.

"No. No, I was just careless."

Standing apart with the women, waiting, Ruth embraced her husband with her eyes. But Nephi didn't see. His eyes were on his father, just emerging from his tent. Awakened from a nap by loud voices, Lehi seemed momentarily disoriented. He hesitated as if trying to take in the situation. As Nephi stood aching for consolation, his father turned back into his tent without speaking. But, close as they were, the son had read the signal. He would go to him for a private conference later.

Nephi gave his father a full account of the accident (he simply missed his footing and fell down a cliff). He made a record of his transgression, and asked forgiveness for his carelessness. The father considered minor injuries and a broken bow of little consequence. Neither of them imagined the repercussions to follow.

The very next day Nephi went searching for the best natural material. He constructed a strong wooden bow, also strong straight arrows. and went out often, using all his hunting skills; but with the breaking of the steel bow it seemed his luck had vanished. Time and time again Nephi came back with nothing. So Laman and Lemuel, Hiram and Heleman were forced to make stronger bows, and go out to hunt. They rarely returned with any game either. Now the family had no fresh meat, while the dried meat and other edibles dwindled dangerously low.

"And it came to pass that they did suffer much for the want of food."

They traveled deeper into the wilderness, the men hunting in vain for game, the women constantly scavenging, looking for plant food. For endless days they trudged, through wind and rain and heat. The days turned into months. Hunger and afflictions ravaged their hopes—and tortured their leader's soul.

Lehi had watched Ishmael stagger (near overcome by weakness), Sariah (with child again in her later years) bent near double with backache, the once plump Anna (now slim and haggard) ever trying to calm her frightened, pregnant daughters... He hurt for his charges. And when one after another complained to him he would soften his general-like orders. Then his conscience began to scream. It was his fault. He had not been strong in holding them to righteousness. So he hardened his requirements again. And their murmuring increased against him—so much so that he finally weakened, and murmured against The Lord.

"And the voice of the Lord came to Lehi...and he was truly chastened because of his murmuring...insomuch that he was brought down into the depths of sorrow."

Nephi came upon his father shaking, and groaning like a woman in labor.

"Father! Art thou ill?"

The son asked the question, but he knew the answer. It was not physical pain that he saw in his father's eyes, but remorse and self-loathing. To the son who idolized him it was like seeing the devil there. Nephi's young shoulders sagged. But born to be a leader he responded in character.

"Father where is thy faith? Arise and fight for it; let not the devil steal it!"

The old man's mouth moved but no words came out. To the son standing over him it seemed that the figure of authority had shrunk. He felt for his burdened father battling against his conscience. But strong in duty he continued.

"Father, thou knowest that the Lord will not let us starve. And I know if you would pray for me—if you would inquire this moment of the Lord whither I should go—I could take again the wooden bow up to the mountain and of a surety bring back food."

Lehi sniffed, looked up briefly, and dropped his head between his knees.

"Please, father," Nephi continued. "Thou hast long been a faithful servant. The Lord is merciful. Surely He will forgive a lapse into weakness out of contrition for those dear to thee. Father ..."

Nephi shifted impatiently. The sun was approaching the horizon. He itched to go and get his bow that he might quickly find a vantage point before dusk—there to watch and wait (however long) until came the opportunity. If he didn't go soon the chance would be lost. He patted the old leader's shoulder.

"Father, I must try," he said huskily, and left to get the weapon.

Nephi knew that his mother, now with Anna, would presently come to comfort him So with a quick explanation to Ruth he grabbed the wooden bow and hurried toward the mountain.

He didn't get far; his father called after him.

The patriarch now stood outside his tent, hands stretched high over his head. With one he waved. The other held the directional ball.

"I am forgiven; I am forgiven. The Lord said look upon the ball."

Nephi ran back. His father presented the ball to him for verification.

"*Look upon the ball, and behold the things which are written.*"

And Nephi "… *went forth up into the top of the mountain according to the directions which were given upon the ball.* And he "… *did slay wild beasts*…" obtaining food enough for all the hungry family.

As they continued their journey a new writing on the ball plain to be read was written and changed from time to time—giving guidance and understanding according to their diligence and faith. Nephi's luck with the wooden bow lasted. His father's strength returned. And all were strengthened for the continuing journey.

However, to each is given a number of years. The body of Lehi's dear friend continued to weaken. It was Ishmael's latter days.

CHAPTER XVII

The little band now traveled on full stomachs. The weather remained good. There were new scents in the air, new color in the foliage. Having been forgiven for his human laps into weakness, Lehi exalted. God's sun upon him again, and those in his care. Life in the wilderness had improved immensely.

So the day the leader recognized the fertile terrain evolving into desert he felt no apprehension. Nor did the expanding cloud of dust ahead worry him. Though it stretched far along the horizon, like the familiar brown disturbance of racing chariots, he knew that could not be. But, only robbers or gypsies would prod their animals to such speed in the desert. He stroked his beard, considering.

"What dost thou think, father?" Nephi asked.

Heavy breathing at his elbow. Ishmael had caught up to them. "Dust clouds of such proportions can only be made by racing chariots!" he said, coughing.

"No, Ishmael. In this unsettled land I doubt it could be chariots."

Lehi recalled that south of Jerusalem they had several times seen similar disturbances of the earth, stirred up by nomad bands. And sometimes when they passed near Bedouin camps. But the family group under God's protection had never been accosted. It was as if they had not been seen, as if God had dimmed the eyes of those who would harm them.

Thus again he did not worry. Whatever it was, God would look after their safety. But their comfort ... As head of the family, that was his responsibility.

"We will stop early," Lehi decided. "We will camp here. And I think we should tarry a while, where there is still grass and water. The goats look thin."

Ishmael nodded with a beaming smile, thankful not only for himself but his family, especially for Abigail. His favorite daughter would soon give birth to her first child, the child she had waited so long for. He had been worrying for her, wanting to insure her as much comfort as much as possible, so all would go well.

Nephi was also pleased by the announcement. The prophet expected him to be at his side constantly. Now he could spend more time with Ruth. He turned to go back to the followers.

"I will start them setting up the tents.

Lehi nodded, saying, "It is early yet; tell them I will talk to them after the evening meal."

He turned his attention back to Ishmael. "My friend," he said, "let us with age upon us rest our weary bones. There's a little shade there by yonder tree."

At the base of the scraggly tree Ishmael lay back upon a clump of long grass and closed his eyes. Lehi first checked out the horizon. Noting that the dinosaur cloud of dust had almost dispersed, he relaxed. But he didn't close his eyes. While his friend napped he watched the activity—and Sari. Standing profile talking to Sam, she looked thinner. Her slim shoulders seemed more bent than usual; and there was the obvious rounding of her late pregnancy. Also, he recalled that his wife had recently been plagued with backaches.

It was for his wife and her friend's daughter, both pregnant, that the good man had decided to stop early. And suddenly it seemed wise to allow everyone a good rest before proceeding to the desert-like country ahead. Yes, they would rest at least three days.

Lehi sighed contentedly, pleased with his decision. He lay back beside Ishmael. As the soft breeze played at his thinning hair, nature's perfume (from swaying honeysuckle) wafted to his nostrils. It reminded him of how Sariah loved flowers. And she had seen so few—so little beauty—since he took her away from her lovingly tended garden. The goodhearted leader decided to extend the three days. They would camp at this place until both of the new ones were born.

And when her days were accomplished Sariah bore a son. Lehi named him Jacob. So great was his joy in her safe delivery, and the momentary peace of the family, that no other name was considered. "Jacob" was *Israel,* the father of the twelve tribes, God's chosen people.

Abigail delivered a tiny girl, which the new father considered a gift from heaven. Zoram could hardly believe her, so fragile, so beautiful. Thereafter, whenever he had no chores to do for his wife, or for Sariah, he would stand and look at his baby daughter, ever waiting to hold her. And when they traveled Abigail's burden was lighter. Zoram would always carry their daughter.

When Lehi felt the new mothers were strong enough he assembled the increased family for departure. Wearing their packs, everything loaded on the burros, they patiently waited for the ritual prayer. Some eyed the barren-looking land ahead, where the ominous cloud of dust had appeared, but there was little tension. Nephi walked around the animals checking their loads (even the goats had loads to carry).

"Good packing," he said to Sam and Zoram.

The young leader smiled at everyone, talked to everyone, making light conversation and joking with the children. Then back to his wife. Together they went to stand beside Sariah. Finally, as the smoke from the dirt-smothered fire dissipated, the patriarch stood before them in prayer. Then Nephi strode out ahead with his father, Sariah and Ruth following behind them.

This morning Lehi set a slower pace than usual, frequently looking back to check on Sariah. "New mother, doth the infant weigh comfortably?"

Sariah nodded. She drew the edge of her shawl farther over the baby's face. A breeze had come up. Ruth lifted her shawl to cover her hair. One bronzed tendril escaped, and kept blowing across her face. The women all drew their garment tighter against the elements. Zoram and Abigail protected their tiny one between them.

Immediately as they started the wind promised to grow stronger. Sariah held her late life blessing tightly, but not nervously. The rocky hills of Judah south of Jerusalem had been much more intimidating. Now a seasoned traveler she did not anticipate trouble in this easier terrain. Nor did she expect to become overtired, not even taking into account that she had more to carry—or by rough calculations, that she was three years older.

Lehi predicted that they would travel many days before finding another comfortable place to tarry. And his prediction proved true. More than many were the days without comfort. Often there were three-day stretches of hot sand and no water. But when at last they reached another place of refuge it was worth the wait. An oasis: green grass, tall trees, and a sparkling spring of pure water that widened into a pool large enough to bathe in.

"We can bathe!"

The women threw down their packs in happy anticipation. Everyone dropped down on the cool grass, Laman and Lemuel already loosening their gritty sandals.

"Wait, my sons," Lehi commanded. "We are all anxious; but we cannot all bathe at once. We must draw lots to decide.

"And," said Sam, "should we not allow the women their privacy first?"

Laman scooted to the edge of the pool and defiantly plopped his feet into the water; but at a stern look from his father, quickly withdrew them.

"I suppose I shall still be gritty at sundown," he mumbled.

By sundown everyone had been refreshed, except Ishmael. Unfortunately the one who most needed the comfort of clean, and rest, had drawn lot for last. Anna attempted to help her husband undress. She would further steady his descent into the water. But Ishmael protested.

"No. Just let me rest. I shall bathe later."

His helpmate stood aside, staring at her husband—for the strangeness in his voice, more than his refusal to bathe as quickly as he could.

"I shall wait," she said.

Ishmael said nothing more. He seemed in a world of his own. Anna searched his face. She was remembering how seldom he had spoken that day, and how often he walked apart from the group. At rest stops he had veritably ignored his daughters. They couldn't understand the change in their jolly father, nor could she. But, secretly, Anna was pleased that he seemed comfortable only in her presence. Now even that had changed. Although he didn't require her, she stayed with him anyway.

Ishmael reclined with closed eyes on the edge of the pool. Anna hovered near. Several times she reached down and felt his forehead. After a while she began loosening his sweaty garments. When he did not protest she dipped the end of her linen towel in the spring and sponged his face.

"I will bathe you." She said firmly.

Afterward, she tried to interest him in food. Ishmael shook his head, mumbling he wasn't hungry.

"But my dear, you need food for strength."

He declined again, raising his voice for emphasis. So after making him as comfortable as possible Anna left her husband to rest. When she returned to check on him, he seemed more relaxed. In the almost darkness the weathered face looked less lined—and faintly lighted.

That faint glow set Anna's heart pounding, recalling a time she saw a similar flush on his face many years before—when a laughing, robust Ishmael carried her then slim body over the threshold of their first house. And her heart ached. If only she could take her loved one home.

She rushed to Sariah.

"My friend, my husband…" She didn't need to finish the sentence. Sariah understood. For a moment the two women clung together in silence. When Anna pushed back and looked up at the taller Sariah her eyes were misty.

"Get thy husband Sariah. I fear that my Ishmael is gravely ill."

"Oh, Lehi left camp. He went out to higher ground, to survey the place, this lovely place. He named it Nahom," Sariah mused, "But he will be back soon, I'm sure." Sariah knew her protector would not remain away long.

Anna returned to Ishmael. She put her hand once more on his forehead. He opened his eyes and smiled at her, assuring her that he was better. So she left her man to his solitude. A little later Abigail checked on her father, when she went to fill her jug for the night. And she sat with him for a while. She gave him a drink, then smoothed his brow, feeling for fever as her mother had done. Ishmael reached up and took her hand.

"Daughter, I am rested, and feel comfortable here. Tell thy mother that I shall remain here tonight."

And sometime during the night Ishmael quietly slipped into eternity.

When at the first light of dawn his wife came to check on him, she sensed the ghostly silence oppressing nature around him. It enveloped her… She approached slowly, and reached down to touch him… Her wails woke the heavens!

Anna's anguish knew no bounds. And her daughters were inconsolable; the older ones also burned with anger. Hannah and Josepha blamed Lehi for their father's death—for convincing him to make a journey beyond his ability.

"Our father is dead and Lehi is responsible," Josepha cried.

"He did not allow enough rest stops," Hannah contended.

But Ruth countered her sisters. "Lehi is not to blame," she said. True, our father was not strong for the traveling; but it was his desire…"

"And it was God's will," Abigail added.

"Well maybe, but Lehi didn't … He shouldn't have …" In cold hollow voices Hannah and Josepha continued their complaints. While Eve simply sobbed.

Sam put his arms around his young wife and led her away. She had grown up too fast. Taken to live in wild, unsettled country while still an adolescent, she'd missed all the city-maiden privileges, all the fun, and perfumed oils, and pretty clothes. Now browned and lean—perhaps as hardened in heart as body… Eve had become old before she blossomed. Sam kept his word to his father; he'd made it more than a year for good measure, before he went into her. But when the girl was able to talk like a woman with her sisters, it was the older sisters (Hannah and Josepha) that she most associated with. For Ruth, of the special love and obligation, gave all her time to her husband and his mission. The tender youngest sister, maturing in an atmosphere of rebellion and bitterness. could not be faulted. She'd learned so many wrong things.

And now she must learn about endings.

Each of Ishmael's family members mourned his death differently. As after they buried him, and departed the place called Nahom, they differently carried the sadness of having to leave him. Anna had rigidly insisted that she would not leave him, that she could not. It was like sacrilege to abandon the body of her lifelong partner in such a desolate place.

Lehi's heart weighed heavy for having had to force her. Also Ishmael had been his lifelong friend. Additionally he lost the constant comfort of his companion. Sariah now spent nearly all of her time in Anna's tent, comforting her friend.

The repercussions from the death of Ishmael were many. Stirred up by their wives (Ishmael's daughters) Laman and Lemuel regressed to their old seditious attitude. So much did they contend against their father that Lehi found it necessary to severely chastise them again. Also, Nephi warned his brothers that God would chastise them if they did not honor their father, and keep the commandments. Still they remained troublesome and uncooperative. Lehi was hurt and worried.

"Oh dear Lord let them not desert me finally, to the point of no recourse,"

But the ominous tide only increased. Laman turned to his old tricks. He assembled his cohorts for a conference. Pacing before them like a gorilla leader bent on murder, lean and hard, with slitted eyes and stringy hair, he also looked like one.

Heleman and Hiram were receptive. Lemuel listened intently, and obeyed like the follower he was, and the gang member he had become. The once twinkling eyes and charming ways having gone by the way of suffering and resentment. Because of their father's mission, they had often gone hungry, had their life threatened, lost friends, missed sewing their oats… The longer they traveled the more their minds dwelled on these facts. *Why must young men's dreams be subjugated to an old man's desires?*

Hiram and Heleman of course never really wanted to leave the city. They had acquiesced to please their father. So after their father died they were wide open to Laman's ideas. And as time passed, resentment increasing day by day, they were primed, and almost ready, when Laman presented his latest plan of iniquity.

"Behold, what I have to say to you I have considered seriously; and many times, even times not in anger. But now my anger does not cool. Listen to me."

Laman liked being listened to. He stopped pacing, and slowed his staccato speech to a dead earnest cadence. With one long leg resting on a cypress stump, he balanced before them and seethed out the shocking words with deliberate slowness…

"And Laman said unto Lemuel and also unto the sons of Ishmael: Behold, let us slay our father, and also our brother

Nephi, who has taken it upon him to be our ruler and our teacher, who are his elder brethren."

Ignoring the gasps Laman quickly added, "It has come to that. It's that, or our own lives are over."

Hiram found his breath first. "What!"

"I'm saying there is no other way."

Hiram and Heleman turned and looked inquiringly at Lehi's other son. Lemuel hesitated. He couldn't quite...but finally shrugged and said nonchalantly,

"Well, this life may never end; we will never have a life if we don't get out from under all their rules and orders."

"But murder!" Hiram swallowed his Adam's apple.

Heleman spoke in a strangled whisper. "But lest we forget," he rasped, "they are servants of The Lord. God talks to them. They have visions..."

"Yea, I know my brother claims it," Laman retorted; "but ofttimes I doubt. Nephi is cunning. He deceiveth our ears; he may deceive our eyes."

Having planted this seed of doubt, Laman expected Lemuel would water it. And he expected right.

"Think about it," Lemuel said. "Would a benign brother seek to rob the firstborn of his traditional rights? Nephi lays hold of Laman's rights, and thinks nothing of it. Our pious brother puffs himself up, and treats us as children. I'm beginning to believe he thinketh to make himself a king over us."

"Yea, so he may do with us as he likes, and according to his pleasure!" Laman added with finality. "We could become prisoners."

Hanging on the edge of conviction Hiram and Heleman wondered how they could they possibly conjure up reasons to justify murder?

But Laman turned on the charm, and finally cinched the full support of his followers. Their warped minds justified doing away with Nephi, and Lehi had little time left anyway... Under azure sky and verdant tree (while enjoying God's gifts of nature) they plotted to take the lives of His servants.

Without warning a bolt of lightning slashed to the ground not two feet in front of them. A deafening crash of thunder followed instantaneously—and there had not been a cloud in the sky!

Quaking exceedingly all four fell upon their faces.

And they "*...were chastened by the voice of the Lord, and did turn away their anger, and did repent of their sins...*"

CHAPTER XVIII

In the days and weeks that followed God's faithful servant Lehi was granted a reprieve from worry. Laman and Lemuel were surprisingly cooperative. Also Hiram and Heleman. For years to come he would enjoy the blessing of full cooperation from his whole family.

But with the sharp turnabout of Laman and Lemuel, remembering how often he had chastened his rebellious sons in anger, the conscientious father began to feel guilty that he had been too hard on them. To those of weak faith, the good man reasoned, he should have been more loving, and more understanding. He prayed for their souls. And for wisdom to teach them.

"Oh dear God teach me how to reach them, that they may not again slip back into iniquity, that I may yet know their love, and that I may kindle a love for Thee within their hearts—that one day I might bring them securely into Thy fold."

The Lord did not answer unto Lehi's satisfaction. It seemed there was no kind way. Those who stray must be admonished strongly, and quickly, *" . . . lest they influence others to rise up against thee."*

So Lehi watched them closely, and tried to control them in accordance with the word of The Lord.

Directions on the ball now led them due eastward. And though they waded through many afflictions there was little complaining. So when Sam and Nephi (neither having ever complained before) came to their father contending against a commandment (the commandment of not cooking food) Lehi was surprised.

"My sons, can you not believe it is yet another indication that our Father in Heaven watcheth over us? Think. If the Lord suffereth us not to make fires, truly it must be for our protection."

"I believe," said Nephi. "But I worry. The women will not eat raw meat. And my dear Ruth is again with child. She grows weak traveling only on the nourishing milk of the goat, and the few herbs we…"

Sam interrupted.

"If the women don't eat meat soon they will not have suck for their children." He dropped his head in his hands. "And father, my Eve also is now with child."

Lehi smiled. Nephi patted his brother on the back.

"Sam, at last thou art blest. I have felt for thee without offspring. Yea, even in the wilderness where feeding one's family is a trial and a tribulation, a man without offspring is poor."

"But, Eve will not be happy." Sam wailed. "She is frightened."

Lehi understood his son's frustration, but spoke to him firmly. "My son, thy young wife has no cause to fear the natural travail of childbirth. And it is her duty to bear sons for you. Have you not counseled your helpmate about her responsibility?"

When Sam did not respond, his father pressed him further. "Perhaps thy wife may now need discipline."

Sam's head jerked up. "I will not abuse her."

The patriarch considered a minute, looking fondly at his son. This was gentle Sam; his wife was very young. He continued quietly.

"Eve is yet of a tender age; I will require that her mother sojourn in your tent to advise and comfort her."

Since the death of Ishmael, Anna (without a husband) had been with Abigail, under the protection of her eldest daughter's husband. Now Lehi decided that the youngest daughter needed her mother. He directed that henceforth Sam would be Anna's protector instead of Zoram.

Sam straightened, as if he had been gifted with the added responsibility. Lehi felt he had made the right decision, but he saw no relief in Sam's face…

"Also, I will send my wife to talk with her," Nephi was saying, "Ruth is strong in birthing. She can do much to soothe her sister's …"

"Yea," Sam interrupted. "But who'll make her eat?"

Nephi turned to Lehi. "Yes father, what about the raw meat?"

"Faith, both of you," Lehi commanded. "I will pray about this, and you must entreat the women again to eat the meat. Even as the Lord fed our ancestors in the wilderness with manna, He supplyeth our food. If in His great wisdom we are not to make a fire—that we not be discovered, that we not be harmed, then I believe in His great goodness, He will give unto me the solution.

And the word of The Lord came unto Lehi, "*I will make thy food become sweet, that ye cook it not.*"

And it came to pass, for the time it was necessary, that the women were no longer repulsed by raw meat. They ate heartily, were strengthened, and continued to bear the many trials and afflictions of the journey without complaint.

Humbly grateful for the blessing, Lehi thanked God continually. And Nephi preached the blessing to the people. "When the children of men keep the commandments of God, He strengthens them and provides means whereby they can accomplish that which He has commanded."

And together, Lehi and Nephi continued leading the little band of believers in accordance with directions given on the instrument provided them.

But was there no end to this barren wilderness? Would they ever again find ample fodder for their animals? Lehi cringed at how little flesh was left on their bones. Still, each time he stood at the head of his weary band, cloak and headdress crested with dust, eyes anchored on the horizon, he managed to speak encouragingly.

Then one day after a short rest stop, when he rose up to encourage his followers and lead them out again, Lehi's tired heart surged. He saw a blur of green on the horizon. He caught his breath, but said nothing. A good leader would not arouse the hopes of his followers without a true knowing. He glanced over at Nephi. The son ever at his elbow hadn't seen it. He'd been looking at the sky.

"Father," Nephi said, "I feel a foreboding; the sky is darkening, perhaps a storm coming on. Should we not make camp early, before it hits? He pointed. "Perhaps over in yonder wash we would have some protection."

Lehi acknowledged the wisdom in his son's suggestion. And while Nephi went to tell the others, and get makeshift preparations underway for protection in the wash, he mumbled a prayer of thanks. He had *not* been hallucinating; he had definitely seen green. He closed his eyes, enjoying a mental picture of the restful color ahead, that they would all soon enjoy.

When Nephi returned to sit with him, believing that his father was meditating behind the closed eyes, he took a thin papyrus roll out of his pouch to mark off the day. As family historian—in addition to recording the most significant accounts of their journey—Nephi maintained a daily marking scroll. Secretly the young prophet had hoped to scribe on metal plates, like Laban's plates of brass, which his father still consulted daily. It would make his record seem more important. But as time passed he'd bowed to the wisdom of heaven not granting the wish. For lo these endless months there had been little to record. And through all these years, he would have had to carry heavy plates. By

Nephi's reckoning, and the daily marking scroll, it had now been eight years since they departed Jerusalem.

Nephi noted the deep lines those long years of worry and hardship had gouged in his father's face. He didn't want to disturb him; he needed rest. But by the look of the sky there was no time to relax. They must soon take cover in the wash with the others. As he reached for his pouch to return the reckoning papyrus a freak gust of wind nearly tore it from his hands. Simultaneously, a powerful blast of sand. Lehi rose up sputtering, brushing sand from his beard.

Nephi shouted, "Look at the sky now."

"Oh, we'll be right in the eye of the storm."

The scattered dome-shaped clouds had multiplied like magic. They were billowing up from every direction like an army of overweight ghosts. The wind had intensified. Father and son, clinging together, rushed toward the ravine. And as they slipped down with the others the threatening cloud ceiling lowered.

There was an ominous stillness. Then a fire-red streak slit the sky, followed by a deafening crack of thunder. Nephi felt the hairs on the back of his neck stiffen. The angry wind tore at robes and pulled at frightened faces. The men pushed their wives and children further down in the gulch. Nephi pushed his father down first. Then seeing that the worst was yet to be, wormed over to Ruth, and covered his wife and panic-stricken son with his body.

Children screamed; donkeys snorted. The tents were rent and ripped from their pegs. Some of the tethered goats broke loose, never to be seen again. In all their years in the wilderness never had they suffered such a satanic storm. It rampaged for hours. And torrents of rain lasted until early morning.

When daylight crept upon the scene, in the calm aftermath, and the warming sunshine, Lehi took inventory.

Surprisingly, no one seemed seriously hurt. And miracle of miracles, he discovered that he had one more soul in his charge—

an addition to Nephi's family. On a soggy soiled mat, smiling up at her husband, Ruth looked like a lily blooming in the mud. In her arms she cradled the new life, which her husband had delivered in the night—in the dark, in the rain.

"Oh my dear Ruth," Nephi kept saying, "art thou really all right? Is the infant? I could not see to find your mother or your sisters. And the roaring storm, their heads covered, they didn't hear me call. I didn't know what to do. But God was with me. And thanks be to God, thou hast given me another son."

Nephi wrapped his arms around his wife and the newborn together, the smell of mud and blood mingling with his own sweat. Then the young father reached over and patted the bulky bundle behind them—his firstborn. Despite being wrapped in wet robes, two-year-old Simon lay snuggled up to his mother, sound asleep. After crying with terror most of the night, exhaustion had come with the calm and the sun.

Ruth lay weakened, but her eyes glowed, her smile strengthening to full beauty. "Oh, Nephi my love my protector," she said. "Thou art my refuge in every kind of storm. I am the most blessed of all women."

Gazing down at the tiny face barely visible through an opening in the wad of wet wrapping, she had recognized the material of the inner folds—that of Nephi's under garments. After delivering his own son he had taken off part of his inner clothing to receive the new life, and give it as much warmth as possible. And he had wrapped his outer robe around mother and baby together.

Lehi's eyes moistened at the scene. Despite the debilitating circumstances all was well with his extended family. He went apart to thank The Lord. Anna and Sariah would tend to the traditional requirements for the newborn (the tender body must be ceremoniously cleaned). The women were already improvising to do their duty. He stopped and looked back: so much to be thankful for: the baby, the delivery, no one hurt seriously… and the infant wasn't even crying. As the old man walked away the deep lines in his weathered face seemed to smooth out.

Everyone now crowding around marveling, trying to see the little one, Nephi stood up and backed away to give them room. Ruth would be attended by her sisters, the baby by the older women. He was not needed. He went to talk with his father.

It was then that Lehi confided his discovery of the previous evening. As Nephi approached him, stripped to the waist of clothing, the old man beamed.

"My son, I am so blessed… here, let me share my cloak with thee—and now another blessing… Look, look where we're going. Look at the green ahead!"

The long walk to that green sanctuary seemed to stretch out forever. The strain of the night before had sapped their energy. When they finally reached the coveted shade it was nearly sundown; they no longer needed it. But the grass padded turf looked like heaven. As one they dropped down upon it, and were soon asleep. The tents would be set up tomorrow. They would bathe tomorrow. And then they would rest some more.

For three days they luxuriated in the cool oasis. And when Lehi led them on they walked in shade. The directional ball had pointed through a thick grove of trees.

At first the forest's cool shade caressed them, and cushioned their feet. A wonderful change from heat and grit. But after a while the heavy hanging branches that blocked out the sun seemed to imprison them. Day after day after day they saw nothing but trees… and often it rained. The dampness depressed them, especially the young. Straining to keep up with adult strides little Jacob began whining. He kept asking his father the same question. When would the forest end?

One morning the child asked the question again, just as they started. Lehi stopped the procession and knelt down to face his small son on even keel. His countenance softened—as it ever did when he looked upon the tender offspring that God had blessed him with in old age—and Sariah past normal productive time. Lehi felt humble. He looked up at Sariah carrying their youngest. The blessings of two more sons had fallen upon him like manna.

"Jacob," he said, "dost thou not like the cool shade?

"Yes father," the boy answered obediently. "It's better than the desert. But I'm tired. And I can't see anything; I can't see where we are going."

"You will soon, my son," Lehi told him. "Soon."

Sariah caught the lilt in his voice. And at the next rest stop she lay down her burden (the younger son—a toddler, heavier than she should carry) and looked at her husband expectantly. Yesterday he had confided (to his wife only) that the trees were thinning. Now he smiled at her and confirmed that the blue he'd glimpsed between the high branches was a distant mountain.

Two hours later the weary travelers emerged from the forest to discover an azure sea, and the earth curving away into a wide and verdant valley ringed with blue mountains. As they came out on the grassy embankment that afforded the magnificent view, Lehi looked around in reverie. He took Sariah's hand. Her dream of flowers had come true; they frosted the meadow in variegated colors. Sandstone cliffs on their left boasted the colors of ore. And below on their right, water that stretched to the horizon. Such beauty and abundance they had never seen.

Lehi and Sariah sat down on the grass and clung to each other, while laughing children and grandchildren tumbled past them down the embankment. The prophet had not heard such laughter since he could remember. Sariah's eyes were overflowing. Anna sat down beside them, staring mute at the view. Nephi and Ruth stood hypnotized. They looked like statues with animated faces. Nephi held his firstborn on his shoulders; Ruth cradled the new son in her shawl. Hand in hand Sam and Eve scrambled down the embankment with the children, Sam cautioning his wife to watch her step. While Laman, Lemuel, Hiram and Heleman and their wives ran after their children, rushing with glee to the sea.

"The Lord has led us to a land of milk and honey," Lehi was saying. "Look, Sari, look. We shall have pomegranates, and coconuts, maybe even dates. I think those are date trees over there."

Sariah nodded, her misty eyes sweeping the panoramic view. "Beautiful, beautiful," she murmured. And when she looked at the great expanse of water it seemed to diffuse into the proverbial sea of glass. The instant Lehi beheld it there had come to his mind a name, "Irreantum," meaning many waters. Lehi named the sea Irreantum.

The leader and his companion stood there above, long after the others.

Sariah kept saying, "How beautiful, how beautiful it is."

"And how bountiful," said Lehi. "I hear the buzzing of honeybees. The berries on the bushes are edible, and ... Oh, blessed be the Lord! I shall call this place Bountiful."

The beauty and the plenty, and the musical voices of his charges rejuvenated Lehi's soul. The plaintive notes of Sam's long neglected flute assuaged his ears. A full bath would complete this rare feeling of well being. After selecting the location for their camp, the ever-on-duty leader took time off to luxuriate in the crystal clear sea. As he emerged from the water he murmured "*my cup runneth over,*" and collapsing on the warm sand he fell into a deep sleep.

When Sariah brought his robe she looked down at her husband and smiled. Wearing only a wrinkled loincloth, gnarled hands clasped across a naked chest, and the tension gone from his face... He looked younger than he did an hour before. Without hesitation, she covered him with the robe and went to be with Anna.

"Lehi has fallen asleep already."

Anna seemed not to hear her. "If only Ishmael could have come to this place.. if only ..." she mused. "Here, he could have regained his strength."

Sariah patted her friend's lean shoulder, fondly remembering her lost plumpness. Anna had also shrunk in height. Time taking its tolls. They sat for a while, friends comfortable together without words. Anna's sigh broke the silence. She said wistfully, "If only Ishmael were with me this would be heaven."

"This must be heaven," Sariah chuckled, "if Lehi can forget to worry and fall asleep before dark."

Soon everybody slept; they slept long hours. And immediately upon rising, even as their mouths watered at the smell of fresh fish cooking, they gorged themselves on berries—as they'd done the night before, along with the children. And the young were not otherwise restricted. Everybody enjoyed unprecedented freedom. Here they could bathe at their pleasure; there was no waiting. And loitering was the rule rather than the exception. When the women washed their spouse's intimate clothing (ragged loincloths and under tunics) the men loitered in secluded coves without covering—allowing the sun to spray it's vitamins over their hardened bodies. It was almost like being warmed by wine. They could only faintly remember wine.

But in this beautiful place they began thinking about it. The idea of planting a vineyard caught fire. They could plant anything now. Laman and Lemuel had already planted wheat and barley, for lo and behold, this time Lehi did not object. The men also felled trees, to build houses for their families, and mined the cliffs of color for stones. In a spurt of energy and high spirits the desert wanderers began building a permanent settlement in the bountiful land—believing it was the land that God had promised them.

Only Nephi knew it was not. He wondered why his father had agreed to the planting and building, but said nothing. And when Sam inquired of him, asking for confirmation, he said he did not know. Since his father had chosen not to tell the people, Nephi could only avoid the subject. But as the piles of sandstone from the quarry grew, and his brothers began enthusiastically building their houses, he became uneasy. *Why would his father allow all this activity, when he knew it meant future disappointment?*

The son could not bring himself to ask. For he realized his father was enjoying the status quo, the relief, the relaxation, as he was. And he sorely needed it.

Both of them intrinsically knowing that all this energy would be wasted, neither would bring up the subject, Nephi opting to wait, and Lehi waiting hopefully… Unlike before the tired leader prayed for this wait to be long. Every aching body and worried mind needed a long rest. And their souls were sick with stress. The compassionate leader decided that being busy and occupied toward a mutual goal was the best medicine he could give them.

Nephi soon realized this. He was learning to become a good leader. But at first it seemed like living in this unfamiliar comfort, almost indolence, had weakened his father. So feeling it was his responsibility, he began petitioning The Lord for answers, going more and more often to pray, and staying longer on the mountain. Sometimes he didn't start the trek back to camp until almost dark. In this peaceful place he felt no apprehension for the safety of his family.

One evening, returning in the dark his breath caught. Ruth stood barefoot in the doorway, clad only in her under tunic. She held her head high, and back—the familiar posture to prevent a tear from falling. Her loosened hair, cascading to below her waist, glinted in the moonlight. With a sob Nephi swept his wife into his arms.

"Oh my love forgive me. I left without telling thee, and I stayed too long."

"Thou has been talking with God?"

Nephi shook his head.

"No. Woe unto me." He whispered, not to awaken his sons. "All this day I prayed, and no word came. I fear The Lord is angry with me."

Ruth pulled him inside, and down beside her on their sleeping mat.

"Oh, woe unto me, woe unto me," he kept repeating. "It's because I'm not worthy. I forfeited the knowing of His will for comfort and pleasure. I have …"

"Sh… sh…" Ruth rocked her husband in her arms. "God will forgive," she said softly. "God will forgive."

Nephi prayed constantly for that forgiveness, while life among the others went on as before, his father seemingly unconcerned about everything.

CHAPTER XIX

"Arise, and get thee into the mountain!"

The surprise of it, like a flash of fire in the darkness. And the relief of it. Like the weight of an ark being lifted from his chest. Nephi rose trembling.

He'd been crouching barefoot at the edge of the sea, playing with his children. Lulled by the gently lapping water and the laughter of his sons, his lead-weight worry was momentarily forgotten. And it was at that moment of relaxation that the voice came to him.

"Simon, come quick; bring thy brother. We go to your mother."

But little Enoch resisted, and pulled back, insisting with all the exuberance of an independent two-year-old that he wouldn't leave the water.

Nephi looked around, and some distance down the shore he saw Sam relaxing alone on the warm sand.

"Brother," he shouted, "wilt thou watch my sons until Ruth comes for them? I go to fetch her."

"Of course," said Sam, nonchalantly. Then noting the tremor in his brother's voice, jerked to attention and came running.

"Nephi, you stagger; what is it? Are you ill?"

Nephi regained his balance, shook his head, then spurted away, shouting over his shoulder. "No, my brother, I'm all right. *All* is right."

He found Ruth making honey cakes, and for the first time was not distracted by the sweet aroma. Nor by the beauty of her fair face, pinked by the heat of the cooking fire. He grabbed his wife's shoulders, and turned her around to face him.

"I left the children near the water; Sam is watching them," he said breathlessly. "I must go; God has spoken!"

Then he kissed her. And before she could find words to respond he was out of the tent running toward the mountain. He turned back, and pointed toward the peak. Ruth reached for his goatskin bag hanging ever ready on the tent pole. She waved it at him and shouted.

"Do not go so far without water."

Nephi meekly returned and took the bag, then hugged his wife, and held her for a moment. "Oh, Ruth," he said huskily, "I think I'm forgiven." He fingered a tendril of her hair, and was on his way, calling back for her not to worry if he was late returning.

Lehi heard the raised voices, and came out of his tent in time to witness his son's speedy departure. He knew what it meant. The word to continue would be given at last. While luxuriating in this place of abundance, waiting, the old prophet had felt guilty for clinging to earthly comforts—and for wishing that this paradise could be the end of their journey. But after the many long years in the wilderness he had learned to wait patiently—having ascertained that The Lord was always *generous* in allowing time for rest and reprieve.

Now, after a good long rest, this reprieve was soon to end. He waited impatiently for Nephi to return, and give him details about the next segment of their journey. Whatever, his responsibility would be lighter—the heavy load of leader would be transferred to younger shoulders. On Nephi's return he would witness that radiating inner light in the gold-flecked eyes of his son. And he would hear "the word" from the one blessed to receive it. Lehi thanked God in advance for the blessing of such a son to carry on for him.

Ruth was also thinking of this as she waited for her husband. She knew that Nephi must first report to his father, but never had she felt so anxious for the news. What *was* the word? What would it mean to them as a family?

Dutifully waiting, Nephi's helpmate paced the earthen floor of the tent hoping and praying that her husband would not tell her they must leave this beautiful place—and each time reprimanding herself for the unworthy thought.

"Oh Dear Lord, forgive me. Thy will be done. Thy will be done."

By the time Nephi returned from the mountain self-criticism and imagined inadequacies had near exhausted her. She lay like a limp rag beside her sleeping sons. But the sound of his footsteps fused her with new energy. She raised up, quickly smoothed her hair, and went to meet him smiling.

Nephi grabbed her. The words almost rushed out before he caught them "The Lord sayeth… But first I must tell my father."

The Lord had said, "*… thou shalt construct a ship, after the manner which I shall show thee, that I may carry thy people across these waters."*

"How, I cannot imagine." Nephi's voice quavered with emotion as he repeated the astounding message to his companion. "I cannot conceive how… I am inexperienced—not a carpenter—yet my faith welled up within me, and I believed. I know in my soul if it is God's will He will strengthen me…"

Nephi rushed on with the telling.

"The Lord hath shown me whither I should go to find the best ore to molten, that I might make the tools to construct the ship, and…"

"Wha…" Ruth had turned white. "Oh, Nephi I fear… I fear…" Her face was suddenly an alabaster mask. "Are you saying we won't be traveling on land?" She was trembling.

But the fire in her husband's voice barely flickered. Having considered the magnitude of the commandment, enhanced by his father's positive response, anticipation had built up within him to near bursting. His faith soared beyond any boundary. *How could his heart have allowed him to doubt? With God all things are possible.* "The Lord will suffer my brethren to help me," he continued, "just as He did exhort them to faithfulness and diligence for many years."

Filled with the spirit and the wonder that he had been given the word instead of his father, that he had been commanded for such a role, Nephi missed the significance of his wife's reaction. He remained completely unaware that something he said had frightened her.

Next morning his enthusiasm had not lessened in the least.

"Oh, my beloved, how blessed we are. The Lord did grant us this paradise, and ample time to rest and enjoy it. He delivered us from the destruction and forthcoming agonies of Jerusalem. He did guide and protect us in the wilderness. And now He doth lead us to a wondrous Promised Land."

Nephi held his wife tight, but with a far away look in his eyes.

"I must now go to my father, that we may make plans,"

Secluded in a grove of sycamore trees for privacy, the father and son discussed the holy commandment in mundane detail. This project God had given them would require faith unshakable, more than was ever needed before. Yet they talked as if the prodigious carpentry job would require only ingenuity—as if it were within mortal capability. And after the conference Nephi went boldly forth to advise and recruit his fellow laborers.

Sam and Zoram responded eagerly, Heleman and Hiram, hesitantly. But true to form the two of lesser faith were emphatically negative. Laman and Lemuel even refused to talk about it. Lolling on the shore, building sand castles with their children, they brushed off the whole conception as if it were a joke.

Nephi desperately tried to convince them.

"God has commanded..."

" Leave us alone," Lemuel repeated.

Nephi bristled. "Listen to me," he barked.

"Listen to *me,*" Laman flared back. "Thou art a fool." He spat the words out. "It's not possible, Even if it were, we wouldn't leave this place. Would we Lemuel?"

"I wouldn't even think of it."

As usual Laman did the talking and his brother echoed everything he said. Lemuel had become his shadow. In the past few years the happy-go-lucky second son had lost his individuality, as well as his mischievous grin. Except for physical attributes—curly hair and chunky, versus straight black hair and lean, the younger brother had become almost a carbon copy of the elder.

As usual Laman, caller of all the shots, ended the discussion.

"I'll hear no more of this. It's a ridiculous idea. Only a fool would believe so few men could build a ship big enough for all of us, let alone sail it across what could be endless unknown waters,"

Hiram and Heleman, recalling past miracles, half-heartedly believed. And they began working, but with their wives protesting—the never-ending contention, they did not work full days, and not every day. Only Sam and Zoram fully supported the project.

That all had not been led by the Spirit to believe and cooperate fully, sorely depressed the old prophet. From his wayward sons' behavior the past few years, he had begun to believe what he hoped—that at last they understood the magnitude of his mission. But now he feared they had just been appeasing him. Biding their time for another break. His heart hung heavy with the thought that Nephi must carry this mountainous load with only the support of Sam and Zoram.

Though burdened with disappointment, Nephi immediately began the project with just two helpers—plus part time half-hearted help from the sons of Ishmael. Sam went with him to the rust colored cliffs to extract ore, and helped make tools. Zoram assisted him in constructing a bellows of the skins of beasts, wherewith to blow fire. Then it came time to fall timber, still no help from Laman and Lemuel. Assistance from the sons of Ishmael still spotty, and unpredictable. Often they all lolled on the seashore together. Although Hiram and Heleman remained curious, without their father's strong faith for influence, they found it hard to swallow what Nephi told them. And as the work progressed, that the shape and form of the ship, every detail of the construction, was being directed by Deity, seemed sacrilegious.

To Nephi it was miraculous. He would not be deterred. He continually preached to the laggards. At night, after sweating all day at manual labor, he worked to spark their faith. Convinced by the spirit that God would turn their hearts if he found the right words, Nephi would not give up trying.

The wayward brothers still would not work. They continued to ridicule him.

"Only a fool would degrade The Lord God of Israel to the mundane position of ship builder."

"Yea, has not the great Almighty more important things to do than to tell you how to cut timbers and pound pegs?"

"That ye are lacking in judgment, we know," said Laman, with an air of superiority, "don't try to make us believe you are a Noah."

Though near exhaustion from physical labor all day, night after night Nephi reached desperately for convincing arguments. He talked to all four of them whenever he could corner them.

"You believe the word on the plates that God directed Noah in building the ark. You believe that He commanded Moses to lead our fathers out of slavery at the hands of the Egyptians, also that He did feed them with manna in the wilderness. Then *how is it that he cannot instruct me, that I should build a ship?* And remember when The Lord suffered that we should not make fires? God said unto our father, *'I will make thy food become sweet, that ye cook it not.'* Didn't our wives thereafter eat the meat?"

When they did not respond Nephi sighed. "O, my brothers, long since, you have been obedient unto our father, and kept the commandments. How is it that you doubt now? Why have you again hardened your hearts?"

The rebels, interpreting Nephi's slump of fatigue as a sign of weakening, walked off while he was still talking.

"Nephi is led by foolish imaginings, just like his father," said Heleman.

"Yea." Hiram agreed. Anyway we'd be crazy to leave this place."

"I don't intend to leave," said Laman, coming up behind them.

With something like his old devil-may-care expression, Lemuel added, "Yea, why should we help him build a ship? *We* are not leaving."

Nephi had followed after them. He caught hold of Lemuel's sleeve. "Lemuel, think. Ye have heard the Lord's voice. He hath spoken unto you in a still small voice, and in a voice like unto thunder..." Lemuel shrugged him off.

"Oh, my brothers, and Heleman and Hiram, my heart is pained, and my soul rent with anguish because of your unbelief. Why is it that ye can be so hard in your hearts that ye cannot believe this.?"

He reached out to put a hand on Laman's shoulder. But Laman twisted away.

When his humble beseeching only angered them. Nephi fell to his knees.

"Oh Nephi, get up," Laman sneered. "Art thou a sniveler or a man?"

"He is not a Moses, or a Noah..."

Nephi said, "I am a servant of God, a man full of the spirit, in so much that my frame hath no strength."

No strength?

Laman's look darted from Lemuel to Heleman to Hiram, to the sea. As if orchestrated, the four of them lunged toward Nephi in unison—they would dispose of their irritation once and for all. Four men could surely hold one under water.

Nephi's voice resounded unto the mountain. He was on his feet.

"In the name of Almighty God, I command you that ye touch me not, for I am filled with the power...and whoso shall lay his hands upon me shall wither..."

The would-be attackers trembled like frightened deer. They stared at him, daring not to lay hands on him. And when Nephi stretched forth his hand toward them, "... *The Lord did shake them...according to the word..."* So strong was the shock, and the power of the Spirit, they fell down before Nephi and were about to worship him. But he would not... *"I am thy brother... thy younger brother; wherefore worship the Lord thy God, and honor thy father and thy mother..."*

And it came to pass that they all began to work the timbers for building the ship. From that day until the ship was completed no one reserved muscle. Although Nephi did not direct the work or build the ship *after the manner of men*, as the strange looking vessel took shape upon the shore no one offered criticism. Bodies ached and brows ran with sweat but there was no contention. Not even when Nephi was not there—when he lay down his mallet and hurried away to the mountain to confer with The Master builder.

Those times the fire of the father's faith inspired the workers to continue. Lehi did little manual labor, age having robbed him of physical strength; but always present he contributed assistance in wisdom and moral strength.

The women also worked on the project. They fetched and carried, braided goat hair with reeds for sails, heated and applied pitch for sealing, in addition to milking the goats, tending the children (and having more). After doing their housewife chores: mending clothes, washing, cleaning, cooking, with the help of their children they also cast nets for fish, picked fruit, and gathered honey. Some wives even built and baited traps to snare the hare for meat—so those who hunted larger game could give full time to the project.

Ultimately every tired worker came to see the wisdom of the Lord's design (and later, to know pride in their fine workmanship). After two years the hardworking families had grown close; all talk of not going having long ago ceased. The fear of Nephi dissipated. His brothers talked to him again. But most importantly, when they looked at the unconventional vessel taking final form they humbled themselves, and gave thanks to The Lord.

At last everybody stood together and gazed at the completed vessel on the shore. Lemuel smiled and clamped a callused hand on Nephi's shoulder.

"Brother, when do we leave?"

"That," Nephi said quietly, "will be revealed to our father."

Together they turned and looked after their departing father. With cloak pulled tight around his sagging shoulders Lehi had started for his tent. Fall was in the air. Although on the southern tip of the desert wilderness winter did not get direly cold, the old man remembered how last year's autumn storms had laced the sea to fury. He was thinking it was about that time of year.... *Would they be commanded to venture upon angry frightening waters?*

Jacob and Joseph running to meet their father ended the worry in his mind. The tender young sons born in the wilderness held Lehi's heart in their dirty little hands. When they dropped their pointed sticks (make believe swords) to take hold of his hands, Lehi bent down and turned them by the shoulders to face the imposing structure on the edge of the great water.

"Look at our ship. Do you like it?"

The youths hung their heads. Joseph smiled up at his father as if asking what he should answer. Jacob, the elder, was braver. "It's funny looking. I do not like it."

The frank retort of the innocent deepened the wrinkles on the weather worn face, but only for an instant. Giving an affectionate boot to both behinds, Lehi said,

"Well, I do, now off with you. Go help your mother with the packing."

For days Sariah and the other women had been preparing food, and packing. Lehi had told them nothing specific, only that it would not be long.

Now, however, when Nephi and Lemuel caught up to him, and asked for a definitive answer, he told them, "Soon."

And the very next morning the voice came unto Lehi.

"*Arise and go down into the ship.*"

CHAPTER XX

The day of loading began in a flurry of activity: children laughing as they ran back and forth between tents and ship; women piling provisions on the shore; the men loading, all working together in harmony.

But before long tension crept in. Lehi noted that the women were not smiling as they were at first. It seemed that they approached the ship more warily with each armful. Many sideways glances at the great bulk on the shore, as if it were a grounded sea monster about to swallow him.

What had enhanced their fears?

Responsibility for their welfare again weighing on his shoulders the old prophet finally left the supervising of the loading to Nephi and went apart to pray.

When he returned, hours later, he fully expected to find the loading finished. For notwithstanding the prevailing tension, everyone had been working. Now, they should be at rest, reflecting on a job well done, ready for his departure sermon. The benevolent leader had been composing it on his way back. With God's guidance he would do his best to put their minds at ease, so that they would have a restful sleep tonight. For on the morrow they would sail!

The picture was not what his mind had painted.

Sacks of seed still stood by the ramp. The crocks of honey had not been carried aboard. And there were miscellaneous piles everywhere. Yet Lemuel, without a load on his shoulders, stood looking out to sea. The sons of Ishmael were talking casually with Laman. Sam was nowhere to be seen.

Lemuel ambled over to his father and said, "Father, my soul soars with anticipation. Traveling upon these great waters will be quite an adventure."

Lehi sighed and stroked his beard. The trip on the water was not an adventure. It was of ultimate importance to the conclusion of his mission. And The Lord had commanded that the ship be loaded *this* day. Had they all forgotten?

Lehi looked around the partially dismantled camp like a shepherd searching for lost sheep. Where was Nephi? Where was Sam. And their helpmates were not to be seen either. He scratched his head. Hannah and Josepha were busy wrapping strips of dried meat in burlap. Heleman now strode toward the ship with an armful of mats, his wife following with clothing. Zoram and Abigail emerged from their tent, loaded. When he turned back to chastise those who'd been loitering Laman and Lemuel surprised him. They were now hefting seed sacks.

But… the day was almost gone. By now the loading should have been accomplished. Had Nephi allowed lagging? Had he gone also to the mountain? All morning he had watched Sam's steady carrying. Had his sensitive son perhaps pushed too hard, maybe strained himself. The concerned father called out anxiously.

"Laman, where is Nephi and Sam?"

Laman shook his head. His wife, Josepha, answered the question.

"Sam went to look for Eve."

"Eve ran away," Hannah contributed, while methodically wrapping the meat. "And," she added, "Ruth cries in her tent."

"And Hiram and his wife argue, while our dear mother tries to rest." Josepha finished the report.

Lehi's mind raced. Ruth crying? Eve gone? Nephi not supervising. The implications left him mute. He rushed to talk with Sariah.

He found her busily patting out barley cakes. The aroma of the freshly baked ones filled the air.

"I feared there would not be enough," his wife said as he entered. "Also, I sent Jacob and Joseph to pick a few more of the plum-colored berries. They like them so much."

"My good woman, thou hast prepared enough food. According to the word we have sufficient."

"But, my husband, I shall not be able to cook…"

"Sari, Sari." Lehi took her busy hands in his, disregarding the flour dusting his tunic. "On this journey, as need be, we will live as a communal family. And I would that you rest from the cooking chore, as Anna now does. Let the young wives prepare the meals."

Pulling a hand free, Sariah pushed at a straying strand of hair, and smiled at her husband. "But a man's bread should be kneaded by his own woman."

Lehi's leathery face crinkled.

"Woman, thou hast kneaded my bread for countless years. Thou hast suffered travail to bear me six sons. Long and well hast thou served me. Surely the Lord will agree to a rest from wifely duties when we are upon the waters."

"Oh," her voice quavered. "How long dost thou think it will be, on the waters, how long until…"

Lehi put a finger to her lips. "Shush. That I do not know. But do not worry thyself. The Lord will be with us. He is ever with us."

Sariah's worry turned Lehi's thoughts to Zoram. He had prayed especially for Zoram today. From the time the loading began, the swarthy little man had faithfully done his share. But every time he carried a load down into the ship he ran back out, bathed with sweat.

Abigail finally told him why.

Before being pressed into servitude this nomad tribesman had never been confined by walls. When going about Laban's big house in the daytime, spacious and open as it was, he had suffered and endured his inherent fear (called claustrophobia). But soon as his master slept, he would escape to the open courtyard. Zoram had always slept outside, rarely even in a tent.

"He prays constantly to overcome these feelings," Abigail told the patriarch, "and he will never complain. Yet so great is his loyalty to the one who gave him freedom he will do anything you ask of him and say nothing."

Equally great was Abigail's loyalty to the kind hearted little man who had married her. While confiding in Lehi, petitioning his prayers in the matter, she had also implored him not to embarrass her husband by telling him that she knew. A woman is not to know her man's weakness.

Lehi told her he would pray about it. Then as it came closer to the time to leave Abigail (in desperation) had proposed a solution: let her family stay.

"Please, I beg of thee; let the family of Zoram stay? I have great fear that if my husband is long confined his heart may fail him. And we will be safe here."

"Good woman," he told her, "I cannot leave you. It is not God's will." And on this final day he assured her that Zoram would not suffer.

Lehi knew that many of his people were understandably apprehensive; that the faith of some had weakened. Now he discovered the strings of many lives under his care were wound to the breaking point.

He went to find Nephi.

Approaching the tent he saw smoke billowing from an unattended cooking fire near the opening. And the scene inside made him gasp. Ruth lay curled in fetal position on the sleeping mat, crying, Nephi hovered over her, repeating her name.

Of all the souls for which God had made him responsible, the wife of Nephi had given him least cause for concern. *Whatever could have happened to put her in such a state?* As a leader he needed to know; but as a father he would not intrude on his son's privacy. He quickly retreated, lest he hear what was not meant for other ears. If it was something he should know his son would tell him.

Reflecting on the scene, regretting having witnessed his son's wife writhing, crying, trying to hide a puffy tear streaked face—and the pain on his son's face, he returned to Sariah. But he told her naught of it. He would not recount even the few words that he overheard.

"I'm sorry; I'm sorry."

Nephi continued coaxing out his wife's full confession. "Oh, my dear Ruth." "Thou art over tired, overworked … I've been so occupied … neglected thee."

"No, Nephi…it's no fault of thine…"

Finally she told him what she had been trying to hide since their arrival—her deathly fear of the great waters.

"Fear?" Nephi stared at her.

Then, gradually, memory began playing the pictures: Ruth, the only one not bathing in the sea. Ruth, climbing the bluff to do her washing in the spring, while the other women washed in the sea. And the hurricane last fall. The angry water swelling thirty cubits high, like an enormous serpent about to devour them, when she panicked, and ran from him—for the first time disobeyed him.

Now he knew why—and at the same time he realized why he didn't know. Flashed back the scene of how she acted when they first viewed the sea, and when he first told her they were to depart from Bountiful by way of the great waters. Twice she'd tried to tell him. But he had not given her the opportunity. He had not listened to the one he loved. Now, on the eve of their departure, she tells him the fear is so strong she dare not exist at the mercy of the sea. She tearfully pleads with him to consider an alternative to traveling on it.

"Oh my husband, I know it's God's plan. But could not His faithful servant request a slight change—that we go around by way of land? No matter how long, to wherever the land may be, I promise never to complain."

"My dear wife, pray for forgiveness. Consider what thou art saying. Would even my father propose to alter God's plan?" He wrapped his arms around her, rocking her gently back and forth and stayed with her—and they prayed together.

Ruth's sobbing quieted. A gentle breeze fondled the tent flap, and floated in to caress them. On the wings of nature the peace of God came upon them. And Ruth's great fear of water drained away. She looked up at the man she loved, quoting a passage from the plates of Laban—about the woman for whom she was named.

"Whither thou goest…"

Nephi went to tell his father. He described the incredible happening, the blessing of God eliminating her fear. Lehi smiled and embraced his son, but said nothing. His heart was relieved that one problem had been solved. But there were others yet to solve, mainly, what was the problem with Sam. Where had Sam gone?

While conversing on other matters they heard a loud voice outside the tent—which solved the mystery.

"Woman, thou hast an asp for a tongue. Let me hear no more," Sam almost screamed at his wife.

Shocked to hear real anger in the voice that was rarely raised, they looked out—and were even more shocked at what they saw. Sam had a vice grip on Eve's arm, and was dragging his runaway wife back to camp. As he jerked her along she looked at the ground, while their small daughter, held prisoner by his other hand, struggled to keep up. Tears streaming down her little face, she looked up at her father as if her world had been shattered.

Lehi's eyes filled with pain. His ears hurt from hearing quarreling. All these scenes of unhappiness tortured his senses. It was his duty to strengthen faith and uplift spirits. He must gather special thoughts for this evening's sermon.

Oh dear God of Israel, help me find words to comfort this splintered family.

As he departed, Nephi looked at him knowingly. "Father, do try to get some rest," he said.

When nature began drawing the evening curtain the loading was accomplished, Lehi was rested, and words of wisdom had come to him. After the evening meal, the little ones asleep, Sariah pulled her shawl around her shoulders, and walked with him down to the sea. Drawing warmth and strength from his companion on the way, Lehi felt confident he could raise the spirits of his charges. As he faced the circle of loved ones who trusted their lives to him, his voice rang with the pure energy of a spirit-filled soul.

"Loved ones, fear not the journey we are about to make, for The Lord is with us. He is ever with us. And we have the instrument He gave us, which ye all know doth point the way, and giveth instructions…."

With his long beard now almost white, arms outstretched to the heavens, voice filled with conviction, Lehi looked like the prophets of old that he revered. And their words flowed from him as if recorded.

"For the way is prepared for all men from the foundation of the world. He that seeketh shall find … The mysteries of God shall be unfolded, as well in these times, as in times of old, as in times to come. For the course of the Lord is one eternal round. His servants He sendeth one after another, each chosen to bring that portion of His word to a time and place, as He desireth… that His children may grow in the knowledge of His laws… And blessed are they beyond measure who keep His commandments…."

Calm settled over the restless group like a protective cloud. Ruth clasped her husband's arm, thinking that soon he would be the one speaking and leading the people. And at that moment she felt a new life quicken within her. A smile spread over her face. She stretched up to whisper in his ear.

Lehi began winding down.

"So we go forth, trusting in God, to the land that He hath prepared for us. Where in accordance with His plan our seed shall multiply greatly … And after many generations God will bring forth the gentiles, also out of oppression… and they will build a great nation on the land, which will be called the land of the free."

And they went to their beds in the land called Bountiful for the last time.

Nephi made a record of his father's words before retiring. It was late when he slipped from the tent, not to wake Ruth, and went to pace the sand beside the odd shaped structure on the shore. Under the stars the giant ship designed by Deity looked even larger. *How could so few men possibly launch it?*

Plagued with the question all day, Nephi sought the heavens.

He stared in awe, Never had the stars shown so brightly. His mind stopped churning. Peace fell upon him. For a long time he stood motionless, watching the sea caressing the shore.

A gentle touch on his arm.

"Ruth!"

Barefoot, but wrapped in a cloak against the night air, she reached up her arms and circled his neck. The cloak fell loose, revealing her roundness. Moonbeams bounced off her hair. Nephi pulled his wife close; he thought she looked like an angel. Angels, however, do not tremble. He grasped her trembling hands and lifted them to his lips.

"Beloved mother of my children, are you ill? She shook her head; the smile didn't quite make it. He led her farther away from the water.

"Dear wife, I thought you were sleeping. What awakened you? Your fear has not returned?"

"No my love, not when thou art near."

He stroked her hair, talking quietly. He said, "I know dear heart it is not your desire to leave this place. And you are yet apprehensive about traveling on the water. But hold strong thy faith. The Lord will be with us. And the land He hath prepared for us is even more bountiful than this."

CHAPTER XXI

"I pray there will be enough water," Sam said to Hiram. They bent down together and eased the last heavy keg of fodder from their shoulders. The dusky cool storage area in the hold of the ship reeked with the mingling odors of fodder, sandalwood, and goats.

Sam sniffed and wrinkled his nose. From the far side of the food storage compartment three tethered goats were eyeing them. Hiram grimaced.

"I wish we could have left them with the asses. Imagine the odor when they've been shut up in here for days, maybe weeks."

"Yea," said Sam, "but think of having milk for the children, and cheese. We all like cheese. Goats give us a lot in exchange for fodder and water."

Suddenly the animals began moving restlessly, and bleating, as if they'd just sensed the strangeness of wood under their hooves. In the semi-darkness Sam and Hiram could see the whites of their large frightened eyes.

"Poor chosen three," Sam sympathized. "The others get to roam free in a verdant valley with the burros."

"Yea," Hiram continued. "Burros are lucky beasts; they can well fend for themselves, even in desert areas. When we were coming to join you and my father would bring more burros, instead of camels, I questioned him. But he said, 'Lehi did not take camels. Burros are more practical for the wilderness.' And I soon saw that."

Sam nodded. "They are also easier to handle."

As the two of them started their ascent up out of the lower section, Hiram became thoughtful. When they reached the main level he said, "Sam, thy father is a very wise man. Or maybe he knew that we would one day cross a great water, and have to leave them behind?"

Sam shook his head. "I don't think so. In all things my father simply bows to God's wisdom."

They hurriedly let themselves down to the shore on ropes. The long thong ladder, prepared for the exit of women and children, had already been rolled up and secured. They would all board by the loading plank.

The assembling families were eyeing the plank anxiously. Sam went over to where Eve stood with Laman and Lemuel and their families, Hiram still with him, still talking. "Now I know also," he was saying, "there was even wisdom in not allowing us the luxury of riding on camels."

Sam nodded. "Desert raiders, or roving bands would steal camels from us. We could have been killed for them."

"Yes, your father, is a wise man," Hiram concluded.

Laman overheard him, and added a comment. "I know now that father is not one of impractical imaginings, as I once thought. But…about the ship..." He hesitated. "I still say, where are the sails? How will we be driven? What if we … I'd hate to be stalled somewhere in the middle of this great sea."

Coming up behind them, Nephi overheard their conversation.

"Laman, I told you, the wind against the taller bulwarks will drive us," Then anticipating the next argument, he rushed on. "Did you forget how they were constructed? Thou knowest we can lower them when it blows too strong. Now quit worrying. The Lord forseeth such things. We will ever be ever prepared."

And on this note of finality he called out, "Now come, all of you and pack your tents; the women have them ready."

And he went to join his father.

Having ceremoniously organized the clan for boarding, according to age and family, Lehi waited calmly with the women and children while the men finished binding the tents into tight, space-saving bundles. But as they were loading them, he became unexpectedly tense. He shouted.

"Hurry. The sky darkens, and the wind is getting stronger. We must soon get inside for safety."

The husbands hurriedly carried their tents aboard, and returned to head their families in formation. All heads bowed for the prayer of departure. Every time they ventured forth the patriarch asked for God's guidance. And this time, for this new kind of venture, the request was of greatest significance. The bright morning fast transforming into a somber autumn day was turning colder by the minute. As Lehi groped for reassuring words, the churning waves surged to unnatural heights behind him. The dark wind-frothed water rushed angrily onto the shore. Fierce gusts tore at the sand beneath the waiting passengers, and shot it into their frightened faces.

Lehi eyed the sky. His robe billowing like a sail in a hurricane, his feet already wet, he decided it was too late for the prayer. Like a giant open-mouthed serpent the whirlwind funneling down from the heavens was about to engulf them.

"Hurry, get inside, get inside!"

The old man was blown backwards into an outcropping on the bow of the ship. He clutched a timber and held on, putting all his strength into his voice.

"Get up the plank. Sari, hurry, get thee and our young ones up the plank."

The whole clan crawling head down up the bowing plank looked like a follow-the-leader line of animals scenting prey. As was proper, the leader would board last. Would there be time?

The sky serpent struck the instant Lehi reached safety, even as the heavy trap door slammed over him. And so great was the force that the ship was set free of the sand. Inside, a jumbled heap of screaming humanity. The bulky tri-level vessel creaked and tipped precariously, then swirled like a top. By centrifugal force the scrambled occupants were swept to the walls—by unseen power the vessel swirled, lifted, and deposited safely upon the sea.

No one was hurt.

When the block of panic melted and senses returned, the passengers felt the cradling of the water, and the mighty wind steadily pushing them. The timbers creaked naturally, the ship tipping only slightly. Tension drained away like run-off. *And they were driven forth before the wind, towards the promised land.*

"Blessed be the Lord!" Nephi shouted. Scrambling to his feet, he raised up his wife and gathered his children into his arms. "By God's great wisdom we shaped and structured a ship that cannot sink. By His great power, we were launched. Though waves reach the sky in this great wilderness of waters we shall sail safely."

"We sail to the Promised Land," they all shouted.

Lehi too was filled with exuberance; but he arose with difficulty—and Sariah's help. For a moment he tested his balance; then he limped to the center of the floor. All eyes upon him, he raised his hand. And all heads bowed for the prayer he had not given back on the shore. In closing he gave thanks ".. for the power of thy forces that launched us, for thy eternal blessings, for thy great goodness. May we be eternally worthy. Guide us now on these great waters as we sail to the place which thou has prepared for us."

In the long years since leaving their homeland, they had lost only Ishmael—and an old man's time comes wherever he may be. They had known hardship and hunger, but encountered no serious danger. The women had borne many children; and God in His mercy had granted that all of them should live. Considering the mortality rate of the time, this was a blessing almost beyond belief.

With soaring faith the leader charged his flock to "give thanks every day."

Each man, woman and child (painting his or her mental picture of the promised paradise) silently vowed obedience. And they all went to their rest happy. The Promised Land was soon to materialize on the horizon.

But after they had been driven forth for many days the strong steady gale lessened. The ship slowed to barely moving. Then the wind ceased entirely. They were becalmed.

Time passed. And more time. Then, after being driven forth again for many days, the land of their dreams still didn't appear on the horizon. The men grew restless. The women were bored. And like prisoners, their movements restricted, their desires thwarted, every personality reacted to the situation differently. Although all were allowed a turn up to the top-turret opening for a breath of fresh air (and hopefully, a glimpse of sunshine) many lay listless on their bunks instead. Although each calm was good for the seasick, it meant they were getting no closer to land. And land-lovers all, the yearning for earth beneath their feet grew to the point of pain.

Robbed of the opportunity for exercise and the adventure of hunting, the men could only try to catch fish. And since it was the only diversion some of the women went with them.

When Laman took his turn working the long line nets from the tiny top cubicle, Josepha was happy to help him. To her it was great fun. Ruth and Eve, for different reasons, would not even go up for air. The wives of Hiram and Heleman, after a few turns with their husbands, decided that a breath of fresh air was not worth the effort getting up there. Hannah would have gone with Lemuel, but he would not allow her… she took up so much space in the narrow cubicle he felt inhibited. And he claimed she hexed his catch.

The friction between them had begun on land. During the sojourn in Bountiful, little to do but eat, Hannah of the beautiful face had swollen to a bulky matron. And Lemuel of the eye that twinkled for beauty felt cheated—if he could have returned to the city there would have been other women.

In the way that Lemuel felt cheated, Nephi felt blessed. As the years counted up his companion had remained slim, like his mother. Even rounded with a third pregnancy, he thought her still lovely. The hard accounting of nature had begun to wear at her outer beauty, but her inner beauty grew. Nephi always wanted her with him. But it fell his lot to wrestle food from the sea without her. Fated to reside upon the water, Ruth controlled her fear of it by mind over matter. The vessel had only one small opening. She couldn't see the water so she wouldn't think about it.

Sam's wife didn't go up for other reasons. The night before their departure Eve had turned rebellious again. Then seasick the first day out and nauseated ever since… By the misery of another pregnancy, and a captive situation, Eve fell into a deep depression. She became uncooperative, and unpleasant. Sam was beside himself. A husband could order a wife, but he couldn't carry her up a steep enclosed ladder in a narrow cubicle—the only way to the fresh air patch of blue (or gray) depending on the weather. Day after day Sam tried reasoning with her. The fresh air would help her. But she became even more withdrawn. Finally in desperation he went to Nephi for advice.

It all came rushing out.

"Nephi, what can I do? She lays like a condemned woman, clinging to the bunk as if she were about to be carried off and stoned. And when I try to help her it's as if she hates me. She doesn't even care for our daughter. And I worry for the unborn child. Tell me, what do you do? How is it your wife glows in a pregnancy? Mine maketh of it a calamity!"

"Ruth worried a lot her first time too, I remember." Nephi said. "But in the later months she relaxed."

Sam just shook his head.

As Nephi looked sympathetically at his brother, trying to think of something helpful to say, the children began to crowd in about them. It was almost time for Sam to give a lesson. This section of the ship, where Lehi and Nephi prayed and kept the sacred records, had also been designated the "schooling" area. Sam's motioned a six-year old to the center of the group. His countenance had changed

"There's barely room enough for them all to sit," he said. "But of course this is the only place." He lifted young Joseph upon his knee. "And of course, the best place—the place of prayer and learning for us all."

"The place is not important, Sam," said Nephi, "only the teacher. Ruth and I, and all the parents, are so grateful for thy talent, and patience in teaching our children all these years. Little Enoch already does his numbers. And Simon scribes commendably."

Nephi smiled at his first born, just entering, leading his little brother close to the teacher. Jacob and one of Lemuel's daughters came next. Sam taught the younger boys and girls together, the older ones separately, in accordance with age and ability. But some of the older ones also came to his sessions for the young. This pleased the teacher. Sam enjoyed the responsibility of guiding young minds. He had now mentally shelved his personal problem; his responsibility must take precedence.

When seven students had crowded into the small cubicle he raised his hand for quiet, and began the lesson. He frowned up at the jiggling ceiling. If it were not for preparing lessons, teaching, and reading scripture to the young ones maybe he would become bored unto rudely roughhousing like those above him. The loud laughing and stomping overhead had become ribald.

Nephi jumped up. “I will go quiet them.”

As Nephi climbed to the upper section the laughing and stomping, crude words and blasphemy, inflamed his ears. And when he ducked through the opening, he gasped. Laman, Lemuel, Heleman, and Hiram were bouncing their wives back and forth between them in a wild frenzied dance—tearing at their clothes, touching wife and sister alike, as if they were paid-for harlots. While adolescent sons and daughters watched. Two of the youngest were giggling hysterically.

Nephi sprang into action like a brawler, blindly knocking Hiram and Lemuel aside to get at Laman. He grabbed his older brother by the neck with both hands.

“Laman! This is a den of iniquity. And thou art the leader.”

With an iron-clamp hold on his neck Nephi twisted Laman’s slim body down to his knees, and towered over him like Thor. The others quieted immediately, cringing back as if in fact the God of Thunder had intruded. But the next instant they all rushed upon him (eight or ten people) and succeeded in wrestling Laman free. Like a spring released, Laman spun around and punched Nephi in the face. The wives and adolescents began kicking him on the shins. Then someone kicked his feet from under him.

From flat on his back Nephi shouted, “ This is wickedness; an abomination to The Lo…” His breathe went out of him. He’d been kicked in the stomach.

“May God forgive you,” he croaked out. “I did not come to chastise for thy sakes, but lest The Lord be angry and smite us. Or that we might be swallowed up in the depths of the sea!”

As Nephi forced out these words, Laman stepped back like a general surveying a battle going well. There was a temporary flash of fear—flash back to another time, and a similar scene. But he hesitated only a minute. That was years ago. Since then his holier-than-thou brother had not always been perfect. Recalling the many times Nephi had been left waiting for "the word," or for answers, he concluded that the usurper did not always please The Lord.

While Laman was busy justifying the action Lemuel and the others had wrestled the victim to silence. Nephi appeared to be completely subdued; he didn't move a muscle. But just for good measure, Lemuel kept a foot on his chest.

"Well, Laman," he challenged, "now what are we going to do with him?"

Laman flipped the hair off his forehead, and threw back his shoulders. His voice resonated with conviction.

"Once and for all we're going to get rid of him. It's got to be done. This time for sure. A younger brother shall not be a ruler over me."

"Not now, or in the promised land." echoed Lemuel.

"Long I have listened to him," Laman went on, "and for years followed him like a lamb—I, the elder, followed a younger brother… But enough is enough."

"It's not right," Josepha stepped up beside her husband for emphasis. And the others chorused, "A younger brother shall not be a ruler over us."

Nephi stirred, and hands no longer pressing on his windpipe, was able to gasp out another warning.

"Think of the consequences of what you are doing. Have you all forgotten by what power we have been protected, and brought thither? Humble thyselves, and ask forgiveness. Thou knowest that I am commanded; that I must preach against unholy actions, as well as wickedness. And truly this is an abomination…"

"*You* are an abomination," someone hissed.

Laman's eyes flashed to the opening, where Nephi had entered. "Quick, I hear someone coming. Gag him." And wrap those cords around him." He looked down at the prisoner. "If we could lug dead weight up to the opening…"

"Oh Nephi!"

Sam had surfaced from below, Zoram right behind him. They rammed the human barricade crying, "Oh my God, my God what have you done to him?"

They were slung against the wall.

Behind the human barricade the clan brothers were frantically wrapping cords around their victim. To the women and teenagers looking on, as they crouched over their prey, they appeared to be in complete control. While in truth, they were shaking inside, expecting…

Nothing happened.

The victim seemed not to be breathing. So extensive was the wrapping of cords, he looked like a pre-done mummy. His blood drained face was barely visible. Yet hearing Sam's voice Nephi opened his eyes and tried to speak again. Laman jerked a shawl from the closest woman and jabbed it in his mouth. Then he whispered something in Heleman's ear, and shouted to his supporters.

"Hold the pious ones. We'll hide him. The ship is unsinkable, and we will have the ball. I will lead. Our father is in no condition to stop me."

And it came to pass that Sam and Zoram were constrained by Hiram and Heleman and their wives, while Laman and Lemuel dragged the prisoner away.

"Helplessly outnumbered, the would-be rescuers could do nothing—but pray.

CHAPTER XXII

"Sam, where is Nephi?"

Ruth had been searching for her husband since he hadn't appeared for the midday meal. When she went to the area of prayer and learning and saw Sam she fully expected to see Nephi with him. But instead, she found Zoram there.

Zoram in the schooling cubicle? Further puzzled to see the two of them sitting bent over, head in hands—not in an attitude of prayer—she raised her voice.

"Sam?" Sam did not respond, or even look up.

"Please, Sam, I have not seen Nephi for more than an hour. And now with a tempest brewing on these terrible waters he surely knows I need him, but he does not come to me."

Zoram's head jerked up, his swarthy face a map of consternation. He attempted to speak but nothing came out. Ruth nodded to her sister's husband, but continued to direct her words to Sam. Sam still didn't look at her, or answer.

Suddenly the floor pitched, steeply. And while she clung to the bastion for balance, Ruth scrutinized the small space as if she expected her husband to materialize. The pitching increased, the timbers protested.

"Oh there is a storm. Nephi!" she screamed.

"Ruth, forgive me," Sam choked out. He got to his feet and reached over to support her. "We've searched the ship; we can't find him."

Ruth swayed. A hand went to her heart. With the other she clutched the wooden partition as if expecting to be ripped from it. Her lovely hair awry, her body swollen with child, it seemed to Sam that she had transform into a strange, aged woman. Gently, he and Zoram seated her at the writing plank (where she had expected to find her husband) before they hit her with the brutal details.

"…And all this time since, we've been searching…"

Ruth crumpled. Her husband had disappeared; the vessel that protected her from the angry sea could be breaking apart… She shook with sobs.

But the next moment, as if ashamed, as if the natural relief of crying was forbidden to one in her position, she straightened. And dabbing at the telltale tears, blurted out, "I must go to his father."

Sam and Zoram went with her, supporting her from possible injury, the floor now tipping wildly. When they reached the cubicle of Nephi's parents, Lehi appeared to be sleeping. Sam and Zoram respectfully retreated. But Ruth could not wait. *He could not be sleeping with this pitching.*

She cried out, "Dear father of my husband, help me. We must pray for Nephi. Thy wayward sons have revolted again; they attacked him, and bound him; and they have hidden him we know not where!"

"Wha … wha … what?" the old man rose up sputtering, and flaying at his covering. Sariah materialized. She had heard. She reached a gentle hand to her husband's brow, and lay the other on Ruth's shoulder. Ruth crumbled against her.

"Oh, dear mother of my husband, I cannot bear it; Sam says they hurt him bad. And somewhere now he suffers; and I cannot go to him."

Sensitive to Sariah's silent strength, Ruth continued to cling to her mother-in-law. Sam and Zoram crowded back into the cubicle. The half-delirious old patriarch stared at them without comprehension. His dark eyes burned like nuggets of coal. Ruth stared into them expectantly—waiting for the voice of authority that would somehow save her husband.

The old man absconded. He slid back down under the coverlet, closed his eyes and shut them out. He had said nothing to them, but Ruth could see his lips moving. She turned to Sariah.

"That my son suffers, tears at his heart," Sariah whispered. To Sam and Zoram she said, "Nephi has served faithfully; God will take care of him."

Ruth's eyes fixated on the moving lips as if *her* life hung on the inaudible words. She clung to Sariah with one hand, and to the side of the bunk with the other. Sam reached over and patted her arm. Then he and Zoram left, to continue searching.

The ship now moved in frenzied jerks, and tipped at even sharper angles. Suddenly it seemed to plunge to the very depths of the angry sea. Ruth turned pale.

"Do not fear," Sariah said quietly. "Did not my son say the ship is unsinkable?"

Ruth managed a weak smile, but she didn't relax her white-knuckle grip on the bunk. There was comfort in Sariah's words and compassion in her soft brown eyes. Nephi's wife felt a warm tenderness for her mother-in-law, like unto what she felt for her children. And it was then that she remembered.

Oh, God forgive me, I left my children unattended.

Sariah quickly released her. "Go carefully, my daughter, remember also to protect thy unborn…"

As Ruth departed the cubicle the voice of Lehi boomed out behind her, strong, stronger than she had thought possible.

"God will not allow the death of my son before his work is done."

The words of authority worked magic. Ruth's heart swelled; her mind began functioning clearly again. She dropped to her knees. For double safety, to prevent falling in the pitching ship, she would crawl back to her children. It was perilous for *anyone* to attempt walking upright. And she must not only protect herself from bodily harm, but the life within her.

Come evening, thankful to find Simon and Enoch unharmed, she kept them with her in Nephi's bed. Usually, she sent them to the community bed. But this night, as the storm raged louder, the mother needed her children more than they needed her. Despite Sariah's reminder that the ship would not capsize, Ruth's recently enhanced fear did not subside. She kept playing over in her mind the many times Nephi had told her that he may suffer, that God might show forth His power—and also, what Lehi had just said. But nothing helped. She couldn't sleep. She needed her husband, and ached to share his pain.

The violent storm continued to wrestle and batter the ship. The oil lamp burned low. Ruth could stand it no longer; she had to do *something*. Slowly, carefully, she extracted herself from chubby, clinging arms and slid her bare feet to the rough hewn floor.

"Mommy!" Little Enoch cried out.

"I want my father," Simon wailed.

The mother slipped back down between her offspring. "My sons, my sons, I will not leave you." And when they had again quieted, she talked to God.

"Oh Lord God of Israel, I know thou art with my husband, thy servant; but I beg of thee, let me be with him too, that I may tend to his wounds… Dear God, let us find him, that I may be with him and tend to him …"

She repeated the prayer over and over unto exhaustion.

When Sam reappeared to check on Nephi's family. He tried to calm Ruth's fears, as he had tried all night with Eve—but with no more success. On the second day of the terrible tempest, due to the constant pitching, there were more cases of seasickness. And now the whole family was near paralyzed with fear—they'd become aware that the mighty winds were driving them *back* instead of forward.

For three days they were driven back. The situation bordered on mass hysteria. Since the out-of-the-blue onset of the mighty tempest, no one had functioned normally. But the wives of the foursome suffered additionally—from the painful weight of conscience. On the morning of the fourth day they came to the food area with downcast eyes. Automatically, out of habit, they began preparing breakfast. With the floor pitching from one steep slant to another the porridge in the community crock (which no one felt like eating) kept slopping over. Hannah, clinging to the table with one hand, mechanically sopping it up with the other, sometimes took a bite. The others couldn't even think of eating.

Suddenly Josepha slammed her fist down on the table, upsetting a bowl of figs, which a quick twist of the battered ship sent flying across the dark floor.

"We shouldn't have done it!" Her high pitched voice cracked. "And I know that I wouldn't have, if I hadn't been drinking."

"Well it's too late now," Hiram's wife chided.

"Yea, if we don't sink, surely we'll starve," said Heleman's wife.

Hannah began to cry. Food was her comforter; she could think of nothing worse—until Josepha reminded her that they had hardly any water left.

A week before Lehi had begun rationing water. Crossing the Irreantum Sea was taking more days than he had imagined. And they had lost time in the calm. It was a wise decision.

But now they were being pushed *back,* and about to be swallowed up by an angry sea. Staring at each other from their anchors on either side of the wooden table the young wives finally faced the gravity of the situation for which they were jointly responsible. Fear of drowning, fear of starving, and guilt gnawing at their insides… They rushed to plead with their husbands, all talking at once.

"Loose him, loose him. Free him. Free Nephi, or we all shall die!"

The sons of Ishmael agreed with the wives. Heleman stepped forward to persuade Laman. "We *must* loose him, Laman. The storm does not cease, and the ball won't work." *The compass which had been prepared...did cease to work. Wherefore they knew not whither they should steer the ship.*

"Yea," said Hiram. "Can that be anything but the wrath of the Lord?"

Laman responded with a haughty look, telling them that strong men should not be afraid of a storm… that he would not be talked into worry…that they were a couple of cowards.

Lemuel listened mute from the sidelines. But his mind raced. He kept his eyes on Laman's face. The women and Hiram and Heleman gave up trying to persuade him and left. When they returned a short time later bringing the aging Anna (who could hardly tend to herself) to join her sons and their wives in begging for release of the prisoner, he weakened. But they had sworn together that they would *never* tell where they hid their prisoner. And Laman held out.

All this was reported to the ailing patriarch. He threatened them with the wrath of God from his sickbed. But aware of his father's condition, relying on his weakness, Laman was not intimidated. So the old man could only censor them in absentia. And pray.

"Oh, Lord God, soften the hardened hearts of my wayward sons that they may conceive what an evil thing they have done, what misery they have brought upon the women and children. Even now their dear mother suffers exceedingly…" Lehi further entreated his errant offspring by messenger to put away their anger and hatred, and consider his offer of clemency "…lest the judgment of heaven be the death of you, and all of us.

Release thy brother, and we all will live—and ye shall have my forgiveness."

This message was given to Sam, when he came to care for his father. And after he had tended to his father, and his mother (Sariah now also have taken to her bed) Sam rushed to report the offer, and plead further, hoping against hope that forgiveness would turn the tide.

It seemed only to fuel the fire.

"Tell the old man to be quiet," Laman sneered. "Or, we will end his misery."

"Do what you will with me," Sam cried brokenly. "Do what you must to vent your anger, but please, do not make an old man suffer. And our mother, in the depths of despair, lies also in her bed. In the name of God, repent of your iniquity. Release Nephi. I beg of you, release Nephi, or show me where …"

"Nephi, Nephi. It's always Nephi. It has always been Nephi." Laman turned on his heel and stalked away with Sam still talking.

Sam spent much time with his mother. She looked so frail it tore at his heart, as the family mutiny tore at her soul. They were both scratching the bottom of the barrel for hope when an idea surfaced in Sam's mind. *Send Jacob and Joseph to the rebels.* The family innocents (their little brothers) might somehow melt the hard core of hate.

But the innocents also failed. Jacob and Joseph loved Nephi, and having heard what had been done to him, approaching their big brothers with fear and animosity, they simply broke down and cried. Hearing this, Ruth was devastated. For she'd been thinking of taking her tender young sons to plead with them, on that same chance—that maybe innocence could soften flinted hearts. But, if the tears of their own little brothers didn't even crack their armor… Hope deserted her. She couldn't help her loved one, nor could his children. And so much time had passed she now anticipated the worst.

What if Laman and Lemuel couldn't bring their prisoner out of hiding, because he no longer lived! Or, was no longer on the ship! Could they possibly have managed to drag him up the narrow ladder to the top opening? Oh, dear God...

Ruth grabbed her children, never to leave them alone again, and went searching for the culprits, for one last try. She found them by following the sound of loud angry voices.

"Shut thy mouth, coward." Laman's voice.

"I may be a coward, but thou hast lost all reasoning," Lemuel screeched. "We are all gonna die if we don't."

The tempest battled ship tipped precariously. Ruth feared she would lose her balance and hurt the children. She trembled at what she was hearing. And then it came to her. If they were arguing they were weakening—they were starting to crack. *Divide and conquer.* She brazenly faced them.

"Yes, you will die. We will all die."

Laman spun around like a wild man. "You again. Woman, get out of my sight." Glaring at Ruth as if she were the sinner who broke God's commandments, he sneered. "And what kind of mother are you, risking injury to your children. Would they not be safer tied in a bunk?"

With Enoch in her arms, Simon clinging to her skirts, she braced against the bastion (to help lighten the weight of the third child, the one carried inside). She looked pleadingly at Lemuel. His outburst had seemed less menacing. But the once twinkling eyes were hard.

"Go, Ruth, get out of here, or we'll ... we'll take care of you too. Then who would watch his holy babes?"

"Well, not our wives."

Laman leered at her as he said this, and reached out and pulled the baby's chubby hand from her neck. With his other hand he gripped the older boy's arm until he cried. As Ruth let go of her safety hold to push at him, trying to free her children, the floor lunged up, slamming her into the wooden partition.

She gasped. Laman released his grip on Simon, and gave her a shove. "Get out of here," he said sullenly.

"And quit heckling us," Lemuel added, "or we will lock you up with him and the two of you can…"

W*ith him.* T*he two of you...* Ruth hardly heard the rest, for with those words hope had re-surged. Nephi was still on the ship; and he was still alive!

Back at Lehi's bedside, she breathlessly enlightened Sam and the grieving parents with her belief that Nephi was still alive—and the fact that Laman and Lemuel argued.

"Now they are divided against themselves, I think they can be overcome."

"By nothing but the power of God will my evil brothers be overcome," said Sam, wearily. He'd had no sleep since watching them drag Nephi away.

The old man spoke—to nobody in particular.

"Soon their fear will become greater, lest they die of starvation and thirst, or be swallowed up in the depths of the sea. Then they will rush to repent of this evil thing that they have done."

Ruth's voice quavered. She turned to Sam.

"Truly, there may be a chance of that happening. I saw fear in their eyes."

Sam took her hands, and pushed her palms together. "Keep praying," he said breathlessly. "I go to get Zoram. We'll search again; somehow we'll find him."

Sam and Zoram came upon them arguing again. Peeking from behind the partition they watched the shadow of realization spread over their faces, that the judgment of God was upon them. "*… after they had been driven back upon the waters for the space of four days they began to see that the judgments of God were upon them, that they must perish save that they should repent of their iniquities.*"

"So…" stammered Lemuel, "we've got to release him. But if we release him now he'll kill us!"

Laman's mouth twitched nervously. "For sure, he'll be angry enough to kill. But… remember he hasn't eaten for four days, and has lost much blood. Wherewith his great strength will not be with him."

"Yea, that's true," Lemuel almost whispered. "And as I think back I also remember … Has he ever done real violence against us?"

"No," Laman had to concede. "Nephi preaches; he fights with words."

"Yea, he may threaten us; of a surety he will preach to us. But also he might forgive us; he might even ask God to forgive us. Unless…"

The ship heaved, and slammed them together. They shoved each other. The eavesdroppers behind the bulkhead held their breath.

"Unless … Unless he no longer lives!"

Simultaneously the conspirators turned and sprinted in the direction of the ship's hold, Sam and Zoram in cautious pursuit. In the shadowy half-darkness of the storage area, hearts beating staccato, they took up their watch from behind a line of huge jugs—and were at last rewarded. Shoving aside the last stone jug of water, the guilty pair began clawing up the floorboards.

Zoram was visibly shaking. Sam steadied him with a compassionate grip on the shoulder. Still, when the perpetrators of pain and evil raised their prisoner up out of the hole, the little man could not contain a groan.

Laman and Lemuel jumped at the sound. Shooting frantic glances over their shoulders, they dropped their prey, and fled.

The rescuers breathlessly crawled across the slanting floor, frantically searching the bruised and blackened face (the exposed part) for a flicker of life. Zoram clawed at the torturing cords wrapped round and round his head. Sam looked for something sharp to cut them, all the while intensely watching for movement of the eyes. They were closed. Blood red showed at the edges. One twitched.

"Oh Nephi, thank God!" Sam choked out.

"Thank God!" echoed Zoram.

Working blindly, their eyes flooded with tears, the rescuers managed to loosen the restricting cords around head and torso. But so tight were the bindings on wrists and ankles the skin puffed over them, purple. The gore-smeared face was gaunt, hair and beard like tangled dirty weeds…

"Oh God in heaven save him, let him live," Sam cried brokenly.

The parched lips moved, slightly—and at that moment Sam realized that the floor was leveling. He jumped up, tipped the keg to steal some of the last precious water, and carefully poured it between the fissured lips. Zoram wiped the blood stained face with the dampened bottom of his tunic. And after a safe interim the two of them raised their patient partially up, offering another small portion of life's sustaining liquid. Sam began massaging his wrists, Zoram his ankles, both of them constantly mumbling assurances. There was still no response.

So, slowly easing one of his arms around each of their necks, they tried lifting him upright. The feet were too painfully swollen to hold his weight.

Letting him down again, on the now almost level floor, they sat holding him between them—naught else to do… They could not carry him; and they would not leave him. One of them must go for help.

Zoram got up reluctantly, his eyes glued on the bludgeoned face. Would this man he almost worshipped, the one responsible for his freedom, still be alive when he returned? With concerted effort he turned to leave.

"Wait! He's trying to speak."

The parched lips were moving but the words were inaudible. Their patient was praying. They waited, and waited. Holding Nephi between them, Sam and Zoram kept looking around the murky chamber as if waiting for a miracle.

Time ticked by like a sick snail…

"Oh Lord God of Israel!" The voice came out surprisingly strong. "Lord God of Israel… Praise be to God." Nephi appeared to be in a trance. He had regained his voice; and his eyes were open, but not focused. Staring alternately at their patient and each other, Sam and Zoram realized that the floor was level. The ship had stopped tipping and pitching… *And it came to pass that the wind did cease and the storm did cease…*

"God bless thee, Sam. God bless thee, Zoram," Nephi said in a normal voice. Then he asked Zoram to bring him the directional ball (and told him the place where he would find it).

When God's servant held the instrument in his hands it worked. Nephi set the course for the Promised Land. Then they hoisted him up between them, and finally, half-carrying, half-dragging, Sam and Zoram were able to bring him up unto the living quarters, to see his wife.

"Ruth, Ruth." Nephi kept calling her name. His loved one would restore him to health; then his strength would return. And all would be well.

But Ruth was not in their cubicle. Nephi's wife was nowhere to be found.

CHAPTER XXIII

Ruth's euphoria from the words of Lemuel, that left her believing Nephi still lived, almost immediately waned. The emotional high evaporated. After taking her children to safety she staggered through the pitching ship looking for Sam. It seemed an eternity since he had left her to search again. When she left her sons in the communal children's bed, with their adolescent aunts, she had assured them their father would soon be with them. Now she doubted.

Frantic with worry, she kept praying, "Dear Lord, be with him, dear Lord be with him until we find him."

The ship jerked sharply, and dropped, throwing her forward. Her extended abdomen struck the protruding edge of a bulwark, for a second time. She muffled a scream, and clung to the offending board. Sweat beaded her brow. The angry sea still wrestled and battered the ship as if it were a chip in a gushing stream. In this vulnerable state of mind and body, without her husband's comforting assurances and support, Ruth's inherent fear of the sea returned with awesome power. She fought for control. Letting go of the bulwark, she slid down to the floor, rolled over on her back and began breathing deeply.

Then, she felt another kind of pain, which frightened her anew. She clutched her stomach. It was not yet time…

Like a child in danger, Ruth thought of her mother. She knew Anna was in no condition to help in a delivery. Abigail would attend to her. But she needed motherly comfort. Warmth and assurance would be forthcoming from both mother and sister, if she could get to them. They also could tell her if it was a false alarm or the baby was truly coming. Holding her abdomen protectively, she rolled over onto her knees and crawled to her mother's cubicle.

"Mother, Abigail" she gasped at the doorway. Abigail was not there; and her mother seemed to be sleeping. *But how could she sleep? How could anyone asleep in this tempest?* Ruth edged toward the still form on the bunk, grabbed onto the side of it, and pulled herself to her feet.

"Mother? Oh mother, no!" she screamed.

Josepha and Hannah rushed in. They grabbed their sobbing sister; and as they pulled her back the stillness of death stole over their faces.

"She's dead," Josepha rasped out.

"Oh dear mother! Oh, mother," wailed Hannah.

Ruth said no more. Death's frosty stillness had already enveloped her. The three sisters stood like statues, staring at the earthly shell of Anna. Their beloved mother's face seemed to have crystallized, but also regressed to a younger fullness. To the grief stricken daughters their aged mother, looking relaxed and peaceful, prompted fond memories of their childhood. As if chained together, they clung to the bunk as one—until another contraction jerked Ruth back to reality. She slid to the floor groaning.

Not until then did Hannah and Josepha realize her situation—or the fact that the floor no longer slanted. On the fourth day, the ravaging tempest had finally ceased. And like the lull before an explosion, the sudden calm was disconcerting. Josepha swirled around looking for the reason, momentarily forgetting her mother. Ruth gasped with another contraction. Hannah, sat down on the floor beside her.

"Oh Hannah, not *here*," Josepha shrieked.

"There is no choice; the baby is coming. Can't you see? C'mon, help me. Hold her. C'mon …"

"No, Hannah, I can't!"

Eyes darting back and forth from her groaning sister on the floor to the corpse of her mother on the bunk, Josepha backed away from the scene like a horrified believer looking on the devil in church. Death and birth together seemed like sacrilege. She couldn't handle it.

"Oh, Ruth, I'm sorry I'm sorry," she shrieked, "but with mother there I can't. I just can't; I can't…"

Hannah looked after her fleeing sister and prayed for Abigail to get back soon, then steeled herself to the duty before her.

"All right Ruth, try to relax, don't worry." With shaking hands she positioned herself for what she must do, and spoke to her sister calmly. "I've never done this before, but you push and pray, and I'll do the rest. I will do my best."

Abigail returned in just a few minutes. She had left her mother only momentarily to check on her daughter—and Eve's daughter, whose care had fallen to her when Anna was no longer able. For Eve still lay inert, ignoring the world. Her young mind unable to cope with the circumstances of the existent reality, she'd simply blocked it out. As all things considered, the frightening dual events had overwhelmed Josepha, Hannah had been blessed with extra strength. But when Abigail came in she was weak with relief—and happy to relinquish her patient to the hands of experience.

With but a glance at the form on the bunk, Abigail whispered, "Oh, dear Mother, dear Mother," and immediately relieved Hannah of the responsibility. But they delivered the baby together. Hannah decided to stay. And in less than an hour she had gained mid-wife experience. Holding the baby in her hands, umbilical cord still attached, she looked at Ruth's tiny daughter with awe. Abigail cut and tied the cord, and wrapped the uncleaned infant in her shawl. Then with the new life squirming weakly in her arms she looked again upon the old life ended.

"Oh dear mother," my dear mother, rest in peace."

Abigail brought the bundle up to her face to blot the tears, then bent down and handed Ruth her daughter. And when the mother had held her newborn for a few minutes she carried the infant away to perform the ceremonial cleansing. Hannah finished tending to their patient.

"Thank you, Hannah," Ruth mumbled. "Thank you. But… the baby… She is so tiny … came too soon. Will she…?"

"Shush… the little one will be fine."

Hannah braced her bulk against the wall and reached out to hold her distraught sister. Ruth welcomed the pillow of her fleshy arms, She had begun to relax when she looked up to see the cubicle filling with people. They showed no surprise at the women on the floor; they'd been told about the birth and everyone had seen the baby. Now they came to see Anna. The whole family crowded in. they shuffled en mass toward the still form on the bunk. The demise of the beloved matriarch had been expected. They had watched her weaken day by day. But expected or not, death holds the power to shock. All in a hush they stared dry-eyed at the body that had harbored the soul of Anna. Crying would come later—followed by the usual self-recriminations and discussions of guilt.

After the tempest roar and creaking timber they'd heard for days the silence seemed eerie. The women on the floor felt forgotten. With just one look at the deceased, Hannah had given her full attention to the birth. Now Ruth was relaxed and resting she wanted to look again on her dear mother's face; she couldn't see it from down among the legs and feet. They were so close she could hardly move an arm to disentangle herself … She nudged her dosing charge.

"Dear sister, could I …?"

Ruth smiled and wiggled from under her arm. Hannah reached up and tugged the closest skirt. It belonged to the wife of Hiram. The couple pulled her to her feet. And Hannah asked them to take Ruth to her bed.

Welcoming the support the new mother, with but a glance back over her shoulder, willingly went with them.

In her non-tipping bunk she rested physically; but her mind raced. Left alone, the newborn in good hands, her sons safe with their older cousins, she tried desperately to sleep. But she could not escape the mental pictures: her mother's lifeless face—and her husband, probably lifeless …

"Oh, Nephi, Nephi…" Her heart pounded in her ears. And the tears streamed.

Dear God where is Sam? Why can't they find Nephi? And why hasn't Abigail brought my baby back to me? Was there something wrong…?

Ruth could be idle no longer. She reared up from prone position like a doe scenting danger, threw off her covering and slid from the bed. She knew not what to do, but the wife of Nephi couldn't lay there doing nothing. Barefoot, in her under tunic, she stood shaking, clinging to the bunk, trying to muster strength. Now the floor was level and the timbers had quieted, but she was weak.

"Ruth!"

Averting his eyes from the half-nakedness of his brother's wife, Sam rushed forward and lifted her back upon the bed. Zoram discreetly withdrew—but was back beside the bunk the second she had covered herself. Ruth looked frantically from one to the other, like a slave girl questioning her fate.

She read the answer in their glowing faces.

"You found him!"

"Yes, yes," Sam gushed. "My dear brother is alive. And I think, I pray he is going to be all right. "We will bring him to you just as soon as…"

Ruth grabbed Sam's arm, and with the other hand reached out toward Zoram. Both men broke into smiles, Zoram nodding, and nodding, as if trying to convince himself that what Sam said was true.

"Oh, thank you, thank you," Ruth cried. "You are my knights without armor. But where is he? Where is he? I must see him."

"You were not here," Sam said gently; "we could not find you. So we took him to Abigail to tend his wounds."

Ruth sobered. "Oh, you saw Abigail? You know about my dear mother?" There was a catch in her voice. "You saw my baby?" Sam dropped his eyes. "Did you see my baby?" Ruth repeated.

"We did," said Sam. He and Zoram exchanged veiled glances. Neither of them had ever seen a premature baby … such a tiny fragile thread of life…

"Abigail was tending to her," Sam added.

"And now my dear wife treats Nephi's wounds," Zoram said. "There are many… We will bring him when …"

"Soon. He will be with you soon." And Sam calmed her mind further. "This night your sisters will tend to the needs of your baby and I will keep Simon and Enoch with me, that you may be beside him all night without interruption."

"God bless thee Sam, and Zoram; you are my dearest friends."

Weak with relief, smiling through her tears, Ruth kept repeating, "Thank you; thank you, for finding him." And when she was alone again she raised her eyes to the dark ceiling, imagining the stars, reveling in her blessings. *Oh how merciful, how merciful the Lord God of Israel. Soon I will see my beloved.* Emotionally and physically exhausted she finally dozed.

And then they were bringing him to her.

"Nephi, Nephi, my love, God has returned thee to me! Oh…" The full impact of his suffering choked her silent: the bruised and blackened face, the puffy purple hands reaching out to hold her... Had she been the fainting kind the good wife would have lost consciousness.

For a moment she held him carefully, allowing herself a fragment of the long ached for comfort. Then reaching for the precious vile of olive oil—the purest, saved for blessings—very gently began applying it to the deep red creases around his wrists, the swollen purple hands, the black bruises …

As his wife treated his wounds Nephi's eyes never left her face.

"My dear, dear Ruth, thou too has suffered much, and the worry, and the travail… and I could not be with you. I pray you're all right. Is the baby…?"

She nodded, tears still streaking her face. She swiped at them with the back of her hand. Crying time was over.

"Our daughter is all right," she said calmly. "Abigail told me she would be. But you, my love, are not."

Ruth kissed the backs of her husband's oily hands, and moved them gently to his chest, saying, "I must save some oil for your ankles."

The gouges around his ankles were even deeper. At the slightest touch pain shot through him. But Nephi had faith that the special oil blessed by his father would heal them. And in the interim his love would be with him.

Nephi motioned for his wife to slide down beside him.

"You need rest, my love." He gently kissed her. "Lay quietly now, and tell me about our daughter."

"Oh dear husband, I do worry for our daughter. Abigail tells me she will live; but she came so early, too early. She is so frail..."

"Have faith dear one. God will not take back the gift He has given. Remember, the Lord said unto my father that his seed would populate the new land. All of his children and his children's children are that seed."

"I know, I know, yet I don't know how. These great waters, they are calm now, but they are endless. When, oh when will we…?"

Swollen fingers touched her lips.

"Soon, my love, soon."

Much relieved, Nephi became drowsy, and drifted into unconsciousness. He slept like a just fed baby, while Ruth continued gently rubbing the ugly grooves, and now and then kissing the puffy purple skin. The appeasing gentle rocking of the ship, the timbers creaking quietly, lulled her into a sense of security. And her love was with her. Completely at ease, she watched the wick in the lighted bowl slip down, suck up the last drop, flicker, and go out.

And come morning, so powerful the love, and the pure blessed oil, the wounds of iniquity were almost invisible.

Nephi appearance was also magic medicine for his ailing parents. His father soon left his bed to command again. And seeing the son she thought must be dead greatly strengthened his mother. However, for Sariah, it would take more time to conquer depression. She had lost her lifelong friend.

"Anna and I had planned… We talked of so many things we wanted to do when we reached the new land. We were going to …" Her voice trailed off.

Nephi took his mother's hand.

"God has called Anna home. Her work is done. Fret not that her time came before yours; think only that she now lives in comfort, and happiness. This thou knowest. And, dear mother, you also know you will see her again."

Sariah smiled weakly. She looked up at her tall son as if she were the child.

"In the new land," Nephi continued, "there will be comfort. We will live in abundance, even surpassing the beautiful land we left."

"I trust there'll be ample food," Sariah mused, "and fresh water, and green grass. My son, will there also be flowers? I do so miss beautiful flowers."

"Mother, I feel of a surety there will be flowers."

"I hope so." She sighed. "All these gray days, I haven't even been able to see land. I dream of flowers. Color would be a treat to my old eyes."

And as Sariah dreamed of flowers, the others each had a special daydream about the new land. But they began to fear they would dream in darkness. Some of the lamps had burned out; others burned precariously low, as did the food supply.

Since the sea had calmed the men had again tried fishing, but with no luck.

On the other hand, their revered leader had risen from his sick bed; the winds were pushing them forward, and Nephi held the directional ball. Hope resurfaced. Faith grew in their hearts again. When Lehi resumed preaching everybody listened—even Laman and Lemuel.

After releasing their prisoner the rebel brothers had hidden themselves. Not even their co-conspirators knew where. They didn't come out for food or water. But after days of isolation (long hours to think) they made a decision. One way to die was as good as another. Thus they timidly emerged, and hungrily went searching for food. Coming upon everyone collected in the open place, giving full attention to their father's sermon, they slipped up behind the group unnoticed. Afire with renewed faith and filled with gratitude—for Nephi's release and miraculous return to health, the return of his and Sariah's strength, the continuing progress of his premature granddaughter—the old prophet called his family together to rejoice…

He caught a glimpse of his elder sons at the back of the crowd. His heart skipped a beat. *His cup runneth over.*

Much shaken, he took a deep breath, and with just a slight pause departed from his script. "… if God grants that my errant sons cometh forth to repent, and ask forgiveness, my cup will be filled past capacity. I shall rejoice to have all my family together."

Nephi surmised that his father knew the rebels had come out of hiding. And after the sermon, said to him. "If my brothers should come forth and repent I too shall welcome the chance to forgive them. For it is my fervent desire also that they return to the fold—that we, that I, may someday succeed in teaching them love. My brothers regress because they have not learned to love. They do not conceive that God is love. And I fail as a teacher until I have taught them that."

Considering these charitable words of the victim (overheard, and reported to them) plus their father's words at the family sermon, Laman and Lemuel gathered the courage to beg forgiveness.

And once again they were forgiven.

However, after forgiving them Lehi also preached to them, as did Nephi. Both expounded at great length on the uplifting lessons of love. And so caught up were the spiritual leaders with the surprising repentance, and their indoctrination of the errant ones, they almost forgot another service that must be performed—a funeral, and a burial at sea. To Nephi's surprise his father (who had so eagerly taken over again) passed the duty on to him.

"I pass the obligation to thee," Lehi said, "as soon I must pass full leadership." For my day is ending. After we reach the Promised Land thou, shalt be the leader. It is God's commandment, and His will."

Lehi pointed a shaky finger toward his son's heart. "And, you, my chosen son, will carry the load admirably. Thou wilt become a great and benevolent leader."

When Nephi told Ruth what his father said, and that he was to conduct her mother's funeral (and burial at sea) she cried out as if in physical pain.

"Oh, no," Her voice quavered. "Nephi, I could not bear to give my dear mother's body to the monstrous sea. I know we will reach land soon. Thy father says so. Can we not wait? You must wait. You must!"

"Dear Ruth, calm thyself."

But she rushed on, the words tumbling over each other. "Oh Nephi, do not do this; you can not do this." She hung on his neck. "Go to thy father, please. Talk to him. Beg him. Though it may be longer than custom when we reach land, still, my dear mother *must* not be sent to a watery grave."

Realizing his wife's agony, knowing the main reason for her panic, Nephi seriously considered. Perhaps to grant the request would not be entirely impractical. Any deviation from tradition usually had little chance of being granted. On the other hand, the son knew his father's heart. The kind old patriarch would make the best decision (all things considered) for the good of all concerned. Nephi also thought of the cold in the hold. It was even colder in the hole below, where he as a prisoner had been hidden. A body could be kept there, preserved and out of sight, for as long as necessary. He promised Ruth he would go immediately and talk to his father.

Nephi found his father atop ship, treating himself to fresh air, and the last red rays of sunset.

"This is good," Lehi said. "I lay abed too long breathing stale air." He drew in a deep breath, and continued taking deep breaths as he stared out over the sea.

"The mist in the air is good for my health, and the beauty of the sea is good for my soul. "

"It's the same for me," Nephi said, "but alas, not for my dear Ruth."

He eyed the darker clouds collecting on the horizon; they would hasten dusk. His father would soon descend to his rest, so he must speak fast. Nephi quickly recounted his wife's request, putting it forth in the best possible light.

The leader lowered his head in thought. For a long minute he stroked his beard. Finally he looked up and met his son's anxious eyes.

"It can be done," he said congenially.

Then all of a sudden the half smile hovering behind his beard spread full.

"My son, my son…"

Something in the tone of his voice… the heightened color in his face… Nephi grabbed his father's arm. "Thou hast received news?"

The old man shook his head no. But he was still smiling. Under the shaggy brows his eyes twinkled. He pointed.

"Look in the far distance."

"Land!"

CHAPTER XXIV

From the high side opening of the tilted vessel the voyagers emerged, blinking and trembling. Enfeebled by lack of exercise, they slowly descended the long thong ladder to the heavenly firmness of land.

Anchoring at the bottom Nephi helped, or pulled, them off. And one by one (man, woman and child) they fell upon their faces, clutching the good earth as if they thought the ground might tilt and slide them back into the sea. Looming behind them, the run-aground ship, like a massive sea monster dying on shore. Spread out before them, the golden future.

The Land of Promise.

Last one down, the old prophet stood shakily surveying the scene—the beauty of the land, and his whole extended family prostate upon it. He collapsed beside them. "It has been accomplished!"

In accordance with His word The Lord God of Israel had delivered them unto a great new land.

Nephi helped his father to his feet, and hugged him. Sariah clung to the two of them, smiling from ear to ear. An emotional prayer rose up from the very depths of the young leader's soul; but he could not yet go apart to officially thank his maker. First he must attend to the flock for which he had been given responsibility—and briefly share the joy of their new home with his family.

After assuring that all were down safe and accounted for, with a nod from his father he gave the congregational prayer of appreciation for their safe arrival. Then turned to his waiting family. Infant daughter between them, young sons at their sides, Nephi and Ruth surveyed their new home.

"It's like a dream. Hardly can I believe it. We made it; we're here. And it's so green, and pretty. And… safe?"

Nephi nodded, contentedly mute. Ruth was bubbling over.

She freed her sons to run on nature's green carpet, and settling her newborn (wrapped in a shawl) safely at her feet, threw her arms wide in an imaginary embrace of the majestic sweep. The picture was embroidered with strange tall trees. She spied a profusion of fuchsia and violet, and her eyes sought Sariah. Then she saw a flash of crystal, a gurgling stream sparkling in the sun on its way to the sea. They wouldn't have to search for water.

Ruth looked up at her husband beaming. "Oh Nephi, my heart is full to overflowing."

Nephi and his wife stood by the stream together, praying their thankfulness. The other voyagers, as each discovered the long-dreamed-of fresh water, ran, hobbled, or crawled toward it. Laman, Lemuel, Hiram and Heleman ran unencumbered—as if blind to their wives and children following. Sam and his family, holding hands together, walked slowly toward it. The parents, supporting each other, were last to reach what Lehi called a miniature river. Yet even before he drank of the water The prophet gave thanks for it.

"Oh Lord God of Israel, great is thy mercy. We thank thee for the safe landing—and within sight of pure water, that we may immediately satisfy our thirst and purify our bodies. No greater was thy mercy long ago, in causing water to flow from the rock for Moses."

When all had refreshed themselves, they lay down on the grass to rest. Nephi then went apart to traditionally, formally thank his Maker. And, as was his practice, made the trip practical. Upon returning he carried a stag upon his shoulders.

"Meat!" Everyone crowded around shouting. "Meat, meat."

The children had gathered sticks; someone sparked a fire. And with the last mite of barley meal Sariah had begun preparing gruel, to tide them over until the men could go hunting…

"But now," Ruth burst out, "now we have meat. Already, Nephi has brought fresh food for us."

Lehi frowned, *Was the perfect wife sinning with pride?* Such a small sin, though. His smile returned. Sariah was the only one who said thank you. As Nephi shifted the weight off his shoulders, her face shone.

"Thank you my son. Thank you."

"Tomorrow, when our men have rested," Hannah quickly injected, "they will find bait to fish."

Ruth's older sister did not speak out of jealousy, only happy anticipation. All the women shouted with joy—and Heleman and Hiram, and Laman and Lemuel, and Sam and Zoram too. All felt in their hearts that they would never again be hungry.

In minutes the wives had the carcass cleaned, and a portion ready to cook. There were more cooks than necessary. Those who'd been listless and shirking on the ship flitted around talking and helping prepare the meal.

The patriarch felt the warmth of inner peace.

Comfortably full, and gratefully satisfied with the whole day, everyone relaxed. Except Sariah. She had been missing her dear friend Anna when suddenly it came to her that she would have additional duties—as matriarch for the whole clan. With Anna's death, responsibility for all the women of the extended family automatically fell upon her shoulders. Thereafter Sariah would advise Anna's daughters (and the wives of her sons) as Lehi advised Heleman and Hiram, when Ishmael died.

And already it appeared she must restrain some of them from gluttony. She put a hand on Hannah's shoulder.

"Hannah, no more; thy stomach will pain tomorrow if you eat too much.

"That's right, sister," said Josepha.

"Yes, all of you." Sariah continued. "Remember, it is wisdom to eat sparingly of meat, especially when your stomachs are empty. On the morrow we will gather berries and …" She smiled at each of the women in turn around the circle. "My dears, in this land of plenty you won't worry about being hungry anymore."

That first night on land, nourished and rested, the frequently at odds members of Lehi's extended family relaxed in a comfortable closeness almost forgotten. As if in honor of the situation, the stars came out in profusion. The air was balmy. Not since they left Jerusalem, had everyone felt so comfortable. The atmosphere of harmony also helped lessen the pain of grieving; they talked together about Anna. Long after the meal some still sat quietly talking.

Sam and Nephi lingered longest. Ruth, with sleeping infant in arms, had taken her sons to bed as soon as they lost interest in the dying fire. Eve left the circle shortly after. Seemingly metamorphosed into her former self, she had surprised her husband by eating.. And she smiled at him as she left to tend to their daughter.

Sam's eyes followed his wife as if she were a mirage, subject to disappear any second. He watched her all the way to the door of Zoram's tent (where Abigail had been tending their daughter). Then he turned back to Nephi.

"This place must be paradise, or another Eden."

"That it must be," Nephi mused. "How blessed we are. This is a great new land—and The Lord hath given it to the seed of our father."

Sam smiled at him. "And now another miracle. Eve talked to me today. I think she's herself again—maybe ready to be my helpmate."

Nephi hugged his brother. "I am happy for thee, Sam. It is a blessing much deserved. I think in this place all of our dreams might come true."

Sam and Nephi talked of their dreams, of the houses they would build… Maybe on this spot, where their feet first touched the land of promise, they would build a great city. Riding high on the wave of good fortune, they imagined becoming as rich in material things as in love and blessings.

That night everyone counted blessings.

They looked up and marveled at the same moon that hung in the sky over the holy city from whence they came, and no longer regretted leaving it. They lost their fear of starving. Those who had panicked at the power of the great waters, or secretly worried about dropping off the end of the earth, lost their fear of dying. The whole clan faced the new life confidently. On the morrow, after they finished unloading the ship, they would put the past behind them.

One part of the past, however, would have to be disposed of first.

First thing upon rising Lehi directed the sons of Ishmael to go back into the abandoned vessel, to the cold dark hold, and bring out the body of their mother. In accordance with tradition (as closely as possible) Nephi conducted the funeral. Then as he had promised his wife, they buried her mother in the good earth. Anna was laid to rest in nature's best offering—in pristine soil, under a great tree, surrounded by perfume and color. The hurt in Ruth's heart was assuaged. Anna's children and her best friend all grieved her passing, but not in excess.

In the following weeks things only improved. Laman's resentment of Nephi seemed fully abated. Having survived his confinement to the ship's closed-in spaces, Zoram bloomed like a lily returned to water; he grew in strength, and appeared to grow in stature. Sam smiled all the time, always talking to Nephi about Eve's turnabout, saying almost the same things.

"Look at her, my brother … She pays attention to our daughter. She ate some berries—and then a good supper. And she listens to what I say."

Eve had truly begun functioning as the helpmate her husband dreamed of. And Sam felt happily sure that when the new child came she would be capable of mothering two.

In the glorious new land everyone had found peace, almost "the peace that passeth all understanding." Month after month contentment reigned, to such an extent that Lehi no longer felt the need to preach sermons. He sometimes preached because he liked to, but the responsibility had been passed on. Well aware that the pride of his loins could handle full leadership the old man slipped out of his worries like a snake slipping out of its skin. That his aging body was weakening did not distress him. He was ready for the great adventure—and fully content that he would leave his people in good hands.

The idyllic days passed into a year.

But like water that never ripples stagnates, after a season of no excitement, no challenge, no danger, the good life loses its flavor. After building their houses and planting their fields (the women took care of the gardens) there was little for the men do but go hunting, which Nephi could always do in shorter order, even after being equaled with a wooden bow. So the others left it to him. Settling down as "house men" happy to lay around and play with their children, the foursome did whatever they wanted to do, whenever they wanted to do it.

Until they ran out of ideas.

One evening walking together for exercise, after laying in the shade all day, the four of them began pooling their thoughts, discussing what they might do for an exciting adventure. The air refreshing, and nothing to fear, they walked all the way down to the sea. And not one of them had come up with an interesting idea.

As they continued along the shore, paying no attention to direction, Lemuel began telling, for the hundredth time, how he didn't get to sow his oats. Reminiscing about chasing girls in the city after workdays in his father's fields, he complained that life had dealt him a dirty deal. The others, ambling along uninterested, were becoming bored.

Suddenly loomed ahead of them the long ignored almost forgotten rotting vessel of their captivity. In the hazy twilight it appeared ghostly, like the ghost of a giant beached whale. But the picture did not shake them as much as the memory of having been confined in it—for so long that they had teetered on the edge of insanity.

About face. They turned, as one, away from it, and started home. They gasped at the view in front of them: the scenic location Lehi had chosen for their settlement, and the high blue mountains beyond it, painted on a background of lighted crimson.

Nature commanded their attention. The magnificent flame in the west awakened their brooding souls. Their minds began functioning. And ideas began surfacing.

Heleman's won the unanimous vote.

"You know," he said, "I keep thinking we might not be the only people here. Maybe there's a civilization somewhere beyond those great mountains. Why don't we go and see?"

All four of them were intrigued by the concept. But Laman's face darkened, wishing he'd thought of it first. Suddenly he pretended that the idea had come to him earlier. And he took over, talking like a philosopher.

Lemuel grinned from ear to ear. His imagination soared. "Yea, if Nephi maketh himself a ruler over us we can flee. We can go wherever we want, pick our own place, and build … "

Hiram and Heleman both nodded. Their eyes sparked.

"Why not." said Hiram. "This land has everything, truly no less than promised. And it's all for the taking."

"There would be no worry providing for our families," Heleman added.

After the landing they all had worked eagerly, tilling and planting. In the first season they sowed all the remaining seed, including the supplement that Ishmael's sons carried from Jerusalem. And it brought forth abundantly. Now they had new seed that they could take with them. They also had building experience.

"We don't need help. And we don't need preaching," said Lemuel. "Just think, no more of Nephi's sermons, no more preaching..."

The more they talked the more they became possessed with the idea of exploring the new land, and building their own city. They began working out a plan.

On the same evening that the four conceived the idea of splitting the family, Nephi and Sam were talking with their father. Eve had delivered a son for Sam. and true to Lehi's prediction, had since performed her wifely duties cheerfully. It pleased Lehi that Sam shared this contentment in his household. The patriarch was further pleased to hear Nephi's report: that he had finished making metal plates from the ore in the new land, and had engraved his father's words upon them, as well as the Lord's commandments.

Nephi said solemnly, "I have received a commandment concerning these plates, that they *should be kept for the instruction of thy people who shall possess this land, and also for other wise purposes which are known unto the Lord, that they should be handed down from one generation to another...*"

Lehi interrupted.

"It is of great importance that you give a full account of this commandment to my people. Thou must preach it as thou will preach all the commandments received hereafter. Remember, it is your responsibility."

Nephi accepted the yoke of problems without question. And his sermons justified his father's confidence. His voice sparked fire. He spoke clearly, radiating faith, wisdom and love—not as a son, husband, or brother, but as God's instrument. Watching and listening to him Lehi thought of Jeremiah. Had his son's beard yet reached the length, had he worn a ragged robe instead of short tunic (considering only the words and the fire) Nephi could be mistaken for Jeremiah.

Years ago, as a young man in Jerusalem, Lehi had hung on the fiery words of Jeremiah. At the end of his days he hung on the words of his son.

"Behold! According to the words of the angel, He cometh, in six hundred years from the time my father left Jerusalem. And the world, because of their iniquity, shall judge him to be a thing of naught; wherefore they scourge him, and he suffereth it; and they smite him, and he suffereth it. Yea, even they spit upon him, and he suffereth..."

When relating this prophecy to the people, for the first time talking about the coming of The Redeemer, and His great suffering on the cross ... the young prophet had faltered in blind agony, almost overcome by emotion. But as time passed greater strength had been given him. The son's wisdom grew like unto his father's. He understood what he read from the sermons of the prophet Enoch, and Isaiah, and things that were written in the book of Moses—which were graven on the plates taken from the house of Laban. Nephi read them also to Laman and Lemuel, whenever they would listen. And happily explained when they asked questions.

"My brothers, it meaneth that after all of the house of Israel have been scattered and confounded, that the Lord God will raise up a mighty nation among the gentiles, yea, even upon the face of this land... And He hath given me knowledge by visions that the time cometh when God will gather his children together... and there shall be one fold, and one shepherd."

All these things Nephi repeatedly told his brothers. With Lehi's blessing he preached to them incessantly—until, too much of a good thing. That night on the seashore the foursome finally decided to flee the preaching. And they began seriously making plans.

But then again fate stepped in.

CHAPTER XXV

Nephi heard footsteps outside his tent. And then a weak voice. He went out, quickly pulled his father inside, and led him to the pillowed chair. Lehi dropped down on it without speaking. His breathing was labored.

"Father, what is it?"

"It is my time." The old man quavered. He took a deep breath before continuing. "First thing tomorrow, I would that you gather my flock together, that I may speak my farewell and give my children their blessings."

Nephi flashed a quick look at his wife for support as he kneeled down beside his father. But Ruth had already courteously turned her back, not to participate in the men's conversation. She gave no indication that she'd heard what Lehi said. But the second he left she went to her husband bearing a cluster of wild grapes and a clay cup of cool water. Then she sat down close beside him.

Aware that his wife had overheard, Nephi smiled at her, and took her hand. "My father," he choked out, "I love him; he is my teacher and advisor. He…" Despite the manly show of strength, a groan escaped. "Oh Ruth, I would that the Lord not take him so soon. I need him. I still need him."

"But he is old," Ruth said softly, "and very tired. God takes him home to grant him rest. And my dear you must see that he is ready."

When Nephi did not respond she gently pressed his arm and added, "My love, thou knowest we all must go the way of the grave."

"I know. And I knew it would be soon, but it's too soon. I need his wisdom."

Ruth touched a barely visible streak of silver at her husband's temple. She had not seen it before. "As great a wisdom will soon be thine," she encouraged, "And God will give thee guidance."

Nephi pulled his wife closer. She gave him strength. They sat quietly together for a long time before retiring.

Next morning he told the whole family, and required that his brothers and Hiram and Heleman prepare a place for the special sermon. He did not notice that their reaction was other than grief (they were almost ready to go, and would now have to alter their plans). Nephi thought of nothing except his beloved father would no longer be with him. Anticipating his loss, the weight of full responsibility weighed heavier on his shoulders. His father had not yet gone, and he felt his confidence slipping.

Nephi made a concerted effort to count his blessings: His good wife, a healthy baby daughter cooing in her hammock, Simon and Enoch laughing at play—a scene of love and abundance. There was hurt in his heart but not a cloud in the sky of everyday living.

"Ruth, my love, let me not ever forget how good the Lord has been to me. I shall count my blessings, and carry on with confidence in my father's trust, that I will serve God with all my heart to the end of my days."

He kissed her on the forehead and went to be with his father.

Ruth's misty blue eyes followed him. "And I shall ever be thy comfort and support," she whispered.

A short time later she gathered up their children and went to the shaded arbor that had been constructed for the farewell sermon. The whole clan had assembled. They all listened with respectful attention—Nephi, with concentration, as if he would be required to repeat the words, as well as record them.

The old man spoke of their difficulties in the wilderness, and of the many rebellions, especially the iniquity upon the waters (and God's merciful forgiveness), of the terrible tempest and being saved from the angry sea, of being given a land like unto paradise where they lived in abundance, free from worry and fear. His deep concern for the welfare of his extended family ever evident, Lehi humbly implored them to always keep God's commandments, and to love one another.

"For behold I have seen a vision, that the holy city has in truth been destroyed. Many of our people have been slain, and carried away in captivity. Whereas we have been blessed exceedingly. Had we not been led out of the city we should also have perished."

He bowed his head in reverence.

"And it has been revealed to me that this land which The Lord God covenanted to my descendants, shall be kept as yet from the knowledge of other nations, lest they overrun the land and…"

He swayed. Nephi grabbed hold of him. "My children," he continued, "hear the words of a trembling parent. Remember to observe the statutes. This laxity hath been the agony of my soul from…" He sagged against Nephi.

Sariah rushed to her husband's side.

"Enough," she said.

Sam stepped up and helped support his father. Nephi and Sam were leading him away when the old man suddenly straightened, turned back, and almost shouted.

"Laman and Lemuel, rebel no more against thy brother. He hath been chosen as an instrument in the hands of God. He has not sought power or authority over you, but works only for your eternal welfare. Listen to him. If he speaks sharply, it is naught but the Spirit of the Lord which is …"

He gasped, as if a sword had pierced his throat and cut off the words. But he had more to say.

"My children, always remember, if you hearken unto the voice of Nephi ye shall prosper. Keep the commandments and The Lord will …"

Again he faltered, and began coughing. Nephi and Sam held him up and led him to his tent. All the family followed. And as Sariah hovered over him, everyone bunched around the opening, waiting, hoping to hear the rest of the sermon. But the voice had weakened to inaudible. His wife fetched him a cool drink and made him as comfortable as possible, then sat down beside him. Sam patted his mother's hand and went outside with the others. Nephi sat with her.

"… must go the way of all the earth," Lehi mumbled.

With that faint uttering the old leader slumped down comatose. Sariah and Nephi, watching over him, concentrated on the faint wheezing sound of his breathing. Outside the tent his apprehensive family hovered like shadows over their veiled future.

When he hadn't moved for half an hour Sariah went out and spoke to them. "Go now, and nourish thyselves." "When my husband's strength revives, that he may continue, I will send for you."

But it seemed the sermon had ended. When dusk brought down the curtain on that fateful day, the deeper darkness was fast approaching. Sariah sent Nephi home also, vowing to call him at any indication of change. Then, by the light of a flickering flame in a dish of oil, her last wisps of hope evaporating, she prepared to watch her life's companion slip away. Flat on his back, gnarled hands in prayerful clasp over his chest, sunken cheeks, eyes closed … There was no movement, except the weak breath barely stirring the white beard. Stretched stingily over his rumpled tunic it looked like limp lace.

Fixating on the beard, Sariah sat unmoving for hours. She didn't leave her husband's side until daylight, when she went to prepare a warm broth—out of habit, the woman prepared nourishment… As she was returning with the broth her breath caught. The cup jiggled in her hands. She set it down just short of spilling. In the increasing morning light the familiar map of deep lines on her husband's face seemed set in marble, the high cheekbones looked like alabaster knobs of wax. She swayed above him like a willow giving way to the wind, not daring to touch him.

The translucent eyelids flickered. He mumbled faintly, "Sariah … my good woman…" He was struggling to finish the sentence. But Sariah didn't need to hear the rest of the words to know what he was saying.

"Call my children."

When all his family were reassembled within and around the tent, God blessed Lehi with strength enough to give the traditional blessings. One by one in shaky voice he blessed his sons: Laman, Lemuel, Sam, Nephi, Jacob, Joseph, and then the sons of Ishmael—and all their sons and daughters.

"Now," he quaked, "I would speak unto Zoram." For the servant of Laban brought out of Jerusalem by the hand of the Lord had become family.

"Zoram, thou hast become as a son to me; and I know that thou art a loving husband to Ishmael's daughter, and a true and lasting friend to my sons… Wherefore thy seed shall be blessed with my seed."

The deed was done. Lehi closed his eyes and lay back inert upon the flower-plumped mat. The pungent smell of crushed fuchsia, hot bodies, and death permeated the crowded tent. The temperature had risen to suffering heights. Sariah sighed, and smiling weakly motioned everybody out. At the sniffling and shuffling of sandals the old man's eyes opened again. Strange pinpoint lights shot from the deep sockets. He lifted a limp hand—and it dropped. Sariah rushed them along, her sons too, "God go with you," God go with you…"

Quietly she said to Nephi, "I need to be alone with my husband."

Watching over the one she had loved all her life (with him for what she knew was the last time) Sariah's mind flooded with memories, good and bad. But her husband had never been the cause of the bad; Lehi had always been kind to her. She'd been blessed beyond measure. There was rarely a break in their closeness. Now he was leaving her. She took a gnarled hand between hers, lifted it to her face, and closed her eyes in prayer.

The stifling heat had not abated with the mass exit. Sariah thought to ease her patient with a sponge bath. But hesitating to disturb him, began fanning him instead. She swished the branch swiftly back and forth, back and forth, staring alternately at her loved one's face, and into space.

"Sari…" She jumped, startled further that the voice resounded with strength. Face alight, Lehi sat bolt upright, without support. "Sari…" he said again. Then a long rattling breath … and the strangely lighted eyes were looking past her.

"Oh my husband …"

Sariah grabbed her husband's hands, and held them until the fire in the eyes faded. Then bowing to custom, sent for the eldest son to close them.

At that exact moment, across the valley on a commanding rise in the foothills, Nephi froze, mallet in mid air. When his mother asked to be alone with her lifelong companion, he'd gone to work on Ruth's new house. Stripped to the waist, sweat glistening on his muscled shoulders, he'd suddenly felt cold to the core—and intuitively, he knew. He threw back his head and cried.

"Oh my father, The Lord hath taken thee!"

This Nephi knew without a doubt. But he didn't know what his mother had done. And he had no idea of the consequences …

CHAPTER XXVI

When called to perform the customary duty of the eldest son on the death of the father, Laman assumed that the breach of tradition (of allowing the youngest son authority over the eldest) had ended. He had been deeply afflicted by this travesty; and the hurt had festered for years. Although temporarily soothed, and periodically displaced by fear, the feeling of injustice had ever smoldered.

Now the dark cloud had finally lifted. When the one responsible was no longer with them (no longer controlling their lives), Laman believed that tradition would be restored—that he would assume his rightful authority. And his mother's action had confirmed it.

He waited until after Nephi conducted the funeral.

While Sam and Nephi still kneeled at the grave with Sariah (the rest of the family returning in solemn procession back to their homes) Laman put a restraining arm on Lemuel's shoulder, allowing the others to proceed out of hearing.

"Our pious brother may be a prophet; at times there is evidence that God is with him. But now that our father is no more I will submit no longer to a ruling against tradition. Our mother honors tradition. She will stand with me."

And I will stand with you," Lemuel vowed. "For surely, on the death of the father the roll of leader falls to the eldest son."

Laman gave his supporter one of his rare smiles.

"But …" Lemuel wanted to know, "what about our plan?" "Does this mean you will not leave?"

The foursome had finalized their plan to depart and explore the country beyond the mountains—they had been ready to leave. Now with the death of the father would Laman still split the family? Lemuel wondered what he would decide to do? He had watched his brother smolder at Nephi's taking over, despite the fact that their mother had called Laman in accordance with tradition. And Laman had held his peace for three days, while Nephi admonished him for lack of reverence, and accused him of shortening their father's life by constant worry over him.

He could contain himself no longer.

During all the years he'd conformed, while burning to remedy the situation that ate at his insides, Laman had noted that Nephi did not always please The Lord. He reminded Lemuel of a few instances…

"The Lord does not sanction pride. And since our father's death Nephi is puffed up with it. He wants to rule over many; if we go he may follow after us and fight to keep us in his flock. To him we're not family, more like subjects, and …"

Lemuel continued the tirade.

"Yea, did he talk as a brother with us in our grief for our father? No. Doth he ever confer with us, that he may consider our opinions? No. He bosses, and orders. He treats us like children."

Lemuel had re-confirmed his support. And believing that Hiram and Heleman would also, Laman felt confident to usurp authority. He called another conference.

"I will take over the leadership. If some do not wish to follow we will go build our city without them, as we planned."

"But," Heleman worried, "Nephi may not allow us …"

"Allow us!" Laman exploded. "Wherefore, we may have to slay him."

And he immediately set to work convincing the others that the drastic action may not only be necessary but was justified.

Lemuel had not expected their break to include killing. Memory of their younger days welled up. *Times they all played together...And he recalled his handsome younger brother working harder than any of them in the fields. He remembered also that Nephi never reported on his sneaked excursions to the city.*

But as enthusiasm grew in the others, with the talk of freedom (and the realization that there would be no more preaching, and no more restrictions) memories of the past paled. Recent recollections weighed stronger. After the death, Nephi had severely chastened Lemuel along with Laman.

Ultimately, they all acquiesced. And a few days later they scheduled murder—for the following Sabbath.

The plotters, and all the members of their families, would absent themselves from the Sabbath sermon. This they knew would anger Nephi, and frustrate him, resulting in a situation that could be enhanced to their advantage. They would then come out of hiding and heckle him, pick a quarrel with him, hopefully make him angry enough to strike first. The rest would be easy. They would have the majority, and the plan—a definite advantage over any of his unsuspecting supporters who would try to rally…

Vengeance at last. Laman had mentally twisted the agreed upon solution to *warranted.* And come the day he would twist it to "justifiable" in the eyes of the spectators. He imagined that some might even become his followers.

On the designated Sabbath Nephi had planned to rest, and enjoy time with his family. After the sermon he would take Ruth and the children to see the house he was building for them. She sparkled with anticipation when he told her. She would prepare a picnic lunch—special goodies for the children, and her husband's favorite honey cakes.

But while kindling the fire (earlier than usual that morning, to bake for the picnic) she heard her husband frantically calling.

"Ruth, Ruth Come. Hurry!"

She rushed to him, shushing him. "Doth thou want to wake the children?"

Nephi grabbed her roughly, silencing her with a look, and whispered intensely, "We must flee. The Lord hath warned that my brothers plot to kill me!"

"Oh, Nephi!" Her arms encircled his neck.

He pulled them away. "Go quickly; tell my mother, Sam, Zoram, all who believe, *all those who would go with me*."

Snatching her shawl, Ruth shot a glance over her shoulder at the sleeping children, and fled. When a man says there is danger a woman does not tarry. And in this case a slight hesitation might mean catastrophe. Her heart beat in her throat; her eyes darted. No one untrustworthy must see her. The wife of Nephi knew not whom she might trust. His brothers planning evil would surely have schemed to lure everyone possible to their side.

Oh dear God, let there not be a battle!

That first fateful day there was no battle (however battles would follow, bloody battles, for generations).

On that Sabbath morning God's early warning disallowed a confrontation. While the rebels and their families hid out (not to be present for the sermon) Nephi and his family, and all who believed in him, made their escape. As commanded by The Lord, they left their Eden near the sea and fled beyond the mountains, taking only whatsoever things that were of dire necessity: tents, food, clothing, and the compass to guide them. Also, the sacred plates containing their people's history and the record of their journey.

The fractured family of Lehi spread out all over the great land, multiplying exceedingly. Those who followed Nephi were called Nephites, and those who followed Laman were called Lamanites. And they warred against each other continually....

And after many wars and many generations all the prophecies of God's servant Lehi were fulfilled.

Because of the endless "bloodsheds" among them, the Nephites were annihilated, and the few remaining Lamanites, having degenerated into iniquity, were overrun by the gentiles. In the latter days the gentiles stole their promised land from them---and built up a great nation, for "*all those who should be led out of other countries by the hand of The Lord.*"

* * * * *

EPILOGUE

Six hundred years after Lehi and his little band of followers were led out from Jerusalem The Savior of the world came, was crucified, and rose again. After the earthquakes, the terrible tempests, and the darkness, the risen Christ appeared … also unto the seed of Lehi sojourning on the Promised Land.

And He taught them. And He said to them:

"Not at any time hath the Father given me commandment that I should tell it unto your brethren at Jerusalem. Neither… that I should tell them concerning the other tribes of the house of Israel whom the Father hath led away. This much did the Father command me that I should tell unto them: that other sheep I have which are not of this fold; them also I must bring, and they shall hear my voice; and there shall be one fold and one shepherd."

Also the shepherd called Jesus told them: "*Ye are they of whom I said, 'Other sheep I have which are not of this fold.'*"

And Lehi's prophesy about the latter days came true:

"It shall come to pass that those of my seed who have dwindled in disbelief will be smitten by the hand of the gentiles… And the nation of the gentiles shall become great. The gentiles shall be blessed upon the land. And it shall be a land of liberty. Oppressed peoples from all the four quarters of the earth and the isles of the sea will come to this land…."

This land, the designated "Land of the Free."

Printed in the United States
54082LVS00004B/7-18

9 781593 303334